MURDER AT THE BIRTHDAY PARTY

The trodden path narrowed, and I fell a step behind Carina. When she abruptly halted, I stumbled into her.

"What is it?" On tiptoes, I peered over her shoulder. Carina stood a head taller than me. Still model material, she'd given up that lifestyle when she decided to have a family.

"Wh-who is that?"

A body lay straight ahead, the upper half of it hidden behind the bushes, the lower half blocking the path. I swallowed the lump of fear that was lodged in my throat. Good grief, one of the guests must have taken a fall, or not. I stepped past Carina and walked toward the extended end of the body.

It was definitely an *or not* moment.

A knife protruded from Evelyn Montgomery's chest. She wasn't asleep, nor was she unconscious. She was dead. . . .

Books by J.M. Griffin

LEFT FUR DEAD

WHO'S DEAD, DOC?

Published by Kensington Publishing Corporation

Who's Dead, Doc?

J.M. GRIFFIN

KENSINGTON BOOKS
www.kensingtonbooks.com

KENSINGTON BOOKS are published by

Kensington Publishing Corp.
119 West 40th Street
New York, NY 10018

All Kensington titles, imprints, and distributed lines are available at special quantity discounts for bulk purchases for sales promotion, premiums, fund-raising, and educational or institutional use.

Special book excerpts or customized printings can also be created to fit specific needs. For details, write or phone the office of the Kensington Sales Manager: Kensington Publishing Corp., 119 West 40th Street, New York, NY 10018. Attn. Sales Department. Phone: 1-800-221-2647.

Kensington and the K logo Reg. U.S. Pat. & TM Off.

First Kensington Books mass-market printing: March 2020
ISBN-13: 978-1-4967-2058-0
ISBN-10: 1-4967-2058-X

ISBN-13: 978-1-4967-2061-0 (ebook)
ISBN-10: 1-4967-2061-X (ebook)

10 9 8 7 6 5 4 3 2 1

Printed in the United States of America

This book is dedicated to bunny lovers everywhere.

CHAPTER ONE

Children scampered across the yard in anticipation of birthday cake and handing their presents to the birthday girl, Adrian Richland. Laughter filled the warm September air that brimmed with excitement. Twelve six-year-old girls surrounded the table set up in the middle of the oval stone patio. I grinned as they anxiously awaited their turn to offer Adrian their gift.

Playtime with my rabbits had ended, as had the puppet show, performed by Bailey Kimball. I was ready to pack up and return to my farm when Carina Richland, Adrian's mother, stepped next to me and whispered, "I have a request before you leave. Please see me after you're finished with the bunnies."

I nodded and set about gathering my furry friends from their folding pen and the run used for events such as these. Children adore petting these social, adorable creatures, which made the extra work worthwhile. Caring for these rabbits at

Fur Bridge Farm, where they reside, gives me a sense of great pride. In the past, I'd been invited to take a few to a local nursing home for elderly residents to enjoy. It had been therapeutic for them and seemed enjoyable for the rabbits.

After the rabbits were caged and watered, I left the van doors open for fresh air and returned to the yard. Many of the children were preparing to leave. Some weren't happy, a few looked tired, others cried while their mothers appeared nervous. Carina's friend Adelle Philby escorted the guests off the property, commiserating with them as they left.

I wondered what had happened in the short time I had been gone that would so drastically change the atmosphere. Mothers grasped their little darlings by the hand, said a quick good-bye, and left for parts unknown. I watched their hasty retreats and scanned the yard for Bun, my very special pal. Alone in the center of the pen, my black-and-white rabbit huddled, awaiting me.

"It's about time you got back. Everyone's upset. The lady of the house looks as if she's lost her mind."

I gathered Bun in my arms and studied the yard. Adrian, a shocked expression on her pale face, was visibly shaken and hovered just inside the sliding French doors to the patio. Birthday presents lay strewn over the deck, and the princess birthday cake, perched in the center of the refreshment table, was untouched and still intact. Decorative paper plates with matching cups tumbled across the lawn, pushed by the breeze.

I whispered to Bun, "What the heck happened?

I was only gone long enough to tend to the other rabbits."

"There's something upsetting, just past the edge of those trees. You and what's her name should go look."

"Uh, okay, Bun. First, I'll put you in the van."

Seconds later, Bun sat in the shaded van with the other rabbits. All the windows and side doors were open for fresh air to circulate. Returning to the house, I'd climbed the three steps onto the patio when Carina rushed forward and grabbed my arm.

Pale-faced, frantic, and a nervous wreck, she demanded, "Come with me. I can't face this alone."

Obviously upset, Carina's face held a sheen of sweat, and her eyes were filled with fear.

"Sure, lead the way." I disengaged my arm from her grasp and accompanied her into the shaded woodland.

Ours is a midsize town. Not a metropolitan city, Windermere was growing steadily. On the outskirts of town, housing developments were spread far enough apart to feature wooded landscaping for added privacy for ostentatious homes. I lived a good distance from my hostess, on a unique rabbit farm, in a sweet farmhouse with acreage galore. I wouldn't live here, but I considered the area interesting.

Bun and I are housemates, we're very close, and he talks to me. I know, it sounds ludicrous. It's not as if he opens his mouth and words come out, rather, he uses a sort of telepathy, if you will. There's no doubt we have a special connection. Due to Bun's avid nosiness, we had recently landed in a situation

I'd rather not have been part of or repeat, for that matter. The one thing I will say is my life isn't boring.

The trodden path narrowed, and I fell a step behind Carina. When she abruptly halted, I stumbled into her. The electrical tension in her body pulsed as she stood in front of me staring at the ground ahead. That's when she started to tremble more uncontrollably than before.

"What is it?" On tiptoes, I peered over her shoulder. Carina stood a head taller than me. Still model material, she'd given up that lifestyle when she decided to have a family.

"Wh-who is that?"

A body lay straight ahead, the upper half of it hidden behind the bushes, the lower half blocking the path. I swallowed the lump of fear that was lodged in my throat. Good grief, one of the guests must have taken a fall, or not. I stepped past Carina and walked toward the extended end of the body. It was definitely an *or not* moment.

A knife protruded from Evelyn Montgomery's chest. She wasn't asleep, nor was she unconscious, she was dead. There was no mistaking the fact that Evelyn had left the planet. I could tell by the blue tinge of her lips, the paleness of her skin, and the fact that there was no rise and fall of her chest. Evelyn wasn't breathing.

Letting out a pent-up breath, I returned to Carina and grabbed her arm, muttering that she shouldn't get any closer. I dragged her away from the woman I'd had words with just over an hour ago. "We have to report this to the police now, right now."

Her legs stiff as broomsticks, it was difficult to get Carina back to the house. It took some doing, but once we were inside, I reached for the phone. The call went through in seconds. I was told police and rescue personnel were being dispatched. Instructed to stay put and wait for them to arrive, I agreed and remained on the line with the dispatcher while rummaging through Carina's liquor cabinet looking for whiskey.

She downed the shot in one mouthful, then hauled in a ragged breath and coughed. Carina's eyes filled with tears and she started to bawl. Not just cry, mind you, but howl. I thought the neighbors could probably hear her.

"Get a hold of yourself," I demanded sharply, my hand over the phone for fear the dispatcher would hear me. It worked, because Carina quieted to a sniffling state.

Her bright blue eyes were now surrounded with dark smudges of mascara that had puddled and sent rivulets down her cheeks. Her perfect makeup job was no longer, and Carina's long dark hair was also disheveled. How the hair thing had happened was anyone's guess. I patted her shoulder and told the dispatcher that the police had arrived. I set the phone down and hurried to the front door.

Sheriff Jack Carver and a few other police officers shuffled into the house, followed by the all-too-familiar rescue personnel. After greeting them, I explained to Carver what we'd found on the wooded path. The tribe of people followed me to the scene where the dead woman lay. In seconds, I was barraged with questions I couldn't answer.

"Do you know this woman?" Carver asked while

the rescue team checked out Evelyn's stab wound, and policemen cordoned off the area with yellow tape.

"Her name is Evelyn Montgomery. She was a guest at the birthday party."

"Were you friends?"

"Hardly, I've seen her around town once or twice, and then here this afternoon."

Scribbling in his little notebook, Carver nodded and asked, "Whose birthday?"

"Adrian Richland. She turned six today."

He cocked a brow at me and asked, "What's your relationship with the Richlands?"

"None, really. Carina called and arranged to have the rabbits at the party. Bailey Kimball entertained with her puppets, but she left before we found Evelyn."

The sheriff turned away and spoke with the rescuers. Another officer stepped over to me.

"I recognize you. You're the rabbit lady, right?"

"Jules Bridge, I own Fur Bridge Farm on Westcott Road."

"I heard you went to the assisted living home where my grandmother has taken residence. She raves about your rabbits. Nice to meet you." The officer glanced up, nodded when Sheriff Carver summoned him, and walked away. The sheriff murmured something to him before he returned to me.

Carver, brought up to speed by the lead member of the rescue team, released them from the scene while officers waited for the coroner's van to arrive.

Rather than look at the dead woman, I kept my eyes on Carver. Not that I'm squeamish, I simply have an aversion to dead people. You can't be squeamish when raising or caring for animals.

"What can you tell me about Mrs. Richland?"

My internal antennae went nuts, the hairs on the back of my neck sprung to attention, and I studied my fingernails.

"I don't know anything that might be helpful to you. Mrs. Richland and I have a business relationship, nothing more. Like I said before, I only saw Evelyn Montgomery once or twice before today. I saw her around town, is all." Not in a million years would I admit I'd had a disagreement with the woman, nor would I tell Carver of Evelyn and Carina's heated argument in the garage before the guests arrived.

I had parked my van in the shade, next to the three-car garage. The closest garage door was open, and Carina had been inside with Evelyn. I'd only heard bits of the conversation, and wouldn't repeat it due to the possibility it might be taken out of context. The chances of Carina not knowing I'd heard the exchange between her and Evelyn were slim. I'd had to make my presence known in order to set the rabbits up for the day.

"You aren't friends with either woman, then?"

Hadn't I made that clear? "That's correct."

"You can go. If there are any other questions, I'll give you a call."

Carver turned toward the body.

I left in a hurry. The rabbits needed care. They'd been sitting in the van longer than I'd anticipated, and Bun was probably upset over what was taking so long. The other rabbits could care less, they're a friendly, happy group who have the run of my farm.

I'm pretty lenient when it comes to their exercise and living quarters. There's no crushing them in cages. It's important for these creatures to have freedom for a great quality of life, and living at Fur Bridge Farm, that's what they get. Instead, each cage was built with a wooden hutch attached. They were large homes for the bunnies, with ample room for them to move about and play.

Carina lingered on the patio and called to me as I left the footpath. She handed me payment for my services. I wanted to say that I hadn't said a word about her and Evelyn, instead I said goodbye.

Closing the rear doors of the van, I promised the rabbits we'd be home soon. I know it seems silly, but rabbits like interaction and enjoy conversation. I climbed into the driver's seat, put the windows all the way up, set the air-conditioning on low, and headed for home. At the end of the driveway, I waited for a break in traffic. In the rearview mirror, I noticed Carver crossing the lawn toward the house. Not willing to hang around, I'd made my escape just in time.

On our way to the farm, I breathed a sigh of relief and told the rabbits we would arrive soon.

"How did it go in the woods?"

I should have known Bun would be curious. "It went fine, the police took over, and I'm sure you saw the rescue team leave," I mumbled.

"The kids were quite active and noisy while I watched all that went on."

"What went on?" I knew this was a gambit to see if we could look into Evelyn's death.

"I might have seen who went in there after that woman."

"Might have? Can you be clear on who you saw?"

"I don't know the names of the guests, Jules. After all, I'm not human, I'm a rabbit. Nobody introduces us to people."

In silence, I slowed the van and turned into the driveway leading to the farm.

Jessica Plain, the vet who had opened a clinic in one section of the barn, strode forward to assist with my passengers and equipment.

I shut off the motor as Jess swung the rear doors open and helped me haul out the rabbits, their run, and the pen. We set the pen and run on a flatbed rolling cart, similar to a platform truck but smaller, and loaded a second one with cages of rabbits. I rolled the first cart into the barn as Jessica began caring for the rabbits. With the rabbits settled in their individual homes, I thanked Jess and took Bun from his cage and set him on the floor.

With Bun hopping alongside me, we entered the house. *"I suppose we're going to look into this?"*

I paused to listen for a moment, making sure we were alone, and whispered, "We most certainly are not."

Bun's nose twitched, his tiny nostrils flared, and his lips drew back a tad showing his two front teeth. I considered it his way of showing disdain over my decision.

"You always say that."

He hopped toward his own room just off the

kitchen, then sprawled catlike on his bunny bed and heaved a deep breath. *"Kids tucker me out."*

I nodded in agreement as the phone rang. Carina was on the line. I was about to say hello, when Carina blurted, "What did you tell the sheriff?"

"Nothing important, why?"

"I know you overheard Evelyn arguing with me today. Please don't tell Sheriff Carver, it might have a negative effect on Adrian and me. We're extremely upset by what's happened."

Aware that Carver would be persistent in questioning Carina concerning the two women's disagreement, I took a deep breath and hoped to allay her fear. "I have no intention of revealing what took place between you. I only heard snippets that didn't make any sense to me. I'm sure Carver wouldn't make much of it, either."

Her sigh was audible and the knot in my stomach relaxed.

"Then I have a favor to ask of you."

Hesitant, I said, "Okay." I waited for the one question I wanted to avoid at all costs.

"Would you investigate Evelyn's death for me? I can pay you for your time. Please say you will. Sheriff Carver has implied I was involved in her death, you know. I read in the newspaper that not long ago it was you who figured out the who and why of what was happening at your farm. I'm confident you could find whoever is responsible for this."

"Sometimes the sheriff is absurd. You couldn't have killed her, you had a crowd of mothers and scads of children running rampant around the yard. There was no possible way you could have committed that crime."

"Thanks for saying that. I couldn't, and didn't, kill Evelyn, but I have to know who did. It's a matter of safety for me and Adrian. Our lives have only recently begun to return to normal after Paul's sudden death in a car accident."

"I know, and I'm sorry you've had such a difficult time of things. It can't be easy to handle everything by yourself." As far as my life went, it could be harrowing at times. I couldn't imagine having a child in the mix. But then, I had Bun, which wasn't a light responsibility, either.

"Give my request consideration, okay?"

Knowing she had no idea what trouble I could end up in with the sheriff for saying yes to her, I reluctantly agreed to think it over.

After I hung up, it was clear that Bun had heard every word I'd said. When I glanced down, he sat next to my feet, his ears in an upright and stiff position. Yup, he'd heard all right.

I waited for him to demand we do as Carina had asked. After our last adventurous mystery, Bun had yearned for another to solve. I hoped it wouldn't turn out to be as dangerous as the previous one had.

"You'll agree to her request, won't you? With my superpowers and keen senses, we could wrap this up in no time."

Really? Superpowers? Had I created a monster rather than a hero? He went on and on for a good five minutes, until I could no longer take his nagging. Eventually, I agreed to look into Evelyn's death to help Carina out. In his usual enthusiastic manner, Bun hopped joyfully around the kitchen.

"Calm down and tell me what you saw while you were in the rabbit pen."

I saw a woman sneak across the yard. She was a guest. I don't recall what she looked like, you know, all humans look alike to us rabbits.

"Take your time and give it some thought, her identity might be more important than you know."

Oh, and another woman went along the path later on. I think that was when the party went downhill because guests began leaving.

"I won't ask what she looked like, since most humans look alike to you rabbits. Should you remember her hair and skin color, or height, clothing and such, you might want to let me know."

Disgusted with this game he played, I left Bun sitting in the kitchen while I went in search of Jessica.

CHAPTER TWO

Tightly wound pockets of alfalfa hay, lined with red lettuce, spring greens, and carrot tops. These treats also had bits of apples and a few raisins tucked in. These delightful goodies filled the stainless-steel wagon Jess pushed up and down the aisles. She'd stop at each hutch to insert one pocket inside.

"Let me help you with that, Jess."

"Thanks, I wasn't going to ask you to give me a hand. You look like you've had a tough day. Want to talk about it?"

"All went well until later this afternoon when Carina and I found Evelyn Montgomery dead on the path between Carina's house and the one next door. The homes there have wooded sections between them with enough privacy to kill someone without anybody being the wiser." I shivered at the thought.

Her eyes wide, Jessica gasped. "Oh my gosh, you just got over one mystery and now there's another unsavory situation that you've been thrown into? Evelyn Montgomery, you're sure?"

"I'm sure. When Bailey left, I should have been right behind her, but not me, I was stupid enough to take my time packing up. Carina had written the check for my services while I dawdled. That's when things took a turn. I'd loaded the rabbits into the van, went back for Bun, and found the partygoers leaving in a hurry. Confused over what had gone awry, I became curious when Carina approached me. She dragged me onto the path, saying there was something very wrong and she couldn't deal with it alone. Can you believe that?"

"Sounds like you need a strong cup of tea and to start at the beginning. Maybe if you talk the entire day through, you'll come up with memories or thoughts that could help Sheriff Carver."

"Good idea. Let's finish this job and then we can chat. By the way, was the shop open today? I wasn't sure if Molly was on the schedule. She's such a great kid and has been doing well, especially since she's had to handle a lot since we set up the spinning and weaving classes. I'm impressed with her organization skills."

"She was here until about two o'clock, then closed up and left the deposit and income tally for you beneath the register drawer. I think she'll shear Petra the next time she comes in. She mentioned a few of our customers wanted her to do their rabbits, too. Before she knows it, she'll have a nice side-business going."

"It's a plus to have her shear and keep the shop open when I'm not able to do so."

We kept the cart moving, each of us taking opposite sides of an aisle to finish the feeding job. We rounded the last corner, gave Walkabout Willy the last goody bundle and then went into the house.

I noticed Bun was fast asleep when I put the kettle on to boil. Jessica set cups, teabags, and the honeypot on a tray. She enjoyed milk and honey with her tea, I took mine strong with nothing added to the taste. I poured water into the cups and set the kettle on the stove. Jess carried the tray onto the porch, while I took gingersnap cookies from the cupboard before I joined her. We relaxed in the two hand-caned rocking chairs and were quiet for a while.

Jess munched a gingersnap and then said, "I can see you're unwinding just by sitting there and sipping your tea. My aunt always said when tough situations arise, a cup of tea is in order. I guess she was right."

"It is pleasant out here, isn't it? Very calming."

"Now, tell me what your day was like."

I heaved a sigh, slurped another mouthful of tea, and leaned my head against the back of the chair. "It began early, before the party guests arrived. Bailey and I were in the middle of assembling our setups. I was closer to the house and garage than Bailey. She felt it would be easier to hold the children's attention if we were separated. Nearly done with the pen and rabbits, I overheard raised voices. It wasn't hard to figure out Carina and Evelyn were in the middle of a spat. I had seen Evelyn stride across the lawn with a determined expression on her face."

"What would they have to argue over? I didn't realize they even knew each other."

"I don't know the specifics of their friendship, or if there was one, but they had one heck of an argument. I couldn't make out the subject of it, but when Adrian came into the yard, they both stopped talking and split up. Evelyn stayed for a while to speak with newly arrived guests. By then, I'd connected the last part of the rabbit run and she approached me."

"What did she say?"

"Evelyn wanted to tell me how happy she was that I entered Petra into the rabbit show she had organized. She discussed how excited everyone would be since this was the first show of its kind held in Windermere. I just nodded in agreement. As she walked away, she stopped for a second, looked over her shoulder, and warned me to keep my mouth shut where she and Carina were concerned or I'd be sorry."

Jessica's snort over the story made me laugh. It hadn't been funny at the time, but in retrospect, I found Evelyn's attempt at intimidation a sad state of affairs.

"She had a nerve saying that to you, but maybe she wasn't aware of all that you have been through. I wonder if she's used intimidation tactics on other people?"

"My thoughts, exactly. Anyway, I stepped into her space and softly told her not to try that again. We argued a bit and she threatened to withdraw Petra as a contestant. I said if she did, I'd go over her head to make sure Petra got in anyway. Honestly, some people think they can do whatever they want."

"Okay, focus on the party. Remember, we want a complete picture of what took place."

"You're right, sorry about the outburst. She pushed my buttons. I think Evelyn Montgomery had a serious mean streak. I, too, wondered if she treated others that way, especially if she thought they had crossed her."

"While you and Petra are at the show, if it continues on, you should snoop and find out. Then report what you find to the sheriff, of course."

I slid a sly look in her direction. "Of course. Fear not, this event won't be canceled. Too much money has been invested in it for that to happen."

A thump on the screen door was enough to let me know that Bun had eavesdropped, again. Undoubtedly using his superpowers. I nearly laughed at the thought and caught myself in time. I didn't want Jessica to think I'd lost my marbles.

"Open the door for Bun, will you?"

Jess let him out and watched as he raced from one end of the porch to the other. After the third lap, he flopped down at my feet and sprawled out. *That felt so good. I didn't get to use the run at the party today. The other rabbits enjoyed it too much to allow me a turn.*

Indeed, he was so put upon. I reached down to smooth his fur, then muttered praise for exercising. Bun perked up and seemed pleased at the acknowledgment.

Jess went inside for more hot water. While I rocked gently in the chair, my taut nerves eased, leaving a sense of calm in its wake.

"I heard what you two talked about. It would be a

good idea when we check things out to report our findings to Sheriff Carver. He should be glad of our help, don't you think?"

I bent near to his ears and whispered softly, "No, he'd be upset. Like I said earlier, we can give it a go and see what we find."

Bun scrambled to his feet, hopped about a bit, and settled into a sprawl. Jess returned with two more mugs of steaming water for tea and a few bits of apple and carrots for Bun.

Watching him snack on the treats, Jess said, "I think you and Bun ought to investigate. I can handle most everything here. Now that Molly has decided to take college classes, she won't be full-time but she has mentioned she can help us both. What do you think?"

"We should discuss it with her. She'll need time to study, and while Ray has gone out of state for college, he was good enough to train his replacement beforehand. Jason Lang is doing quite well and appears to enjoy the job."

"Then that settles it. You'll be free to investigate while Petra rakes in all the prizes at the show. With her lovely fur, she's bound to be popular with the audience. I've heard it's going to be a hit with the community backing the show."

"Are you sure the three of you can do all the work entailed? I know how busy the clinic is becoming, and Molly has been of great help." I shook my head. "It may be too much for all of you. The kids have classes and work crazy hours that don't always fit our schedules." I leaned my head against the chair, rocked a few times, and said, "I'll give it some thought and if we can work out the logistics,

I'll go ahead with the idea. If not, I won't. It wouldn't be fair to you, the help, or the bunnies."

"Good enough. We'll have a sit-down with the kids when they come in. Both of them will be here on Monday."

"You know you want to investigate this as much as I do, so don't play coy, Jules, it's unbecoming."

Annoyed, I swooped Bun up in my arms saying it was time to get back to work. After entering the house, I freed Bun and went into the barn with him walking a good distance behind. I spent a couple hours doing odds and ends that hadn't been done in my absence. All the while considering if these jobs weren't tended to while I looked into business that wasn't mine to look into, then who would do them?

I stopped short while sweeping the floor. Was I ticked off at Bun for being fresh to me? Or, was I angry because he was right in saying I wanted to investigate Evelyn's death? I heaved a sigh, chose the latter, and emptied the dustbin before telling Jessica that I would be in the house. She poked her head around the clinic door casing and gave me a thumbs-up.

Silent, Bun stood in the doorway of his room. He didn't budge when I motioned for him to come into the kitchen.

"You were rude to handle me roughly and you didn't talk to me while we were in the barn, either. It's as if I was having a time-out. I'm not a child, I'm a rabbit. You need to apologize."

Hands on my hips, I stood my ground. "You were fresh. I'm the one who should get an apology."

Ears lowered, tips nearly touching the floor, Bun turned away, and slowly crept to his cushion where he plopped down.

"I guess you aren't interested in what Jessica and I have decided, then." I hadn't moved an inch, but studied my broken, and in need of a serious manicure, fingernails. I waited, and waited, and waited some more. When Bun didn't comment, I left him to his mood and rang Carina.

She answered immediately.

"Hi, it's Juliette. I wanted to let you know that if I can figure out a schedule with my staff, I would be happy to help you by looking into Evelyn's death."

"You'd really do that for me? Oh, Jules, I would be so grateful to have you help us. The sheriff makes me nervous. I would never harm anyone, no matter what, and I have Adrian to think of. Paul's death has been so hard on us."

She was babbling. I held the phone away as she went on and then she suddenly stopped.

"I'm sorry, I do babble when I get excited. This is such good news, though, I can't help myself. When will you start?"

"As soon as I meet with my staff on Monday. If they're willing to pick up a few more hours, then I'll begin. If not, we'll come up with an alternate plan, okay?"

"You are wonderful, I knew it the moment we met. Feel free to call me anytime, I'll do what I can to assist you. Not shovel rabbit poop, though, not that. Please don't ask me to do that."

I snickered. "You needn't worry about the rabbit poop, it's under control. I will keep you posted as I gather information. Take care, Carina."

"Thanks." The line went dead. I hung up and started supper. Bun had entered the kitchen. Still solemn, he watched me prepare veggies.

"I didn't mean to be what you call fresh. I know I'm outspoken at times, but I'm never mean."

"I'm sorry if I hurt your feelings, Bun." I reached down and smoothed the fur on his head, ran my hands over his long ears, and tapped him on the nose with my fingertip. "I would be lost without you."

"I know. You're the best friend a rabbit could have." Lighthearted again, he hopped across the kitchen, checked out the newspaper rolled up in the basket, sniffed the flowerpot leaves, sneezed, and then said, *"We'll get to the bottom of Evelyn's murder. Don't you worry about a thing. We've got this."*

Supper was a simple affair. Veggies, burgers, and blueberry pie for dessert. Jessica cleared the table when we'd finished eating, and loaded the dishwasher before she left for the night. She'd moved back into her own apartment after we'd solved the last mystery. There was no need for me to have a live-in for safety in numbers any longer.

I bid her good-bye and watched as she drove away. There was still enough daylight left for a brief walk. I slipped Bun's sling over my body and leaned down for him to settle inside.

"Let's go to Lake Plantain."

"I'm not sure we have enough daylight left to go that far. We'll give it a try, I know how much you like it there, and the lake is beautiful at this time of year."

Snuggled in the sling, Bun poked his head out to enjoy the ride. Thankfully, Bun didn't weigh much and the sling wasn't cumbersome, which made a good stride easy. We, or rather, I, walked every day, weather permitting. Bun usually enjoyed the trip to and from the farm as much as I did.

We sat near the edge of the lake for a while and then began our homeward jaunt. About a half mile from the house, Sheriff Carver's cruiser slowed to a crawl beside us.

"Everything all right, Juliette?"

"Sure, Jack. How about you?" What this was about, I could only guess. I'd play along until he made his purpose clear. I had no doubt he'd once again warn me not to become involved with Evelyn's murder investigation.

His car slowly idled alongside us until I came to a stop. He shifted the car into park and told me to get in.

"I'm not finished exercising yet."

"It's getting dark and you won't arrive home before it is, so please, get in the car. Besides, I need a cup of coffee and you can make it for me, if you would." His attitude light, I wasn't fooled for a minute when I looked into his eyes. The man meant business.

Bun and I slid onto the front side passenger seat. I buckled in and enjoyed our ride back to the farm. Jack said little, except that his wife was waiting for another yarn sale and was wondering when that was going to happen. She'd also decided to take a spinning class.

"I'll let Molly know when she comes in on Monday. The classes have been successful and she will check to see if there's an opening for Meredith."

Parked at the front walk, we went up the stairs and I unlocked the door. Bun hopped out of the sling when I leaned down and headed to his room. He stopped just inside the doorway and squatted down. He wasn't about to miss a thing.

While the coffee perked, I handed Jack the cups and put the sugar and cream on the counter. "You don't mind sitting on the porch, do you?" I asked.

"Not at all. Meredith and I enjoy ours. So often you see people with huge porches added to their homes and never once do they use them. Such a shame, really."

The coffee finished perking and I took the loaded tray outside, set it on the small table between the rocking chairs, and took a seat. Jack did the same.

Thoughtful for a moment, he sipped his brew and then said, "I know you won't be able to help yourself where Evelyn's death is concerned. I also know I can warn, threaten, cajole, and beg you not to get involved, but it won't do me a bit of good, so I have an offer for you."

Astonished by his admission, I sat in wary silence and drank my coffee. What kind of offer? He had me dead to rights about Evelyn and what had happened to her. I couldn't deny that. I turned to look at him. He stared back, his expression intense.

CHAPTER THREE

I set my cup on the wooden tray. Something was up. But what? With anticipation, I asked, "What offer?"

"It seems that you'll be attending the rabbit show, am I right?"

"Petra has been entered as a contestant. Why?"

"I'm short staffed for the next couple weeks and could use eyes on everyone and ears to the ground while you're there. As a rabbit owner and farmer, you'll be in a perfect position to see and hear things we officers can't. What do you say, will you give me a hand or what?"

Fearful this was a gambit to see if I planned to look into things on my own, I hesitated. Thinking fast, I said, "I'm not sure I'll have the time. Petra will need a lot of care and gentle handling while I'm at the show. What is this really about?"

"Like I said, I have two men on vacation and another was injured in a foot chase. He tore his Achilles tendon and is out of work for who knows how long. I'm not crazy about asking for your help, but frankly, you're the best bet I have to discover whatever there is that can aid in my investigation. It's apparent Evelyn had issues, she was mean-spirited, threatened folks and what not. She had enemies, lots of them. What do you say? I'm not joking here, I mean what I've said."

"In that case, I'll help. I don't want to end up in a situation like the last one, though. I'd never been so scared in my life."

"I understand that, Jules. You're not to take any chances, or get into trouble, either. Keeping your eyes open and ears to the ground would go a long way in finding who committed the murder."

"Okay, we have a deal."

"Great. I hope I don't regret this, but it's the only solution I could come up with in these circumstances. Thanks for agreeing and for the coffee. I should get home, Meredith will be waiting."

As Jack drove away, I gathered the cups and tray and went into the kitchen. Bun sat near the kitchen table, his ears upright and his whiskers all jittery. He had heard. Again.

"He needs us, doesn't he? He can't do without our services, huh? I thought as much. He now realizes what a dynamic duo we are."

"I'm sure you're aware of his reason for asking us to snoop. Don't get all puffed up and overconfident with a sense of how great we are at detecting. It will only come back and bite us in the behind."

"I know you like to keep a low profile when it comes to our abilities, but really, you have to admit, we are very cool."

With a chuckle, I pointed to his room. "Time

for bed. I'll check the other rabbits and return shortly."

"Okay, if you need me, just give a yell."

The rabbits slumbered as I walked the aisles taking care not to disturb them. At the moment, all was well at Fur Bridge Farm. I gave a last look around before entering the gift and yarn shop, which was neat as a pin. A few handspun hanks of washed and dried yarn awaited winding. I set up the winder and swift to get started. The hank lay uncoiled across the countertop, ready to be mounted onto it. I gently wrapped the hank onto the swift that resembled an umbrella without its covering. Once it was set, I threaded the yarn onto the winder and began the process. There have been customers who prefer electric winders, but I've found hand cranking offered more control over how the yarn ended in a ball. After I'd completed rolling the hanks, I tucked the cushy balls into separate cubbyholes that held the same colors and type of wool.

Luscious-colored yarns were soft against my fingertips, leaving me to wonder why I didn't take time to knit or crochet. With the amount of work the rabbits were, I wouldn't give them up for anything and knew I wouldn't have enough time to devote to knitting. I turned to the bank deposit and paperwork Molly had left for me to handle.

Her day in the shop had been profitable between sales and registrations of new students interested in the art of wool spinning. Once the deposit was ready to go, I gave the building a once-over to make sure all was well, and then promised myself to spend time with Molly as she taught the students the basics of spinning and wheels. She'd taken a crash course from one of her mother's friends, which had been a godsend to me and the farm. The more she engaged the students, the more her guidance in class was talked about, which drove novices in to see what it was all about.

Once in the house, I checked on Bun and prepared to drive into Windermere to make a night deposit at the bank. It was a relief that I needn't drag Bun along, he was fast asleep.

With an effort to make little to no noise at all, I crept from the house and headed into town. It was fairly late, with few cars on the road, leaving me to scoot up to the night deposit box and slip the pouch inside it.

The ride home went smoothly. I turned into the drive and parked the car in its usual spot. Stars hung in the sky like tiny lanterns and the moon's face was clearly defined. I sat on the porch until mosquitoes discovered I was there. I made a hasty entrance into the kitchen for fear of being eaten alive by the tiny vicious bloodsuckers.

Walking past the phone, I noticed the message light blinked on and off and pushed the button to play the message. The voice belonged to a woman who said she was following up with people who had entered their rabbits for the show.

"My name is Vera Benedict, and I'm the senior organizer for the upcoming rabbit show. I hope I'm not calling too late, but since Evelyn has passed away, my workload has doubled. My purpose for calling is to ascertain whether you definitely will or will not be showing your rabbit, eh, Petra." Papers crinkled in the background before she left her phone number and asked that I call her in the morning.

From the tone of her voice, the harried manner in which she spoke, I assumed she wasn't happy to have Evelyn's work added to her own. It was understandable, this type of venue took careful planning and a crew who would carry their own weight. Not long ago I'd held an open house here at the farm to drum up business for me and Jessica. It had been quite a task, and we had been exhausted at the end of the day. I couldn't imagine setting up a slew of days, staff, entertainment, vendors, and all the rest of what was needed.

As the sun rose on Monday, so did I. An early start allowed me to address the many issues of being a farmer, even though I use the word *farmer* lightly. I didn't farm in the grower sense of farming. I raised rabbits instead, and though the job is fulfilling, the work is full-time. Fortunate enough to have a small, part-time staff, I had to be flexible concerning their schedules. They were teenagers, after all, and in school. Jason Lang, the newbie, had taken over where Ray Blackstone had left off. A bright young man of sixteen, he was responsible and took his duties to heart. He liked the rabbits and they responded to him. Rabbits are sociable animals, and even the rescued rabbits that had been brought to me were happy with him. His thoughtful manner brought a positive response from animals and humans alike.

Molly had the most experience of the two. She

worked hard, and had entered night classes at the same college Jessica had gone to for training as a veterinarian. Pleased with the way Molly had stepped up after the debacle we'd had earlier in the summer, I hoped her paycheck matched the amount of work and enthusiasm she exhibited. I didn't want to lose her if I could help it.

Jessica arrived as I fed the rabbits and cared for them. She pitched in to help, saying her first appointment wasn't until nine o'clock. Surprised, I asked why.

"Mr. Lindstrom has a dentist appointment. He likes to bring Ringer in early, but couldn't change his dental visit. His appointment starts a crazy day that will go on until late this afternoon. I'm swamped. Maybe when Molly comes in she'll be able to reschedule appointments so I won't be backed up if an animal has an emergency. I'm so terrible when it comes to appointments and that end of the business."

"I'll do my best to be available should you need me. Just give a holler, okay?"

She nodded and started to empty fecal trays. Of all the tasks I handled, it was my least favorite. But then, who would enjoy it? She must have caught my look because she grinned and said, "Stop dragging your feet and get over here. The sooner we get this over with, the better. I know how much you dislike this but it must be done. Isn't that what you preach to the help?"

"You're right. It goes much faster when there's someone to give me a hand. Thanks for that. I appreciate it."

We worked steadily for at least an hour or so to

get rabbits set for the morning. Then Jess and I cleaned up in the sink after removing our heavy work aprons. She went toward the clinic and I said I'd make breakfast if she hadn't had any. She gave a thumbs-up and went on her way.

We'd eaten, I had fed Bun, and then Jess and I sat on the porch in the cool morning air, sipping coffee.

"Jack came by when I was out with Bun yesterday. You're never going to guess what we talked about."

"Don't tell me, he wants you to stay out of his investigation or else."

"Wrong. He heard that Petra was going to be in the show and said that while I'm there, I should see what I can find out about everyone involved with it and how Evelyn was viewed by all and sundry."

"You're joking. He did not ask you to help him. I don't believe it for a second. Why do you really think he wants you on his team? He's always adamant about you staying out of police business."

"I know, I thought the same thing. At first I thought he was trying to catch me out about giving in to Carina's request. I didn't mention her and he didn't either, so it's safe to say he doesn't know about it. He's very interested in Evelyn and her background, how she handled contestant owners and fellow workers, and what people thought of her. Jack is of the opinion that Evelyn wasn't a very nice person. I could have told him that, but knew better than to say a word. I finally agreed to ask around without looking like a sleuth."

"That should be interesting to watch. When you

get into that mode, it's evident you won't stop until you achieve your goal." Jess checked her watch and leaned back in her chair, rocking slowly. "You will be careful, won't you?"

"I promise. After what happened to us this summer, I've learned a thing or two about safety. By the way, Petra is doing well with her tricks and acrobatics. She's so funny. I saw her do a few things at the birthday party Saturday. The kids cheered her on. Our training might pay off yet."

"Let's hope so. She's been so cooperative, even if she does get a snack when she gets the hang of what we're trying to teach her. She's quite smart."

Bun, who had nosed his way out by through the unlatched screen door, came forward, his ears straight up.

"I'm pretty darned smart, too, you know. I could have learned those tricks in half the time, that is, if I'd wanted to. Not wanting to be a show-off, I felt it better that Petra be the one getting the kudos."

Leaning down, I ruffled his fur. "Bun's pretty smart. It's too bad he isn't going to enter the contests to win. I know he could have managed to take home the winning ribbons. Petra will, though."

Sprawled on the porch, Bun watched a plump bumblebee flit from one flowerpot to the next in the unhurried way bumblebees have. *"I'm like the bee. He surely has superpowers to find the best flowers and get the most out of each one. He's brilliant. I have the same ability. Mine include far more important things than prize winning and adoration from a crowd of strangers. That's not what I do. Mystery solving is what I specialize in."*

Unable to make a snide remark about how humble he could be, I held back my laughter and gave his ears a light tweak. He eyed me for a second before he followed the bumblebee's progress. I'd made a comment without uttering a sound, and knew I'd hear about my actions later.

The sun was rising higher by the moment, meaning we had to get back to work before long. I cleared our breakfast remains while Jessica went into the barn to ready Petra for her morning workout. The dishwasher full, I pressed the start button and was about to join Jess when the phone rang.

"Hello?"

"Good morning, this is Vera Benedict. I hope I haven't disturbed you. I will be in town today and wondered if we could meet to go over a few things. I realize this is your first show, and want you to get the most out of it."

Quick to sum up my responsibilities for the day, I agreed to meet and invited her to the farm. Vera asked for directions. Once we set a time, she hung up and I went to work.

Ecstatic when going through her paces, Petra had gotten quite good at fence and hoop jumping, along with racing to the finish line. Her long fur ruffled as she ran. It was beautiful, silky, and so very soft. I'd have to let Molly know she couldn't be shorn until the event was over. If Petra was a contestant in a beauty pageant, I was certain she'd win first prize.

Jessica offered Petra treats after she completed each thing on the list while Bun watched with a running monologue. You'd think it was a horse race, not a rabbit competition. I petted Petra after she'd leapt over the final hurdle.

In the playground with the other rabbits, Bun ran through the clear tunnel that wrapped around the barn walls and out through a thin trapdoor to the outside tunnel into another playground outside. Racing through it gave the rabbits much needed exercise. They were never just left in their cages, not here. It was one of the reasons Fur Bridge Farm had a great reputation.

A knock sounded on the gift shop door. I hurried to let Vera in and welcomed her to the farm. She gazed at the yarns, goods, and spinning wheels set up for class, then asked if she could see the rabbits. Knowing her intention was to see if they were well cared for, I gladly invited her in. Walking through the barn, we discussed the rabbits, their care, and then Vera focused on the playground that led into the exercise area.

Tall, gangly, and frazzle-haired, Vera had a bold personality, and her love of rabbits was as apparent as mine. A frank woman, she didn't miss a thing. Zoned in on Petra, she asked if she could pet her. I fetched the rabbit and handed her over.

"She's quite wonderful. Is this the rabbit you have entered?"

"Yes, we've been training her to handle the rigors of the competition."

"Your reputation precedes you, Juliette. I can see why your rabbits are so popular. They have everything they need, including comfort and love. It's written all over your face."

It's the first time I'd been complimented by someone who adored these critters as much as I did. "Thank you, they are wonderful and keep Jessica and me quite busy."

Entering the barn, Jess reached out her hand and shook Vera's. I introduced them and mentioned Jessica's clinic just off the gift shop.

Talking about the clinic as she led Vera into the waiting room, Jess explained, "You're welcome to take a tour. Mine is small with a couple of examination rooms and this waiting area. I've only been open for business for a short while, but I'm quite booked up with appointments. As a matter of fact, here comes the next patient." Greeting the dog and her owner, Jessica said good-bye and led them into a room.

We returned to the gift shop, sat, and talked about the show. Vera went over the rules, the setup, and how competitions were held. There was no doubt her organization skills were amazing. I made a few notes on a pad I'd taken from the counter and when there was a brief lull, I said, "I am so sorry about Evelyn's unfortunate death. I know she worked with you and the others to make the show the best it could be. You must miss her." Okay, so it was a gambit, so what? I wanted to know how Evelyn was thought of by those who worked closely with her.

"Thank you for those kind words. Evelyn didn't deserve to die, but she was a mean-spirited woman who treated the show's participants and workers poorly. Even the vendors weren't fond of her."

Startled a bit Vera's outspokenness considering she'd only just met me, I realized she was indeed frank. Our meeting ended when Vera received a phone call and talked while she left the shop. As I turned I noticed Mrs. Slade and her dog walking along the path from the clinic. She said hello and opened the SUV's passenger door for Lady to jump in. With no other patients waiting, I went to see Jessica.

"How did the meeting go?"

"Vera is an interesting person. I was taken aback by her when I offered condolences over Evelyn's death. As Sherlock Holmes would say, 'the game is on.' Vera told me how the people who work at these shows and those who participate in them didn't like Evelyn. I guess she was quite rude and rotten to everyone. I know she threatened me at Carina's, so I shouldn't be surprised her attitude ran over into other areas of her life."

We walked into the barn, returned the rabbits to their cages, and I scooped Bun off the floor.

"That was enlightening for you then, and it's a great place to start your investigation. Was Evelyn married?"

I shrugged and said, "I'll ask Carina, she must know. I'll give her a call later."

With a glance at her watch, Jess said, "Got to get back to the clinic, I think my next patient is about to arrive."

"Sure, let me know if I can help in any way."

CHAPTER FOUR

"*We could always find out where she lived and check it out by being sneaky and such. If she isn't married. I heard that woman, Vera whatshername, say Evelyn was beastly to others. I'm sure someone wanted her dead, if not lots of people. We might have our work cut out for us.*"

"I thought so, too. After Vera made it clear how much Evelyn was disliked by so many, it seemed a reasonable assumption. Luckily, I'll be there with Petra, that way I won't look weird if I ask questions."

"*I don't mind going with you.*"

"Having to handle Petra will be enough. I'll engage the entrants by walking the show floor with her in tow. She doesn't mind being carried, which is a plus."

His disappointment evident by the drooping of his ears, Bun's whiskers jittered a bit before he admitted it would be difficult to deal with him and Petra at the same time.

We went into the house. I gave him some fruit and veg to snack on and filled his water tray to keep him occupied while I called Carina.

She answered on the first ring.

"Hi, Carina, it's Juliette. Do you know if Evelyn was married?"

"No, she was single. Why do you ask?"

"Just wondering. Knowing that leaves out the possibility of her being killed by her spouse. I'll be attending the upcoming rabbit show that's scheduled to take place here in Windermere, and have found out Evelyn, who worked for the show organizers, wasn't liked very much. There's a chance she might have pushed the limits of her power too far and was killed because of it. I'll keep you posted."

"Do that. Thanks, Juliette."

I set the phone down and looked down at Bun, hunched at my feet, awaiting confirmation of whether the woman had been married. I said she hadn't.

"Then the show is the best place to look for the killer. I do wish I was going. Maybe if I hadn't refused to . . ."

"Don't think about that. You never would have liked being a contestant. You'd be unable to use your superpowers to investigate if you were exhausted from all that would be demanded of you. If I can somehow take you with me, then I will."

Skipping around the room, Bun came to a stop when Sheriff Carver knocked on the door.

"Hm, I wonder what he wants now."

"Me too," I murmured, and answered the door.

"Hey, Jack. Come on in. Coffee?"

"No, thanks, I stopped by to make sure all is set

for you to attend that rabbit show. You will be going?"

"Petra is ready to compete, and I've decided how to chat up the other contestants and the vendors. The help shouldn't be a problem either. I'll figure it all out when I get there. Oh, the organizer and I met this morning. When I offered my condolences for Evelyn's death, she told me how viciously she'd treated everyone at those shows. I guess she wasn't popular with anyone. I don't think I would enjoy living that way. What makes people cruel, Jack?"

"There are many reasons, but some folks just like to push people around and use their power to do it."

"Oh. Well, we're ready for this little adventure with Petra and at least I won't have to put up with Evelyn."

He eyed me for a second, ran the brim of his police hat around in his hand, and then softly asked, "Did she try to boss you around at the party?"

"Be very careful in answering that question."

"Not at all. She never came near the rabbit pen or the children, for that matter. I have no idea why she showed up at all. She was just there when I arrived at Carina's." Hoping I sounded as innocent as a newborn kit, I watched Jack's reaction closely.

"Those furry little critters do keep you busy."

I noticed Molly and Jason had arrived, and said, "I have to get back to work. If this investigation thing is going to take place, I have to ask if the high school kids can work extra hours."

"I'll see you around, then, Jules." He put his hat on and left.

Bun and I went to greet the help. They were chatting and grinned happily when we caught up with them.

"Jason has a request," Molly blurted.

I looked at him and raised a brow. "What?"

"Can I work more hours? My classes are only half days, and I could use the experience, and the money. I really like this job, Jules."

It was as though manna from Heaven had dropped at my feet.

"I'm pleased to hear that. I wanted to ask both of you to help me out by working extra hours." I raised a hand when Molly opened her mouth to speak. "It would only be temporary for you, Molly, unless you want more hours. If you can't take on anything extra, I completely understand."

I turned to Jason. "You certainly can have more hours. Why don't we go into the shop and figure what works best?"

Jason grinned. "Thanks, Jules, I appreciate the opportunity."

Her face beaming, Molly said, "Me too. College is expensive and my parents can't afford the extras I need for my classes. Thanks a lot."

Scheduling their hours was easier than I had anticipated. They made note of their new schedule, and then went to work.

Before I left the shop, I asked, "Molly, do you think you could fit one more person into one of the spinning classes?"

She thought for a minute before checking the student list and looked up with a grin. "Who wants to join the fun?"

"Meredith Carver."

"She's such a nice lady. Spends a fortune here on yarn and oddments, too. I'll call and let her know there's an opening." Counting the spinning wheels, Molly nodded with a look of satisfaction on her face. "We have one that isn't being used. Mrs. Mason had to drop out. She and her husband leave for Italy sometime this week and they'll be gone for at least a month. Meredith has perfect timing."

With that agreed upon, I left knowing Molly was more than capable of handling just about anything that came her way. I would make sure she wasn't in over her head with all the responsibilities she'd taken on.

Four days before the rabbit show began, Jessica walked into the kitchen, her face filled with concern.

"What's wrong?"

"Come take a look at Petra."

I followed Jess into the barn and watched her take Petra from her cage and put her on the table that held a weight scale. Petra sneezed, her eyes were as runny as her nose, and I was sure she had a common bacterial respiratory disease, better known in rabbit circles as *the snuffles,* that can be treated with antibiotics.

"Would that be a case of the snuffles?"

"It would. You know what this means, don't you, Jules?"

A voice from behind me said, *"She won't be competing."*

"She won't be competing?" I repeated Bun's words with disappointment.

"No, it's important that she begin treatment right away and be made as comfortable as possible, so she can get well. No playing with the other bunnies until she feels better."

Disheartened by Petra's circumstances, I agreed with Jessica. "Okay, I'll call Vera and let her know Petra can't attend the show. Let's get her started on medication, and I'll do what I can to make sure she's comfy."

"Deal. I knew you'd feel that way, and that you were looking forward to the show and Petra's chances of taking the show's best ribbons. Sorry, Jules."

"It isn't anyone's fault. She's come down with, um, uh . . ." I snapped my fingers a few times, searching my brain for the answer. "An ear and sinus infection?"

With a broad smile, Jess nodded. "I'll run tests on her to make sure she isn't having an allergic reaction to something. I really don't think she is, but we should be certain."

Jess removed Petra from the table and took her into the clinic. I sanitized the table and then followed Jessica, as did Bun. Jess was far enough ahead to not hear me, so I whispered, "You should remain here. She might be contagious and I wouldn't want you or any of the other rabbits to become infected."

He backed away, turned, and ran up the walk toward the house. For once, Bun had taken me seriously. I wished that would happen more often.

In the examining room with Petra, Jess had

begun to draw blood, then check Petra's eyes, tear ducts, and nasal passages. She stepped back, placed her equipment in a stainless steel bowl, and washed her hands thoroughly.

"She must be kept away from the other rabbits. If she tests positive for the infection, she could spread it to the others, or we could by passing the bacteria through handling her and then touching the rabbits. We could also carry it on our clothes. I'll set her cage up in the last cubicle, away from the others, and we'll make sure she doesn't pass this on. That is, if she's infected. If it's only an allergy, then she can be left near the others."

"Thanks, Jess. I appreciate your being on-site. It makes things easier all the way round."

"The test results should be ready soon, so feel free to wash your clothes and disinfect shoes, scrub your hands well, and get on with whatever you were about to do."

Hoping and praying Petra had simply developed an allergy, I did what Jessica advised and left the building through the shop entrance, then entered my kitchen by way of the front door. I undressed and tossed the lot, including my sneakers, into the washing machine, then showered and changed into a new set of work wear as well as a pair of fresh shoes. Never let it be said that I put my rabbits in danger of becoming ill. They were too dear to me for that.

From Bun's room, I heard, *"Is it safe to come out now?"*

"It is. We won't go near Petra until we have her test results. I'll go into the barn to start feeding and cleaning, and will avoid Petra's cage. I want you to stay in here, okay? All equipment and the tunnels will be washed down before the other rabbits are allowed out of their cages."

His ears drooped. *"I hope Petra will be okay. She's a fine rabbit and Molly really loves her. I'll do as you ask, but tell me what Jessica says."*

Walking into the breezeway, I said over my shoulder, "I will."

Glad it was still early, I got started and worked feverishly to catch up. Usually, the rabbits are fed, and their cages are freshened up by now. I hurried through the cleaning process, after filling water bins and handing out lettuce-wrapped food pockets. The rabbits jumped toward them as I hooked each one to individual cage ports. I added timothy hay and food pellets as I made the rounds.

By midmorning, I had finished the first part of rabbit care. Since Bun would be lonely, I went into the house, made a pot of tea, and sat on the porch with him at my feet. The phone in my hand, I dialed Vera's number.

"Vera Benedict, how can I help you, Juliette?"

"Hi, Vera, do you have a minute to talk?"

"What's going on?"

"I have to withdraw Petra from the show. She's a bit under the weather, and I wouldn't want to take a chance of her becoming worse or infecting any of the other contestants. She just started feeling poorly this morning."

"I'm sorry to hear that, it's very disappointing. I do hope she recovers soon."

"Me too. Jessica is treating her now. I'm grateful for your understanding."

The phone line was silent for a moment, causing me to wonder if she had hung up, until she suddenly started speaking.

"There's a position open if you'd be interested in taking it on. One of my show judges had to bow out due to a family emergency. He's had to leave for Iowa or some such place. If you'd be willing to step into his spot, I'd appreciate it. I can go over the rules of the position so you'll know how to judge the games and then the rabbits themselves. What do you say?"

My interest piqued by the offer, I quickly accepted. "I'd be happy to do that for you. Can I bring my pet rabbit along? He's very well behaved, and won't get in the way."

"That will be fine. Be here the day after tomorrow and I'll show you around. You will need a complete explanation of what the position entails. I'm pleased to think you can be a judge, you have such a great reputation and your rabbits are marvelous creatures. I'll see you around eleven that morning at the Windermere Exhibition Hall. Don't be late."

The call ended and I leaned toward Bun, who had heard every word I'd said. He probably heard what Vera had said as well, but unsure, I whispered to him that he could accompany me to the show.

"I won't have to compete, will I? Cause if I do, you can count me out."

"You'll be my second pair of eyes and can keep your ears to the ground. That way we'll be aware of all that goes on. Can you do that?"

"Sure can, and I won't even have to work hard at it. Superpowers and all, you know what I mean?"

"Mm, I do."

I heard Jessica call my name and shot out of the chair to greet her at the door as she came through the breezeway.

Breathless, I asked, "Are the results in?"

"They are. I'm happy to say Petra does not have an infection, she has an allergy. I checked her cage before coming in to tell you and noticed she has a new toy. Since we haven't been feeding or treating her any differently, and nothing else has changed, other than the toy, I feel it's safe to say she's developed an allergy to it."

"She's not seriously ill and isn't contagious?"

Jess shook her head.

Delighted and relieved by the news, I hugged her. "Can Petra go back to her cage, so I can feed her? She must be hungry. I saved her food pocket."

"She's already there, and I gave her the pocket. I also cleaned her cage and added alfalfa hay, too. She's going to be fine. I wouldn't recommend she go to the show, she might not feel up to it. I'll keep an eye on her nasal passages and eye ducts in case they become clogged."

"This is such wonderful news. I've been so worried about the idea of having snuffles spread among the other rabbits, and Petra being ill. Are you hungry? You've had a busy morning."

"Yes, on both counts. Is lunch ready?"

"No, but sandwiches will do, won't they?"

She nodded cheerfully.

I gathered sandwich-making supplies while Jess set the table.

Over lunch, we chatted about how Petra's allergy issue would be dealt with. Then I related Vera's offer on judging the competitions.

"I'm able to take Bun along, the students will fill in the hours I'm away, and this presents the perfect opportunity to investigate Evelyn's background. She could have been killed by someone from the show, not necessarily one of Carina's friends at the birthday party."

"This will be exciting for you. Stay out of trouble, it's the only warning I'll offer you. Don't worry about the workload here. I'll help out in the mornings before you leave. I bet Bun will enjoy the goings-on and watching the rabbits engage in the games."

"It will be interesting, especially since I don't have to get involved in them."

"I'm sure you're right, Jess." I looked at the clock and realized it was time for the rabbits to exercise. We turned toward the barn as the phone rang, and I motioned Jess to go ahead without me. The caller ID listed Sheriff Carver.

"Hello, Jack. What's up?"

"Not much in the way of finding Evelyn's killer. Have you made any progress?"

"None to speak of. The rabbit show begins in a few days and since my rabbit won't be competing, I've been asked to be a judge. It'll give me a better chance to scope out contestant owners, the workers, and even the vendors."

"Just be careful. I don't want any problems like you had the last time you investigated a death."

"I promise not to be foolish. I still get rattled when I think of what could have happened to me and Bun. What did happen was bad enough."

"Good, I'm glad to hear you'll be sensible. Oh,

uh, my wife tells me she's been accepted into the wool spinning class that Molly Perkins teaches at your shop."

I heard his hearty sigh. "Juliette, you'll put me in the poorhouse one of these days."

"Jack, you would never deny Meredith anything, so stop whining."

He snickered and said good-bye. I went in search of Jessica.

CHAPTER FIVE

Low-beamed and sprawling, the Windermere Exhibition Hall bustled with activity. With Bun tucked inside his sling, I murmured for him to stay put and behave.

I hadn't planned on jumping out and running away like an out-of-control marble. I'd have thought you would give me more credit than that. " Bun's whiskers jittered a tad as he craned his neck upward to look at me.

I smoothed the fur on his head and went indoors. The hall was a perfect venue for this type of event with all the rooms large enough to hold just about anything. The rabbits would undoubtedly enjoy the space for their contests. We took in everything as we strode through the crowd. Energy filled the air as attendees worked to make the most of the assigned spaces.

Beyond that was another, larger room designated for vendors. By this time, Bun rambled on about vendors and competitors alike, insisting we'd gather information from all of them. I had reached the same conclusion and wasn't above using Fur Bridge Farm to inveigle my way into everyone's confidence. The more information and gossip, the better.

Returning to the entrance, I noticed recently arrived rabbit owners and vendors stood in line to receive instruction packets and name badges. During the comings and goings, I became aware of the differences in the rabbit owners. Their attire and attitudes caught my eye first. Some were well-heeled and had haughty attitudes, while others dressed comfortably and acted down-to-earth. I wondered if the Westminster Dog Show was like this and hid my grin at the absurdity of the idea.

"You're laughing, I can feel it. What's so funny?" Bun followed my line of sight, and instantly realized why I had laughed.

"You compared them to the Westminster show? Don't be ridiculous. This show beats that hands down."

Now who was being ridiculous?

Many entrants hailed one another like old friends, while others raised a brow, and peered down at them for their frivolity while remaining aloof. I'd have been one of the friendly ones, no snobbery for me.

Bun, still fascinated by it all, kept up his monologue as though I couldn't or didn't see what took place. I didn't mind, since he often noticed details that I didn't, or couldn't, as a human being.

We found Vera at the edge of the hall commanding her workers to do this or that. I stood by until she was finished. After a brief hello, Vera ordered an escort to take us through the building to introduce me to the vendors and entrants. She looked back at me and said, "I'll see you afterward, I'm overwhelmed right now. Evelyn couldn't have chosen a worse time to . . . uh, never mind." With that, she marched off like a drill sergeant.

My escort explained the system used for setting up the show, where help could be found if needed, and then introduced himself as David Murphy. We shook hands, he peered at Bun and then smiled.

"That's a beauty of a rabbit you've got there. Showing him, are you?"

"No, he's just along for the ride. No pun intended."

A chuckle followed, and he began to initiate my meet and greet when we reached the first rabbit station. More than half the stations were set up with rabbits in hutch-style cages, eating alfalfa hay or snacking on delicious morsels of some kind. Other owners were in the process of unpacking to settle their rabbit and merely nodded when we arrived at their spot.

After that, my kind, middle-aged, portly escort steered me toward the vendor room. His black hair, laced with white strands, flowed past his shoulders. He wasn't handsome, nor ugly, just showed signs of exhaustion instead. I wondered if he worked all the shows and decided to ask.

"I do most of them. Vera is a hard taskmaster, but she has to be or chaos would take over."

We'd reached the vendors, who were ready to sell a variety of goods to everyone. Bun almost swooned when viewing the tempting displays. Not just bunny snacks, mind you, but rabbit beds (like those used for cats), rugs, toys, games intended to entertain rabbits, along with feeding dishes and a slew of water containers. There were plenty of items to ask about and possibly purchase once the tour with David ended. Engaging vendors over their merchandise would fit in perfectly with my plan.

On our way back to the main hall, David veered off to the left, guiding me by the elbow. The room had a sign designating it for competitions. Pointing out the judges' stand, David explained the importance of unbiased judging. He needn't have worried, I wasn't friends with any of the rabbit owners, nor was I attached to their rabbits. That's about as unbiased as I could be.

"Winners are awarded after every competition and the best-of-show rabbit is determined on the final day, an hour before the show closes. Welcome to the crew, Juliette, I'm sure you'll do just fine."

"Thanks, I appreciate your confidence in me. This is my first judging experience and I find it all quite interesting."

"Oh, it will be that and more," he said. The hint of mischief in his eyes caused me to wonder if there was more to the world of rabbit shows than what lay on the surface. Hm.

"Before you leave, what position did Evelyn Montgomery hold here?"

"A responsible one, like the rest of us. You have to work hard to maintain a show."

Okay, so was this guy a politician, or simply good at sidestepping an issue he'd rather not discuss? I chose the latter, since he in no way looked or acted like a politician.

Gently, I mentioned how sad it was that such a vibrant woman had been killed.

I must have hit a home run. He looked me straight in the eye and remarked, "She will not be missed by anyone here. Not the contestants, the workers, or the committee."

"I'm surprised to hear that. I was under the impression Evelyn was a mover and shaker in this business."

"The only thing she did was make everyone miserable." He hesitated, and then said, "You seem like a sincere person with good sense, Juliette. Take my advice and refrain from asking questions about Evelyn that might be misconstrued and your intentions misread."

Taking his warning to heart, I looked down at Bun and then said, "Thank you for the advice, David. I appreciate it. I apologize, I was so shocked when I found Evelyn's body, well, never mind that, I'll keep questions to myself."

David nodded and left me on my own. Instantly, Bun and I returned to the rabbit stands, giving each one our full attention. It was then that I mentioned ownership of Fur Bridge Farm and that Jessica Plain had set up an animal clinic. I recommended her services and asked questions about their contestant. My gambit worked, as with any pet owner, answers were freely given with profound preening over their pet. This might not be Westminster, but by golly, these folks adored their rabbits. Just like I did mine.

Curious as to why I hadn't entered a rabbit, I said her allergy had kicked in and she wasn't up to competing. The answer seemed to be accepted, so I offered it to anyone who asked. Having established a rapport with many of the rabbit owners, we made our way through the showrooms.

We slowly made the rounds as Bun harped on asking questions about Evelyn. With care to avoid being seen talking to the rabbit, I took a seat on the nearest bench, pretended to cough, and lightly covered my mouth with my hand. "First off, we've been warned against doing so. Secondly, it wouldn't be smart to begin our friendships with these people by jumping into Evelyn's death immediately upon meeting them, and thirdly, we have time to find out what we want to know." I had given a slight cough between the first, second, and third reasons why we'd wait.

Not one to be put off, Bun said, *"Let's check out the vendors. They have some cool products. Did you see those beds? They might answer our questions, too."*

Rising from the bench, we wandered the showroom and viewed merchandise by way of the left side of the room. Perusing the materials offered to make rabbits more comfortable and happier, I stopped at a booth to read a brochure on why this or that was the perfect must-have for any rabbit.

"I think I need that bed, the blue one over there." His right ear pitched to the left, drawing my attention from the brochure.

While the salesman was busy convincing a couple that his products were allergy-free and the best-made in America, I whispered to Bun, "You aren't getting a new bed."

"Jules, I really need that blue bed. Mine is lumpy and uncomfortable. Pleeeaaase?"

That was the moment when the salesman turned

his attention to us after he handed the couple over to an underling. I offered him a smile and a firm handshake, using Fur Bridge Farm as a way to start a conversation. After all, if the man saw me as a rabbit farm owner, then my credibility would climb, and his brain would make a *cha-ching* noise when he figured I had money to spend.

I was right in my assumption. I could tell by his greedy smile and peering eyes as he looked at me and studied Bun.

"I'm happy that you returned to my booth after your tour with David. Fur Bridge Farm has a spotless reputation. You must be proud of that."

Wow, he'd covered all the bases in one fell swoop.

"I am very proud." Looking at the beds Bun was determined I buy, I pointed out the blue one. "Could I get a closer look at that bed?"

"Certainly." Elvin Werfel, according to the name on his badge, slid the bed onto the counter and stepped back, waiting for me to look it over.

The fabric was soft and smooth to the touch, unlike the corduroy bed that Bun slept on—and yes, he is quite spoiled. It would be a nice addition to his comfort.

His nose working overtime, Bun's whiskers bobbed up and down as he sniffed in the essence of the fabric. *"Nice, very nice, indeed. I think you should get this for me."*

"The fabric is very nice and the bed appears to be well made. Was this manufactured in America?"

"It certainly was. My company is built on American-manufactured merchandise. We don't carry any merchandise from outside the US."

Well, crap. I didn't want to buy it on the first day. If it had been manufactured outside the country, then I could have begged off from the purchase. There is nothing wrong with merchandise from other countries, it's simply a matter of personal taste. I liked to support what was American-made and that's all there was to it.

"That's great to know. We have two days before the show opens, and I'm a judge for the games, so I'll be around all week. If you don't mind waiting until the end of the show, I'll buy one of these beds from you. Thanks so much." Before he could reply, I sped across the room and stopped at another booth.

The same pillow-style beds were stacked on a shelf behind the salesman. In contrast to Elvin Werfel, this man was dressed in khaki jeans and a plaid shirt, his sleeves rolled up to his elbows. Wavy brown hair and a smile the size of Utah set the outfit off completely. Jim Brody's image reminded me of a country living ad, which was bound to draw in those who weren't of the hoity-toity group. Elvin probably handled that bunch.

I glanced at the badge pinned to his shirt and saw his company name and logo, You Need It, We Got It, beneath his name. I ordered from You Need It quite often and was satisfied with their service. He read my name badge, and then asked if he could pet Bun.

Before I could answer, Bun said, *"Of course he can. I'm feeling a bit rejected right about now."*

I nodded, and watched as he smoothed Bun's furry head, and then ran his hands over Bun's ears. This part of the petting was one of Bun's favorite things. I had asked if his ears got itchy, but he had said no, that he liked having his ears rubbed. When Jim drew his hand away and then shook mine, Bun's eyes, which had been closed, suddenly popped open.

"You're from Fur Bridge Farm, aren't you?" Jim asked.

"Yes, I do a lot of business with your company. It's a pleasure to meet the man behind the scenes."

"How are things at the farm?"

"Better than ever. My rabbit numbers have dwindled a bit from people selecting a rabbit for themselves, though. I will probably get more if the rescue people need me to take any they've rescued."

His brows rose a tad as a look of surprise crossed his features. "I wasn't aware that was part of your rabbit care practices. How does that work?"

I gave him a brief explanation of what took place, how the rabbits arrived and what Jessica and I did to acclimate these poor souls into our farm. I must have said the right thing, because he withdrew a folder from a briefcase that was on the chair behind him and handed me a packet of information.

"I would like to offer you the opportunity to apply for a grant from my company. It must be very expensive to handle all that comes your way, especially with those creatures who have been abused. If you fill out the forms, I'll take them back to the office with me and put them in the right hands."

Astounded by Jim's offer, I readily took the packet and tucked it inside the sling, behind Bun.

I lingered a while, discussing his company and their stock. He, too, only supplied merchandise made in America. "To my knowledge, we sell nothing but the best to our buyers. I firmly believe that though it might cost a little more, American goods can't be beat. My representatives and I choose our stock wisely, or at least we try."

"Mr. Werfel said he only carries American-manufactured goods, as well. Is this a new trend for companies?"

He glanced over my shoulder, took a quick look at the booth I had mentioned, and then snorted. "Elvin endeavors to buy the best, but he does trade with several companies that manufacture overseas. I don't. If it isn't made in the States, then I refuse to carry it."

"Nice to know."

"Have you resided in Windermere for very long?"

"All my life. Why?"

"You must know Meredith Carver, then. She's married to Sheriff Carver."

"I know them very well. Meredith is a great customer. She buys the handspun yarns I carry in the gift shop at the farm."

He reached toward the shelf to his right, and pulled what appeared to be a knit baby beanie from the shelf. "Were you aware that she hand knits these for pets of all kinds? Even rabbits?"

I could tell my jaw dropped and quickly closed my mouth. "She never said a word." I took the hat and studied the design she'd knitted. I recognized the yarn as having come from my own shelves and was quick to say so.

Jim nodded. "Please let her know I was asking after her. She's a pleasant person."

"I will. She's enrolled in a yarn spinning class at the farm. Maybe this will be the way she uses the yarn she'll spin."

He leaned forward and murmured, "Her husband is investigating the death of a woman who worked with this show organization for several years. Did Meredith tell you about it?"

Rather than my having to bring Evelyn's name into the conversation, an opportunity had presented itself. Grateful for it, I sent a silent thank-you to the powers that be.

I murmured, "Evelyn Montgomery was my contact for this affair." I waved my hand around at the show. "Meredith doesn't usually talk about Jack's police work, I'm not sure he discusses it with her."

"That's a possibility."

"Was Evelyn easy to work with?" I hoped my expression was as innocent as my question sounded to my ears.

"Not ever. She barked orders at everyone and was obnoxious, too, but she liked the rabbits."

Bun's whiskers jittered. *"That seems to be the overall opinion. Now, are you going to buy a pillow bed or not?"*

I ignored him and wondered if a tirade would follow because of it. He began to complain once I handed the knit beanie back to Jim. I resettled the sling to let Bun know I heard him and wasn't pleased.

He suddenly stopped mid-complaint, his ears all jittery. A clear sign he'd heard something I hadn't. But then, I hadn't paid attention to what was said by people walking the room. My focus was on any information I could gather from Jim without seeming pushy.

I glanced at my watch, said a hasty good-bye, and promised to stop by again. It was way past lunchtime and Bun's jittery ears meant he might have seen or heard an important tidbit.

We left the room. I found a bench and again pretended to cough with my hand lightly covering my mouth. "What's up?"

"People are talking about you taking Evelyn's place. One of them said you should be careful not to end up like she did."

My heart began to hammer against my rib cage. Here we go again, another dangerous situation.

As if he could read my mind, Bun said, *"Surely you knew there would be some level of danger involved?"*

My head tipped downward, again I gave a light cough, then whispered, "Mm, I suppose you're right. Did you see who made the remark?"

"No, it was a man with a deep voice."

I rose from the bench, petted Bun's head, and said aloud, "It's time to return home." I made our way to the front entrance, considering what Bun had heard and realized we must be discreet when speaking of Evelyn's demise for fear we would enter dangerous ground.

My car sat in the staff section of the building's lot. I opened the passenger door and let Bun out of his sling. He hopped into the front seat, then the back seat, and then back into the front. He hadn't gotten to exercise all day. Closing his door, I went around the front of the car and got into the driver's seat.

"It sure has been a long day. I'm exhausted and quite hungry."

"I'm hungry, too, we'll eat as soon as we get to the farm. You're lucky to have had a free ride all day. My feet are tired, I can tell you that. That building is much larger than I thought and walking it with you in the sling is tiring."

"I'm not that heavy. Besides, my being with you shouldn't bother you in the least."

Certain he was insulted by my remark, I explained I hadn't mean it that way, but meant the day seemed to go on forever.

Mollified, Bun stretched out on the seat and closed his eyes. The moment we arrived at the farm, he jumped up to peer out the side window.

CHAPTER SIX

Several cars sat outside the gift shop. All was quiet until Bun and I entered the building. Spinning wheels hummed as they spun hanks of wool into yarn. Their whirring faint, but noticeable. The sight of such glorious colors caught my eye. Some newly spun yarn was ready and had been set aside for washing. Molly slowly walked the room, keeping an eye on the progress made by the students. Meredith Carver was one of them.

I waved to Molly when she noticed me and then went into the barn. Bun jumped from my arms and raced through the breezeway. I heard the sound of the leather flap as it slapped against the edges of the wooden door after he dove through it into the kitchen. Similar to a dog or cat entry flap, I had fashioned mine of leather to secure it at night should Bun decide to go walk about.

Bun rarely did that anymore, now that he felt safe in his life. He'd been abused by his former owner, and was rescued from dire circumstances.

After Jessica and I had worked with him for some time, he had relaxed and become part of my household, buddies in the best sense of the word. Not long after he came into my life, I realized he could indeed talk to me through telepathy. At first, I'd thought my marbles had gone astray, but eventually reality set in and we've communicated ever since.

His bowl filled with food, I set fresh water alongside it. I left Bun to eat and had a quick snack before I returned to the barn.

A schedule attached to a clipboard hung from a nail in the wall next to the phone. I scanned the list and readied feed for the rabbits as Jessica came in.

She hauled a bag of pellets from the shelf, and asked, "How did it go?"

"We've had an interesting day. I met the owner of You Need It today. He offered me the chance to apply for a grant from his company. I left the packet in the car, but will fetch it and take a look later. The farm could use grant funds."

Her eyes widened. "Are you in financial distress?"

"Not at all, it's a matter of keeping money coming in for repairs to be made without a bank loan, should they be needed."

"Whew, I was worried for a minute."

By this time, we had fed the rabbits and were at the fruit, veggie, and water refill stage. The rabbits feasted on their meal. Even Petra munched away.

"Petra seems to feel better. I can't begin to tell you how relieved I am that her ailment wasn't associated with snuffles."

"She's a lucky one."

Having returned to the front of the barn, we organized the bags of pellets and then worked on moving the bales of hay to create space when a delivery would arrive. We'd cleaned our hands and heard the chatter of women, a sign the class had ended. I looked at the clock, it was going on five o'clock.

"Shall we join the students?" I asked Jess, and opened the door.

We stood at the door's edge and saw everyone compare one another's efforts to spin a skein of yarn. I gave Jess an elbow in the ribs and pointed to Meredith.

Captivated by the yarn spun by the student next to her, Meredith spoke animatedly. I swear her hands were moving as fast as her wheel had. "Your work is so lovely, how long have you spun?"

"About two months now. Molly's a good teacher, very patient and she's willing to help out when we all get stuck and have no idea how to rectify the problem."

"She's wonderful, she really is." Meredith turned toward Molly, who was headed in my and Jessica's direction. When Meredith saw us, she came forward, waving her hand in greeting.

The two women stood side by side, both talking at once. I raised a hand and they went silent, then glanced at each other with a grin. Molly motioned for Meredith to speak first.

"Thank you. I have enjoyed this class. I won't have to give up my seat if the other student returns, though, will I?

Before I could say she wouldn't, Molly said, "Not

at all. You're a natural, Mrs. Carver. I'm very pleased at how well you did, it being your first class, and all."

Meredith became flustered, and her face turned a deep shade of pink. "I must get home, I want to tell Jack all about the class. I know he'll want to hear what I've learned so far."

Jess and I nodded at the same time. It was possible we both thought his wanting to hear all about the class was the last thing Jack might have on his mind.

Meredith drew me aside. Molly and Jessica wandered the room looking at all the spinning stations and the progress made. I gave Meredith my full attention, especially when she asked, "Were you at the exhibition hall today?"

"Yes, I'll be judging the contests."

"There are vendors at those events, too. You'll have a chance to speak with Jim Brody, he owns You Need It. You must have ordered from there, am I right? Well, anyway, he knew Evelyn better than most since she worked for him part-time. They weren't romantically involved, of course, he's simply adept at getting people to gossip or tell him anything he would like to know. He could be a good place to start your investigation. You are investigating, aren't you?"

Unwilling to admit I'd already spoken to Jim about Evelyn, I said, "I often order supplies from Jim's company. As for gossip, I'm glad you mentioned that. I'll see what I can find out from him concerning Evelyn. She was certainly on the low end of the popularity scale with rabbit owners, the staff, and show organizers." I put my hand on her arm and softly said, "It's important that I help Jack with Evelyn's death."

"He mentioned you agreed to be his eyes and ears. Most people won't tell an officer anything." She patted my shoulder lightly. "You're a sweet person, Juliette. Be careful, okay?"

Having had her say, Meredith took my nod as her answer and left for home. The other students had gone out the door during Meredith's chatter. Molly, who had tried to cover a yawn, and Jessica appeared worn out.

I said, "It's time for both of you to go home. I'll put things in order. Thanks for your help, Molly, and you, too, Jessica. I hope these extra hours aren't going to be a problem."

Both women shook their heads and went on their way. I straightened the shop before I tended to the cash register. I hadn't expected a deposit, and was pleasantly surprised that Molly had filled out a deposit slip and clipped money to it. Her neat handwritten receipts stated who bought what and for how much, who had paid for this class and who had paid a month in advance. Happily, I took the deposit bag and drove to the bank.

It was after hours for the bank. I slid the bag into the night deposit drop-off and drove away. I caught sight of Carina's car in the library parking lot as I waited for traffic to stop. I parked next to her car and went inside to search her out. Seated at the far end of a long table, Carina whispered to her daughter as she ran her finger across the page of a book.

I slid into a chair next to them and waited for Carina to finish with Adrian. When she had, Carina looked at me. In silence, her eyebrows rose, her eyes widened, and I took her expression as a question of what I'd found out. I beckoned her to follow me to an empty alcove. She nodded and told Adrian where she would be.

We stood in Adrian's line of sight for a whispered update. "It is apparent Evelyn was unpopular with the people she worked with as well as those who entered their rabbits in the show. That dislike should have made her change her ways, but it didn't. Instead, from what I understand, she was more domineering and miserable than ever."

"I'm not surprised. Do you have any idea yet who might have killed her?"

"Not yet, it's early days. The show officially opens tomorrow, everyone who needs to be in attendance, will be, which means I might get a better idea of who disliked her enough to kill her."

While she listened, Carina hadn't taken her eyes off Adrian. She glanced at me, gave me a nod, and whispered her thanks before she returned to her daughter while I walked alongside.

"Adrian has to read several books for school, and we've put it off until now, so here we are."

"I'll leave you to it, then." On the way home, I mulled over how hard it would be to find Evelyn's killer, or if I even could.

Bun sat facing the door when I walked into the kitchen. I swear I'd seen him tapping one foot when I'd entered the house with the grant packet tucked under my arm.

"You were gone a long time. Where were you?"

"At the bank and the library. It's nice to know you missed me."

"I never said I missed you, but now that I think of it, I guess I did. I woke from my nap and you were gone."

"Bun, you know I'm never far away."

"Do we have to leave early tomorrow?"

"The show opens at eleven in the morning. We have to be there by ten. Do you want to stay home or go with me?"

"There's no leaving me behind. I can hear things you can't, sense what you might not, and help you to stay out of trouble." With a sniff of his sweet little nose, he continued, *"Of course, I'm going."*

"Perfect. I didn't think you would make me do this by myself. You have keen senses, which makes a huge difference in an investigation such as ours."

Pleased at my response, Bun rubbed his head against my ankle and then asked for a snack. I gave him one that I hastily put together and left him to it.

The packet of information lay on the table. I opened it and sorted through multiple sheets of paper. Gosh, this wasn't going to be easy. I leaned back in the chair, browsed each page again, and started to read in earnest.

The clock struck the hour. I realized it was eleven o'clock and I hadn't finished reading the entire set of documents. I persevered until just past midnight. The pages were completed, folded, and stuffed into the envelope they had come in. There was little hope of the company issuing a grant to Fur Bridge Farm, at least that was my opinion. If it came through, fine, if not, fine. Well, maybe not fine, but I wouldn't lose any sleep over it, either.

*   *   *

My internal alarm went off before the clock alarm sounded. I stretched, yawned, and arose in a bleary-eyed fashion. The smell of perked coffee and fried bacon meant Jessica had made breakfast.

Dressed for barn work, I'd only combed my hair, washed my face, and brushed my teeth. The rest could wait until the rabbits were cared for. The table was set and fresh coffee poured by the time I got downstairs.

"You have a late night, or what?"

"I stayed up to fill out the grant forms. I don't think the grant will come through for the farm, but at least I tried." I shrugged a shoulder and swigged down the coffee, scalding my palate, my tongue, and my throat.

"Here, put some sugar in your mouth. It will help with the scalding you just gave yourself." Jess shoved the sugar bowl across the table.

"Oh my, this isn't any way to start a day. We have lots of work to do, so don't be clumsy, okay?"

I nodded and rolled granules of sugar around in my mouth until they dissolved. Surprisingly enough, the burn lessened in a few seconds.

"Now, eat your breakfast. After chores, I'll need a hand in the clinic before you head out for the day. Oh, Molly will be a half hour late, but Jason will be here on time. I played the messages left on the phone in the barn."

"Glad they called. I can handle the chores alone. You needn't help me." I spread cashew butter on toast and slathered blueberry jam on top and ate an egg, before I called it quits.

"Great breakfast, thanks, Jess." She was still eating when I pushed my chair away from the table.

"I'll be in the barn," I said over my shoulder. As I passed Bun's room, I noticed Jessica had already fed him. Okay then, this was a good start to the day.

I'd done double duty by filling the food and water bins as I made my way up one aisle and down another. With cages on each side of the aisles, it took a little longer using this method. It was the way I had started out when I first opened my business. Some cages were empty from rabbits that had gotten new homes. I made a mental note to check on their circumstances once the show was over.

"Are you finished yet?" Bun hopped alongside me as I filled the last dish with food.

"I am. Now for the poop trays."

"Ugh, those stink. How do you stand it?"

I gave him a look that said he needn't ask, watched him hop off toward Jessica's clinic, and then follow her back as she entered the barn.

"I loaded the dishwasher and cleaned Bun's room. Sorry I got waylaid. I'll help you with the hoppers."

"I don't mind doing it, really. Get your clinic ready for the day, I'll be in shortly."

Jess shook her head as I wrinkled my nose and cleaned a poop tray into the hopper. "Come in when you're done, then."

Wearing a huge rubber apron and heavy rubber gloves, I scoured and sanitized each tray as I went. The last tray slid underneath the rabbit cage as I said, "Sure thing."

Removing the gear, I hung it on a rack nailed to the barn wall and washed the gloves in the sink before I moseyed on into the clinic. Grunts and groans emanated from the last exam room.

"Wait a minute." I rushed in to lift one end of the heavy examination table Jess struggled with.

"Glad you're here. I can't get this over to the other side of the room by myself."

"Why didn't you tell me you wanted to move this? I would have hurried through the chores."

"Just give me a hand now, will you?"

Together, we hauled the table across the room.

"Anything else you want a hand with?"

"Now that you mention it, I have supplies that were delivered while you were busy."

Again, we made short work of the job. We went to the front porch of the house and Jess took a seat while I brought out glasses of orange juice.

After a huge gulp, Jess asked, "What did Meredith say last night?"

"She told me about Jim Brody being a vendor at the show. She implied he knows everything that goes on there because people gossip with him and tend to say things they might not share with anyone else. Sort of like when women go to the hairdresser. I read somewhere that hairdressers and barbers know more about the lives of their customers than anyone else. I guess it's the same with Jim Brody." I grimaced while thinking about people who shared their secrets.

"Wow, remind me to button my lips when I have my next haircut. I do hear some stuff I'd rather not while sitting in the stylist's chair. Customers have no clue who listens to what is said, or if anyone is familiar with the person they've gossiped about. I think you might have an ally in Jim Brody.

Take note of what he says and sort out what's true and what isn't."

"I've considered doing just that. We'll see what I can find out before Sheriff Carver comes by and nags me for information. It's hard to believe he's asked for my help."

"He knows you can get people to talk. Besides, he probably thinks you'd be up to your neck in clues that might help him if he had only asked you to gather them in the first place."

"We'll see how that works out. The rabbits should be ready for playtime. Let's put them in the pen and then I can shower before Bun and I leave. Could you let Molly know I need an inventory of what's in the shop?"

"Will do."

We set the rabbits in the pen. I opened the small door that allowed entry into other places they could explore without getting away. Walkabout Willy was fond of getting away from us. Not that he would know what to do if he took a jaunt into the woods. I feared he would end up as a predator's next meal.

Showered, changed, and ready to go, I packed Bun's snacks, my lunch, and a small water container in the Bun Bag my mother had sent me, and gathered Bun into his sling. Mom had seen the bag in a market and while it was supposedly for bread and coffee buns, she thought it a fitting gift for Bun. He thought so, too.

CHAPTER SEVEN

Our driving time into Windermere was filled with speculation on how to further our investigation into Evelyn's background and follow it up to the day of her demise.

"Remember, it's opening day, and sporting competitions are bound to keep us judges busy. As my-ears-to-the-ground detective, you'll be in a great position to hear and see what I can't. I'm depending on you, Bun."

"I'm up to the job, don't you worry for a second about that."

Assured that he wouldn't go off on his own, I was grateful for his abilities.

"My exemplary wits will be in play from the minute we arrive to the minute we leave. I bet the killer will be in the audience, what do you want me to do if he or she is?"

Conscious of Bun's overconfidence, I hesitated to answer, then said, "I'd like you to report your findings to me. I wouldn't want you to come to harm, Bun."

"That's doable. I won't take any chances, honest."

Once inside the contest arena, I found the space had been reduced. Areas were blocked off, and seating was restricted because of it. Rabbits aren't large animals and the reduction made it less intimidating for these sweet creatures, as well as less of a possibility any of them would wander off.

I took my place at the end of a long table, with the panel of nine judges. Each of us had large cards, with numbers printed on them, stacked in front of us. When a rabbit had completed his or her skill, we would hold up our numbers and they would be noted by the announcer. At the end of the competition, the numbers would be compared and the winner announced. I couldn't help but be excited. The rabbits were beautiful, and I looked forward to the events.

"There sure are a lot of contestants. I think that brown-and-white one is going to win. He's very attentive. You know, one must be focused to meet any challenge."

Words from the wise. I applauded the contestants as they paraded past us and the crowd of onlookers and then watched them line up for the first skill.

I scanned the room, peeked down at Bun, who was doing the same, and centered my attention as the first rabbit displayed his jumping ability. He was very good at it, and when the bar was raised for the third time, he soared over it, his ears flying backward. The fourth time around, he caught the tip of his right foot on the bar, but sailed over the bar anyway.

The audience had given a loud "aww" when he'd touched the bar, but gave a loud round of applause for the rabbit not slowing but increasing his speed to finish. We had held up our numbers. I glanced down the row, saw the majority had given the creature an eight, and that I had held up a nine.

The day went on in this manner, with a break for lunch around one o'clock in the afternoon. I fed Bun, poured water into his container, and sat quietly on the edge of our stage while everyone else stood in line at the food vendor's to order lunch. I leaned down and whispered, "Did you hear or see anything out of the ordinary?"

"Not this morning. I have high hopes for this afternoon." Bun continued to nibble his fare as I pulled a sandwich out of the Bun Bag carryall. After we'd eaten, I connected a leash to Bun's collar, much to his dismay, and said he only had to tell me when he wanted to ride in the sling.

"We'll walk around and listen. If you're in the sling, you might not have as much of an advantage as being on the floor. If you feel uncomfortable, let me know."

"Good enough."

Off we went, to make the rounds of every stall and vendor we had time for. Rabbit handlers guided the animals into their cages to rest prior to the next set of skills. One man pointed his finger at another, nearly poking the tip of it into the man's chest. I sidled closer and heard the pointer accuse the other man of cheating.

"Seamus, you don't know what you're talking about," the man responded.

His voice deep, Seamus accused, "You gave that rabbit somethin' to hype him up, so he'd be the fastest contestant. I know all about your shenanigans."

The man shook his head and started to turn away when Seamus grabbed his shirt. "I'm not done talkin' to you." Burly and heavy-handed, I wondered if Seamus McKenna had been a schoolyard bully who hadn't outgrown that bad habit.

His hand was disengaged from the man's shirt by David Murphy, my escort from the day before. Fascinated by the way he defused what could have become an incident that included fisticuffs, I realized it was time for us to move on. With a light tug on the leash, Bun and I drifted away, seemingly unnoticed.

"I was nearly trampled when people surrounded those two. I think the sling is a good idea. There were a few of the onlookers who were betting on them. I guess this guy, Seamus, does this sort of thing all the time. I heard a woman say she was disqualified from the competitions last year for fighting with another rabbit owner."

"Hm, very interesting," I murmured, and perused goods at a nearby vendor stand. I knelt and opened the sling for Bun. He nestled inside, and popped his head and the tips of his two front paws out of the opening.

I smoothed his ears and scratched his forehead. "Better?"

"Very much so."

I noticed the time and then heard an announcer say the games would get underway in ten minutes. We started toward the arena and were jostled by people returning to their seats.

At the table once again, I put my cards in numeric order while Bun crouched on his mat, which

I'd set at the end of our table. Doing so would enable him to acquire more gossip and hear any remarks that might be pertinent to Evelyn Montgomery. Eventually, he focused on the rabbit owners and switched back and forth between them and the audience. I gave up trying to figure out what he was doing and settled on my own job.

Around three o'clock, a fifteen-minute break was announced. Some folks left their seats, and all the judges left ours, as did Bun. He and I went out into the sunshine, walked the area, and then sat on a stone bench for a little while. Bun filled me in on the impressions he'd gotten and said it would do us well to remain cognizant of each rabbit and owner.

I ran a hand over his fur and asked, "Why?"

"I think it would be worthwhile. They are a chatty, competitive group, that will turn on one another in a flash. We saw that this morning, right?"

"Uh-huh."

We returned to the judging platform in time for the next skill set, a race to the finish. Five fleet-footed rabbits zoomed the undersized oval track, which reminded me of those used by NASCAR drivers. On the second lap, two rabbits collided—one flipped head-over-teakettle and landed with a thud, while the other jumped the wall that was supposed to keep the animals contained. The crowd jumped out of their seats, some shouted for the race to end, while others urged the judges to repeat the race. In the end, the audience became a tad unruly.

Shocked by their behavior and that of the contestants, I watched as they now ran wildly about to catch the rabbits that had followed the one who had raced off. I concluded it was a blessing Petra wasn't involved in these games. The judges, all ten of us, stood and gaped at the melee before us. It was then that I noticed Seamus. He elbowed his way onto the track, swept a rabbit into his arms, and ran for the door.

The man he had accused of drugging his own rabbit raced after him, shouting his name. Our game room had fallen into utter chaos. Fearing Bun would take off after them, I scooped him up and sat in my chair.

"Did you see that? It's shameful how that rabbit careened into the other one. Good thing Petra isn't here."

I nodded and said nothing. The other judges talked among themselves and decided to call the games off for the remainder of the day. One of them spoke to David Murphy, who hurried to tell the announcer, who in turn, repeated the decision and said the final game from today would take place first thing tomorrow when the games resumed.

People booed, shook their heads, and went on their way, some saying they wouldn't be back. Those who approved of the decision walked off with smiles on their faces as they chattered away like nothing had happened. I wondered if the dissenters were all talk with an added touch of disappointment and asked David about them.

"This sort of thing happens all the time. These animals aren't professional racehorses, they are rabbits. The audience will return tomorrow, hoping for another such commotion." He snickered over their departure, or at least I thought that's why he did so.

"I don't find it the least bit funny. The owners were unprofessional and that poor rabbit could have been injured."

"You're right, he could have been. I apologize. I know you're a rabbit farmer and care about your critters."

I agreed and left the arena for the vendors' gallery. Goods that weren't on display the day before caught my eye, along with Jim Brody, who waved to me from across the floor.

Wending our way to his booth, I greeted him and surveyed a slew of goods I hadn't seen on my last visit.

"I see you've been busy resetting your booth."

Bun's head appeared from within the sling as Jim said, "We sold quite a lot of merchandise this morning during the game breaks. It was somewhat crazy in here after they were called off, too. I heard various stories. What really happened?"

I gave a rundown of the race and let it go at that.

"Did you bring the grant paperwork with you?"

"Sorry, I walked out the door without it this morning. I'll try to return it to you tomorrow." It had occurred to me that having my attorney look it over would be smart on my part. After all, grants weren't my field of expertise.

"That's fine, you can always drop it off at the office, if you want. Excuse me, I have a possible customer and my helper is taking a break." He left me to view the goods and listen to Bun whine about a new bed.

Having had enough excitement for one day, I began to make our way to the exit.

"Stop and look at something while I listen to that guy over there. I believe he's talking about Evelyn."

We hadn't quite reached the end of Jim's booth. I reached out, plucked a bed from the stack, and pretended to read the information on the tag. When Bun didn't let me know he was finished eavesdropping, I placed it on the stack and picked up a feeding tray, and gave it a once-over. Bun's ears seemed to vibrate, then stopped.

"Get a move on, right now."

I did his bidding and we left the hall. While we crossed the lot my car, Bun began to speak and then hid inside the sling, his whole body aquiver. Surprised by his actions, I gazed the entire lot and saw Bun's former owner, Margery Shaw, on course toward us. What madness would she present this time around?

Margery, a miserable sot, had mistreated Bun due to his ability to speak. She often accused of him of being the spawn of Satan, but truly, Bun was fortunate to have this gift and have me to listen to and believe in him. We were both lucky, I guess. We'd found each other, and I refused to put up with Margery's foolishness.

"I see you've got that demented rabbit with you. He can talk, you know. I heard him, many times."

I gave what I hoped was a sympathetic look and remarked softly, "Margery, you know animals can't talk. Have you seen a doctor for those hallucinations?"

She was angered by my implying she had such a disorder, and her eyes fairly snapped with it as she stepped closer. I held my ground. I had been through worse than what Margery could hand out.

"Don't you dare call me crazy."

"I never said that. You think Bun can speak, and I know he doesn't. I've even had my veterinarian look him over to make sure."

She grabbed the sling, Bun squeaked from fear, and I reached for Margery's hand. In a second or two, I'd peeled her thumb from the fabric and yanked it backward, causing her enough pain that she instantly released the sling from her grasp. I wanted her to think twice before she acted that way again.

Her cell phone in hand, Margery shrieked at me. "I'm calling the police. Sheriff Carver will arrest you for assault. You almost broke my thumb."

"Go ahead, call him. When he arrives, I'll let him know you tried to harm Bun."

Her face reddened with anger, Margery stuffed the phone into her pocket and stomped off toward the building.

I snorted at her attempt to harm Bun, then reached inside the sling for Bun before I opened the car door. "Come on, you're safe now. She can't hurt you, not now, not ever. I promise, Bun."

"You can't be sure of that. She is a wily, cruel person. You see that, don't you?"

"I do, but I'm wilier than she is. We escaped a near-death experience this summer due to being clever, didn't we?"

He didn't speak for a moment, he just huddled on the seat. At least he wasn't shaking any longer.

"You're going to be fine. We'll go home and you can have a special treat, okay?"

"Okay." He edged closer to me, giving the door quick glances as though he expected Margery to return.

The door locks clicked when I started the car and shifted into gear. I backed out of the parking spot and went home.

After a couple of minutes, I urged Bun to tell me what he'd heard. "Was that the same person who discussed Evelyn the last time?"

"The voice sounded the same, so I would say it was that guy Seamus. He was with two other people. They didn't agree or disagree with him, they listened and then moved on before he could get worked up. As they passed by, I heard one of them say the man held a grudge, and it didn't bode well for the show organizers, or anyone affiliated with them. Does that mean us? We're affiliated, aren't we?"

Unwilling to scare him more than necessary, I asked a question without answering his. "What was Seamus going on about?"

"He harped on the games being fixed, and said the rabbit who ran out of control had been trained to do so. Bets are being made between owners and show attendees over who will win each contest and take best of show."

"Glad to know that. Sheriff Carver will be interested in those shenanigans. Does this guy have a rabbit that competed, and is he set up in the rabbit owners area?"

"I'm not sure. Since you didn't answer my affiliates question, I assume that would be a yes?"

"We'll have to be careful, and look out for each other. It's the best thing we can do. I'll keep

Carver apprised of what we've learned and see what he thinks. You know how protective he can be where civilians are concerned." Worried that we had taken on more than we could handle, I took into account that Bun hadn't refused my suggestion to share our findings with Carver. I realized we might both be in for a rough time if we weren't alert.

"I'm glad I came to this show. You might have bumbled around, not knowing who was what. Fortunately, my hearing and keen wits will be how we find Evelyn's murderer. I'm certain the killer is at the show."

"I'm not as sure as you are, but it sounds plausible." I turned into the long driveway, drove under the FUR BRIDGE FARM sign, and parked in front of the barn.

"I have to check with Jess on how the day has gone, do you want to go ahead into the house?"

"I'd rather visit with the other rabbits, if you don't mind. I miss them. They're really a good bunch, you know."

I gave him a gentle pat on the head, smoothed his ears, and opened the door. He hopped out of the sling and went into the barn to see his friends.

Jessica was gone for the day. Molly and Jason were settling the rabbits in their cages. Having finished exercising, the rabbits were ready for snacks and a rest. From the look of both kids, I figured they might need one, too.

"Job well done. Thanks so much for your help, I know you have classes and homework to do. I'll take it from here. Oh, uh, Molly, did Jess say if she'd be returning?"

"She had to pick up a special medication for Mr. Roman's dog and drop it at his home. She'll pick up dinner for you both."

"Great, thanks. I'm beat. What a frantic day."

"Too many rabbits in the same place," Jason remarked, and tucked his jacket under his arm.

"We'll see you tomorrow, Jules."

They got into Molly's car and drove away.

"They make a cute couple, don't you think?"

I turned and gasped at Bun.

Chapter Eight

After supper the evening before, I'd phoned Jack Carver to give him the information Bun and I had gathered. Before he could say a word, I added my theory that Evelyn's death was somehow linked to this event. He said we'd talk in person very soon and hung up. He could be short at times, it was usually because someone was close by and he didn't want them to know what was up.

Bun and I had begun day two of the show and entered the game room earlier than the other judges to prepare for the first session. The rabbit race that had failed the day before would take place within the next hour. I sipped coffee I'd bought at a concession stand while Bun happily chomped away at his fruit and veg snack.

I wondered if this was what moms felt like when they had small children and carried incredible amounts of supplies and incidentals. I used the oversized Bun Bag for food and water bowls, a small pad for Bun to sit on, and I had folded the sling to fit as well. Small packets of Bun's chilled food and my own sandwich were in a lined cooler bag that filled the rest of the space. Not exactly packhorse material, but it seemed darn close.

Fans arrived, found their seats, and got comfortable. Rabbits and owners came next, followed by judges. Surprised that I was already in place, they offered smiles and brief greetings. The judges hadn't made much effort to be friendly, but then, neither had I. Yet.

I searched the audience for Seamus, in case he had withdrawn his rabbit, if he had one, from the rest of the games. I didn't see him. About to turn my attention to business, I caught sight of Jack Carver dressed in street clothes, rather than his uniform. A closer look at the crowd showed no one had noticed or paid him any mind. If the fans were from out of town, they probably wouldn't know he was a lawman. Only local folks would be aware of who he was.

He watched everyone and everything closely as the rabbits lined up for their race. We, the judges, focused on the rabbits, hoping all would go well. From what David had said, mishaps weren't unusual, but I had been concerned over it.

The announcer gave the go-ahead and the rabbits took off, making their first turn around the track with no issues. They kept going until they had done five laps and the flag went down. The first, second, and third rabbits were scooped up by their owners and held up for cheers from onlookers. The rabbits who hadn't placed were consoled by their owners and given a treat. With a sigh of relief, I noted who won what place by scribbling the numbers pinned to the petite harnesses of the winners.

The owners took the winning rabbits back to their cages to rest while the next two events took place. When a fifteen-minute break was called, I noticed Sheriff Carver stared in my direction. He tipped his head toward the rear of the room and we met him there after the crowd had emptied out.

"Are you undercover?"

"Just taking a day off."

"Like that ever happens, Jack."

"Do you know who is betting on the rabbits?"

Before I could say a word, Bun said, *"There are three people in the fourth-row booth of the rabbit room. They take bets from anyone willing to put cash in their hands."*

I repeated what he'd said.

"You saw them do that?"

"Yes, we can show him, Jules."

I glanced at my watch. We had time and I said, "I can show you who they are, we should be able to get there and back before the games commence. Come on."

We walked from the game room into the rabbit stations. Guided by Bun, I showed Jack where they were. "Are you going to bet? I see money changing hands at that booth to your right." I didn't point it out, but Jack was smart and followed my line of sight.

With a nod, he left me and Bun on our own and

slowly made his way to the stand. He petted the rabbit and remarked upon it. I was uncertain what he knew about rabbits, but Jack was no fool and had likely read up on them beforehand. Bun and I returned to the judges' table.

The games went on until early afternoon before another break was announced. Bun and I went outside to sit on a bench to have our lunch. I'd packed his bowls and slung the backpack over one shoulder and Bun walked beside me on a leash.

"What a brilliant move by the sheriff to go undercover like that. While I'm not crazy about him, I can see why he's so good at his job."

High praise from Bun since he rarely gave Jack credit, let alone admitted he was brilliant. I handed him a small portion of lettuce leaf and bit into my sandwich. His food and water bowls had lids clamped on tight to prevent spillage. I opened them both and set them on the seat for Bun.

I glanced up to see Jack sit on the bench that backed ours. I didn't utter a word, but kept eating and tending to Bun, who knew Jack was behind us.

"I placed a bet. The guys from the station will arrest these people for gambling at the end of today's show. There are more plainclothes officers here at various times, so you'll be safe. I would rather you didn't go any further in my investigation. It would be too dangerous for you and the rabbit."

I looked at Bun, leaned low, petted him, and murmured, "Good to know about your men. After what we heard yesterday, I was nervous." I refrained from saying it was too late for me to cease and desist. I had promised Carina and would keep looking for Evelyn's killer whether Jack liked it or not.

Sheriff Carver rose and entered the building. Fans went indoors for the afternoon games as I stored Bun's bowls. We, too, hurried to arrive on time. We all filtered into the area set up for the remaining contests.

The games would end around three, if all went well, and I'd have time to chat with rabbit owners and employees before the day was done. With only one more day to go, I wanted to poke around, or the killer would get away. This was my one chance to make serious headway into Evelyn's death. I didn't want to waste the opportunity.

One competition followed another while I considered what Jack had said. Did this mean I didn't have to report to him any longer? I thought that over and decided to keep what we learned to myself until I had enough evidence to present to him.

"I think the sheriff is wrong to shut us out of the investigation. We have proven our value to him and he should appreciate us more."

"Mm-hmm."

"I know you can't talk to me, but we should keep looking for Evelyn's killer."

I reached down and gently tapped his head twice to let him know I agreed.

"The games have become monotonous. I want to search for the killer, not watch this. And, it's too noisy for a nap."

After the last game of the day ended, Bun and I congratulated the winner of each competition as they filed out the door wearing brightly colored ribbons. We followed the lingerers out and strolled toward the rabbit stations. In their section, I stepped to the side while I watched two women arguing.

Bun, who scrambled around inside the sling to get a better view of the happenings, settled down and said, *"Well, isn't this something?"*

Accusations were hurled from one woman to the other and back again until the situation escalated, and a shoving match took over. I drew closer, yet remained far enough away to stay clear of them both. More shoving and foul words followed. Fearful a fistfight was in the offing, I was prepared to intervene when I heard Bun say the sheriff was on the other side of the room and had seen everything.

I relaxed when I saw Jack, who nodded at a plainclothes man standing opposite him. I remembered he'd said there were other cops in attendance.

The officer strode through the crowd. Brave man that he was, he stepped between the women and admonished them for their actions.

"Break it up, you two. There's no need to behave like children. You're upsetting the rabbits and making a spectacle of yourselves."

The more aggressive of the two women refused to back down and said, "Mind your own business."

Security personnel arrived in time to save the day. They moved in to disperse onlookers and handle the two women's differences, thus saving the plainclothes policeman from having to produce his badge and blow his cover. I grinned over his statement that the rabbits were upset. It was likely he had no inkling of what rabbits felt. Bun's ears had flattened and then flipped up again when he'd heard the cop say it, and I took it as a sign of Bun's sense of humor kicking in.

Bystanders loitered until they were ordered to move on. Bun and I were adjacent to the sheriff, the other cop, and the two women. Our vantage point was perfect. We could hear what was being said by others and the two offenders.

I glanced over my shoulder. The booth behind us was attended by a young man who beckoned to me.

"That sure was poor behavior for two adult women, don't you think?"

"It was indeed. Do you know them?" I asked.

"They attend every show and come to blows each time. Too much jealousy if you ask me." He shook his head.

I saw his badge and asked, "How do they get away with such disruption, Colin?"

"Miss Montgomery always kept them under control. Last year, one of them threatened her with violence. She said Evelyn should mind her own business or she'd pay for her nosiness."

Colin Bedford's eyes flicked back and forth, as though he expected someone to walk up to the booth. I wanted him to share more of what he knew and encouraged him to continue.

"Which woman was that? I want to stay as far away from her as I can."

His mouth opened as Jack stepped next to me. I never got my answer. Colin and Jack began a conversation on what type of food he recommended for his rabbit, since Colin's rabbit appeared so healthy.

I bid them farewell and went in the direction of the merchandise vendors. I stopped to chat at several booths, purchased all natural rabbit toys from each, and ended up at Jim Brody's booth, where I pondered a bed for Bun.

"That was quite the brouhaha, wouldn't you say?" Jim remarked.

"This has been an eye-opening experience for me. I never realized there was such jealousy among owners or the competition between them, either."

"Those women have disliked each other since they met."

I touched the light blue bed that Bun had found to his liking.

While he shared the benefits of it, Jim said, "Personally, I think if owners and contest entrants can't behave professionally, they shouldn't be allowed to participate in the show. The majority of them are great people, with a love of rabbits, and enjoy the chance to show them off. It's a shame when people like those two women create an atmosphere that can ruin an event such as this. Evelyn never allowed it to get as far as it did today."

As he paused, I jumped in with a question. "How well do you know these rabbit owners and helpers?"

"They attend the same shows every year, so I know them very well."

"It must be nice to see them every time. Good for business, too, I bet. I'll take that blue bed if you have a huge bag I can carry it in. As you can see, I have Bun and a backpack to deal with."

"You're really buying it for me? I'm so happy, I could jump out of this comfy sling and run around the room."

I hugged the sling a bit closer while Jim put the purchase in a huge plastic bag with handles. I held out my credit card. "Evelyn must have been quite brave. How did she manage to keep the peace?"

Jim returned the card and smirked. "She wielded her power over anyone foolish enough to push their luck." He leaned in close as he lifted the bag over the counter. "She was a miserable person, and was rude and overbearing toward the entrants. Even the hoity-toity group steered clear of her."

"Really?" I remarked in awe. Fake though it was, my awe came across as believable, because Jim warmed to the subject.

"She would threaten to have them disqualified. I have to say her one saving grace was her affection for the rabbits."

Sympathetically, I said, "It's such a shame she was, uh, killed. Do you know of anyone who would want to harm her?"

"Be careful, don't push too hard."

Leave it to Bun to remind me of that, when he would be the first to not push, but shove as hard as he could. Rabbits, ya gotta love 'em.

"I can think of a few who held grudges against her. The two booths in from the right side of that entrance over there, for instance." He chinned in that direction so as not to lift a finger and point. "I'm sure they wouldn't harm her, though."

I'd followed the direction he alluded to and noticed Sheriff Carver had entered the room. It was time for us to leave. Before I made a run for it, I asked, "Evelyn worked for you, didn't she?"

He gave me an odd look and nodded. "She did, albeit briefly."

After offering my thanks for Bun's bed, I walked past Carver with a nod.

CHAPTER NINE

Day two had proven to be informative. With one
more day to go, I was positive I could make
enough headway to prove Carina hadn't committed
the crime Jack thought she had. Even though he
was interested in the show folks, I knew he would
maintain his belief that Carina could have been
the culprit.

*"You know, that Brody fellow could be mistaken about
the people he pointed out. If Evelyn was as miserable to
them as she supposedly was to everyone else, there's no
telling what they might have conspired to do to her."*

"After dinner tonight, we should compile notes
on what we know, and have heard and seen. Let's
keep it concise since we're dealing with lots of possibilities and gossip."

"I think that's a smart idea. What's for dinner?"

"You're having what everyone else is."

"And that would be?"

"Whatever Jessica and Molly have put together.
It will be scrumptious, it always is."

He lay still and quiet for the remainder of the ride home. I had managed to tucker Bun out with all our investigative efforts. He awoke upon arrival at the farm. Cars were lined up just as they were for the last spinning and weaving class.

Jess met me at the door and whispered, "Sheriff Carver wants you to call him." She lifted the Bun Bag from my shoulder onto hers.

I went in and let Bun loose, then removed the sling. "Thanks," I said in recognition of her message and taking on half of my load. I set the bags of purchases on the floor next to the barn door and watched students intent on their creativity. The weavers sat at their small rigid heddle looms, wending their shuttles to and fro, then tightening each row.

Molly joined Jessica and me, then motioned us into the barn. We followed her lead and waited as she closed the door.

"I have some news, though it might not be so great for you, Jules."

Jess and I looked at each other, then back at Molly. Prepared for the worst, I said, "Okay, go ahead."

"There was an article in the newspaper about a murdered woman named Evelyn Montgomery. She worked at the show you are judging at, Jules."

"I know. There's more, isn't there?"

"Well, um, there is. She was seen with Carina Richland's husband before he died. I only know this because my sister, Emily, used to be a waitress at a restaurant in Jasper. She also knew of Mr. Richland because Emily's friend used to babysit for the Richlands. Emily would wait until the couple left and then join her friend while babysitting the Richlands' daughter. She said he and the dead woman were all cozied up at that restaurant."

"Whew, I'm relieved that's all you wanted to tell me. It is good news, but bad at the same time. I'm working to keep Carina from being accused of Evelyn's death. Please don't tell anyone that, and I mean, *anyone*."

Her smile, as always, lit up the room. She crossed her heart with two fingers, and promised not to breathe a word. Having said what she thought useful, Molly returned to her students.

Bun came toward us, his ears twitching. A sure sign he had heard every single word. Before he could expound upon his views, I asked Jessica if the rabbits' meals were ready.

"They are. I prepared them in between patient appointments. Petra is fine, by the way. Her allergy has taken its leave, and she's her old self again. The fare for dinner is a mix of orchard and oat hays, followed by a portion of mustard greens and pansies. Dessert consists of a couple teaspoons of apricot bits."

"Yummy for my tummy. Yippee."

I gave a thumbs-up. "The rabbits will be happy with that menu. I appreciate your help. One more day to go, and then I'll be home to handle things. Thanks."

"You can make our dinner. I have late patients today. The last one will be here by five o'clock." Jess glanced at the clock, then left me and Bun on our own.

"I'll put your new bed in your room so you can take a rest if you want."

"I'd rather go into the run tunnel to exercise, if you don't mind. That kit nap I had on the way home refreshed me."

A kit nap, huh? Kits are what baby bunnies are called. Bun cracked me up when I least expected it by using *kit nap* rather than *catnap*. "Get going, then."

After lifting him into the tunnel, I fed the rabbits while he raced to the end and back again. By the time I had doled out the last meal, Bun awaited me. I retrieved the shopping bags and Bun Bag from the shop before we entered the house.

Bun checked out his new bed. Sniffing it, he placed his front paws on the fabric and kneaded it like a cat would. His final move was to hop into the center of the huge pillow to snuggle into it. His approval was obvious. Pleased that I'd made his day, I prepared dinner.

While a pot roast, potatoes, onions, and carrots simmered in a pan on the stove, I wiped my hands and answered the phone. Carina was on the line.

"Hi there, I was going to give you a call later tonight."

"I'm glad I caught up with you. The sheriff hasn't been around, but I think he assigned an officer to follow me."

"Are you sure?"

"When I take Adrian to school and pick her up, I see the same car and driver. I went to the market yesterday and he was in the parking lot. When I walked toward his car, he took off."

"I'll see what I can find out and get right back to you."

"Please do. I don't like it, but being stalked is

much more sinister. I'll be here for another two hours before Adrian goes to dance class."

I hung up and dialed Jack's number. He answered on the first ring.

Without niceties, I asked, "Do you have an officer keeping track of Carina?"

"Why do you want to know?"

"She thinks she's being followed or, even worse, possibly stalked."

"Adam is assigned to her. Now that he's been seen, I'll remove him from that detail. How did she come to her conclusion?"

"Good golly, he couldn't have been more obvious, Jack. If you want to tail her, don't let the officer sit in front of her house and take off when he sees her at the grocery store."

"And, you know all of this because?"

"We spoke on the phone. I wanted to know if she wanted to bring Adrian over to see the rabbits. She mentioned the situation and is quite rattled." Ashamed of lying to Jack, I knew he could probably see through it.

"I see. Let her know the police are keeping an eye on her for her own protection. After all, the murder was committed on her property and the victim was one of her guests."

"You're kidding, right? You aren't watching her on that account, you think she killed Evelyn."

Silent for a minute, Jack said coolly, "You don't know what I think, so don't assume."

"Fine, I'll let you go then."

In a snit, I slammed the phone into the charger. He could annoy me in no time flat. Jack Carver had that cop thing down to a science. I walked into his trap every time he used it to get under my skin. He hadn't wanted to say more, so he'd made his remark knowing full well that I would get snippy. Geesh, would I ever learn?

The news that Carina was under surveillance to assure her safety was taken well when I offered Carina the sheriff's reasons behind it. With a sigh of relief, Carina went on to say she was certain the sheriff had figured out she couldn't have killed Evelyn.

I wanted to tell her to rethink that, but I didn't. Instead, I shared what I'd learned at the rabbit show and how Sheriff Carver felt the killer was somehow connected to it.

"Thanks, Jules. You don't know what it means to me to have you on my side." With that said, she hung up.

The table set, Jess and I ate supper after she had closed the clinic.

We chatted over our individual happenings of the day. Jessica mentioned Molly's ability to handle the shop and classes, work in the clinic if needed, and then help Jason with the rabbits. "She doesn't get flustered. It amazes me that someone her age can compartmentalize what comes her way and deal with it accordingly."

"She's a winner in my estimation." Pleased that Molly could shoulder responsibility without a meltdown, I considered her an asset to the farm.

"Is there a raise in her future? She could use the money."

I calculated what I could afford and shook my head. "I can't afford to pay either one of them more. I wish I could."

"What if you received Jim Brody's grant?"

"I haven't turned in the application yet. I've never had a grant like that one and I'm worried there might be a loophole in it somewhere."

"You should have told me. I'll take a look at it if you'd like."

Happy over the offer, I rose from my chair. "I'll go get it."

Handing it to her, I watched as she pulled the sheets of paper from the packet. "What are your concerns?"

"That there may be a way for Jim's company to take over the farm or influence the operation of it."

"Okay."

Other than the sound of paper rattling, Jessica was silent. I'd expected a running stream of thoughts from Bun as he huddled in his doorway, but there wasn't a peep from him. The table cleared and dishes loaded into the dishwasher, I walked to the mailbox at the end of our driveway, and took the mail inside.

When I sat at the table to look through the mail, Jess shuffled the papers and folded them neatly.

"You have no need for concern. It's a straightforward grant. You won't have to pay it back, but you will have to give reports every six months until the money runs out. Give this to Jim tomorrow, I think he's an upstanding guy. If you still have doubts, ask Sheriff Carver about him and his business. That man knows everything about everyone."

Tucking the application into the envelope, I added it to the Bun Bag for delivery in the morning.

"Should the funds be granted, I can offer both kids a raise and do the small repairs that have been put off until I could save enough to pay for them."

"Good. I should get going. Thanks for the meal."

After Jess was gone, Bun and I sat on the porch to watch twilight descend. I'd brought a notepad and pen with me to write our findings.

"She's very helpful, isn't she?"

"Indeed, she is. But you're helpful, too. Now, we should organize the information we've gleaned. I also have to consider how to let Jack know anything new, without him becoming angry."

With what I thought of as a snort from Bun, who hadn't sneezed or sniffed. Rather, it sounded somewhere between the two.

"After he said we were out of his investigation, I wouldn't give him the time of day. He's totally unappreciative of our talents."

"He wants us to be safe, is all. I was shocked when he asked me to be his eyes and ears in the first place. If his boss knew he had involved civilians, he'd be in hot water."

"Go ahead, rationalize it any way you want, but in the end, the result is the same. We're on the outside looking in, even though we're in a better position to get people to talk to us. Look at what we were told today. I bet no one offered that information to the sheriff."

"You could be right. Anyhow, we will continue on our own and Jack can do his best by himself. Let's get what we know down on paper. You dictate, and I'll write."

"We're a great team, you and I. We should open an investigative service. We'd get rich, though I have no use for money."

He didn't, but I could use all I could get. A job as an investigator wasn't on my to-do list even if it would please Bun. I wrote furiously in the light from the porch lamp as he talked. Night had fallen, all was covered like a dark blanket had been cast over the land. The longer we sat out here, the cooler it became.

The last word written, I suggested we go inside as it was chilly. I had no idea what time it was. I yawned and stretched, tipped my wrist to see my watch and found we'd been at work for two hours.

Shuffling through the door, I locked up for the night and went into the barn to check that all was well. The rabbits rested. The shop room was neat and clean. No odd bits of yarn or hanks littered the floor.

A note from Molly was on the countertop. She'd made an inventory list, left totaled sales slips clipped together, and gave me a rundown of the progress made by the students. The note ended with a question of how many additional small spinning wheels we could afford and asked where could they be set up. She also suggested we acquire one or two more looms. I smiled at her business acumen, and knew quite well she could fill the room with spinner and weaver students given the chance.

I left the room, thought over her requests, and heaved a sigh. Tired to the bone, I was delighted the show would end soon, and hoped to procure Jim Brody's grant. I walked through the breezeway and turned my mind to the mystery surrounding Evelyn's life and death.

By all accounts, the woman was disliked with a lust for power that she cruelly wielded in her favor. What had Paul Richland seen in her? Why would he take interest in a mean-spirited and brash woman like Evelyn?

I stood still, my hand on the doorknob to the kitchen. Had they been involved? Or was that how it seemed to a young woman who waited on them at the restaurant? Had the episode been misread? Hmm.

CHAPTER TEN

Day three of the rabbit show started with Bun and me conversing with rabbit owners, using Fur Bridge Farm and Jessica's vet clinic as segues. It worked well until I realized odd looks came our way. Maybe I had pushed too hard for answers that people were reluctant to give.

I hurried to the game room, ready to take my place on the platform when Vera Benedict caught hold of my sleeve and tugged me aside.

Soft voiced, Vera said, "Stay away from the competitors. It will appear that you're choosing favorites. While this is your first time in this position and all, I insist you refrain from contact with them."

"I see, you're right. I hadn't really given that a thought. The rabbits are so beautiful, I'm drawn to them. It won't happen again, Vera, I promise." The entire time I talked, my concern grew over how I would garner information on Evelyn if I couldn't speak to rabbit owners.

Vera accepted my word before saying the games were about to begin and left me to take my seat. The first round of games went off without a hitch. We took a break while employees readied the room for the next event. Bun and I went into the foyer only to be approached by Jack Carver.

"Were you getting a lecture from Mrs. Benedict? You didn't look too happy."

"Bun and I made the mistake of visiting the rabbit owners. I wanted to promote Jessica's clinic and the farm. My attention could be misconstrued as showing favoritism when I'm a judge." I shrugged a shoulder and rolled my eyes. "She's right, I guess. I'm new at this and it could be seen in that light."

"It could also be seen as information gathering, and not just by me, but by the guilty."

"Okay, okay, I get it. You said my part was over. That's good enough for me. Some of these owners give me the shakes. Especially after those two women went at each other. Criminy, I was shocked by their unprofessionalism."

With a narrow-eyed stare, Jack said drily, "I bet."

"I've got to get back to the games. See you later."

The day proceeded with onlookers' cheers, high spirits, and shouts to their favorite rabbit to win. All said, the games were eventful for everyone but me. Afraid I wouldn't achieve my goal of catching Evelyn's killer, I tried to concentrate on the rabbits, their wins and losses. By lunchtime, Bun and I were ready for some privacy outside where we would eat.

On our way out, Bun asked, *"Will you give Brody that grant paperwork?"*

I was swift to veer in the direction of Jim's table where he watched people idly shop. I caught his eye and offered him the grant packet.

"Ah, thank you for returning this." He tucked it into a section of his briefcase and closed it. "You'll hear from us within a week or so, we meet next Wednesday."

"Great, thanks for the opportunity. I appreciate it." I bid him good day and sauntered away with my fingers crossed.

We took the same bench as before to eat lunch. Bun busily munched on his hay mix, fruit, and veggies. His food and water containers full, I was confident he wouldn't babble. It's annoying to be mistaken as often as I was.

"I was thinking, we should take a ride to Evelyn's house. You must know where she lives."

I chewed a mouthful of tuna fish sandwich and wondered why we hadn't done that right after Evelyn's death.

"It was only a thought."

"Mm-hmm."

Strands of hay waved about before they disappeared as Bun steadily chewed. It reminded me of slurping spaghetti noodles as a youngster. The utensils and supplies repacked, we walked the grounds awhile before we went inside.

Crossing the foyer, I was stopped by Stephanie Driscoll, a rabbit owner, who asked in a quiet tone if I would accompany her to her rabbit stand. When I asked what was wrong, she told me she didn't know, but I should go with her. Wary, I followed Stephanie, filled with angst over what she wanted. We arrived to find her rabbit, a crowd favorite and multiple winner of the games, sprawled across the bed of hay in his cage.

Advising her to stay with the animal, I went to notify Vera. We rushed back to the stand.

Vera peered at the rabbit and then stepped away from it. "I think we should get a veterinarian in here to examine this rabbit. I'll put a hold on the games until we get this straightened out."

"I can recommend my vet. Jessica Plain can tend to this."

"Call and ask her to come here right away." Vera gazed at people who had stopped to gawk. "Move along, there's nothing to see."

Much to my surprise, they dispersed. I called Jess, asked her to come as quickly as possible, and gave her a description of the rabbit's condition.

"I'll be there shortly."

While we waited, I asked Stephanie a few questions about the rabbit to save Jess time before the examination. His breathing shallow, the animal looked peaceful. Fearful of touching him, lest he be infected or contagious, I kept my hands to myself. I had to think of Bun and my own animals' welfare first and foremost. Any germs I brought home could prove detrimental to their health.

Jessica, escorted by David Murphy, examined the rabbit thoroughly. "I don't see signs of external injury. I recommend blood tests to find out more."

Given permission, Jessica opened the satchel she kept for house visits, and used a syringe and empty test tubes to draw vials of blood as Stephanie, Bun, and I watched. By this time, Stephanie wrung her hands.

Jess turned and said to Stephanie, "Bring the rabbit to my clinic, I can care for him better there while the tests run. I'll wait for you outside."

"Okay. I'll be right with you."

I took Jess aside and murmured, "Do you think he's seriously ill?"

She shrugged. "I won't know until I have test results. I'll be in touch."

Murmurs in the room ran rampant. I spoke loudly to capture everyone's attention.

"The tests results should be in soon and we'll be notified immediately. Until then, please keep your rabbits caged."

Owners milled around, opinions between them spoken in undertones. It was impossible to hear what was said, and I couldn't very well intrude without arousing suspicion.

An hour later, my cell phone rang, which silenced conversations. I listened to Jess explain Stephanie's rabbit had been drugged, not poisoned. He would be fine but unable to participate in any further games. I glanced to my right. Vera had returned and stood at my elbow.

"I think you have a desperate rival among the group of owners, Jules."

"I'll pass that on to Vera. She's right here with me."

"Take care, you've ventured into treacherous territory."

"See you later." I ended the call and whispered Jessica's findings into Vera's ear.

Vera walked to the center of the room. She turned in a complete circle to study each owner and announced the test results. Waiting a moment for the news to sink in, she then said, "If the person who committed this crime doesn't come forward, the police will speak with each of you upon their arrival."

Many rabbit owners stared at the floor and nervously shifted from one foot to the other. The arrogant, hoity-toity group sniffed their disapproval and then turned away, while others, less well-off, appeared horrified by the accusation that one of them was to blame. I guessed it hadn't occurred to them that the rabbit hadn't taken the drug by himself. Appalled at the cruelty of drugging a rabbit, I began to ask questions.

Vera, who had been adamant that I should steer clear of these people, stood aside to let me continue my interrogation.

My effort to get a sense of where each entrant was, who they were with, or if they had any alibi at all, was met with dismissal. Emphatic in their right to not answer me, the well-heeled owners seemed to view my interference as they would a pesky fly, and shooed me away.

Annoyed to no end, and horrified that an animal as sweet as a rabbit would be treated in such a heinous way, I warned them.

"If you don't answer my questions, you'll have to explain your actions to Sheriff Carver." I made certain I was heard and understood by all. Even though I surmised Carver hadn't yet been called, and my and Vera's threats were empty, only we knew it.

The owners had closed ranks, and grudgingly responded to my questions. Staffers and helpers alike insisted they hadn't seen anything unusual going on. Disappointed by it, Vera gave them a narrow-eyed glare as we left the room.

"You did very well in there. I'm impressed, Juliette."

"It didn't amount to much, though, did it?" I leaned closer and whispered, "Has Jack Carver been called?"

"I believe he's on his way. This sort of situation not only damages the image of our shows, but also puts honest sportsmanship in question. To think a contestant would harm a rabbit to win a prize is unacceptable." Her phone beeped. Vera rolled her eyes and griped, "I'll talk to you later, I have a call to make."

We parted ways. Bun and I veered toward the game room. I'd left my sweater and the small pillow I carried for Bun on my chair while we had lunch.

We walked the empty corridor. I heard my name whispered and turned to see who it was. The young salesclerk, Colin, who had spoken to me after the altercation between the two women, furtively beckoned me into one of the curtained-off areas. Curious, I followed him.

He stepped close to whisper, and I bent toward him to listen. "I know who tranquilized the rabbit. I also know who killed Miss Montgomery."

I stared into his face, but his attention was on what was behind me as he backed away.

"Watch out, watch out," Bun warned, too late.

I was shoved hard from behind, and my arms flailed. Unable to catch my balance, I fell forward and struck my head on the corner of a wooden crate. Pain seared through my head, and all went temporarily dark. Dazed, I lay still with my eyes closed and listened to Colin argue with another man as they rushed off.

"Jules, wake up. I need you."

I thought I had heard Bun, but, fuzzy-headed, I wasn't sure. Footsteps receded. Hoping they were truly gone, I peeked through my eyelashes, saw I was alone, and rose. I staggered, unsteady on my feet. The area looked the same, except Colin and his ally were gone and so was Bun. The realization hit me like a brick. Frenzied, I searched behind crates, in corners, and called Bun to come to me. I was alone, all alone.

It took some doing, but I made it to the game room and reached for the door handle when the door swung inward. Wobbly, I fought to stay upright. Sheriff Carver reached out and grasped my arms. He led me to the nearest seat.

"What happened, Jules? " He pushed my hair from by forehead and whistled. "That's quite a lump you've got there. You should see a doctor to make sure you don't have a concussion."

I brushed his hand aside, and asked, "Maybe later. Have you seen Bun?"

Jack shook his head. "Can't say that I have. I was looking for you, though. Vera mentioned you went in this direction when she saw you last. Tell me what happened to you."

I went over the attack, then asked if he was sure he hadn't seen Bun.

"This has something to do with Evelyn and the tranquilized rabbit. Otherwise, why would I be attacked? They must have taken Bun."

"Who took Bun?"

"Colin and his sidekick. Didn't you hear what I said? I came to and heard them argue. Colin was upset over the attack, his pal told him to shut up, that they had to get going. When they were gone, I searched and called for Bun. He wasn't there. He wouldn't go far, especially without me." The more I said, the more I believed Bun's life was in jeopardy.

"Stay calm, it won't do any good to fret. He'll be fine. He's undoubtedly scared and has hidden somewhere. Focus on the events from when Jessica took the rabbit to her clinic right up to now. Tell me every detail you can remember, including smells, sounds, everything."

As much as I wanted to search for Bun, it might be more helpful if I did as Carver asked. The possibility that I'd remember an insignificant detail prompted me to comply.

With the game room empty of people, rabbits, and most importantly rabbits competing, I gave Jack as accurate an account as possible of what took place. "I can't think of anything else, other than I will never even entertain the idea of ever being part of an event like this." I glanced at the sheriff. "Things are always different behind the scenes, aren't they?"

"That's for sure. You got a good taste of it, too. In competitions such as these, you'll find most owners are vicious when it's time to win. Their worst tendencies take over and cause everyone grief. I'm sorry you got involved."

I ran my fingers through my tangled hair and

slumped in the chair. "I have to find Bun. I can't leave until I do. Thanks for being here, Jack."

We walked the corridor, side by side. I peered into every room, behind each curtained-off area, and softly called Bun. There was no response. My anxiety grew over his disappearance with each passing moment. I drew a deep breath, let it out slowly, and did it again to keep from losing what little perspective I had left.

By the time we entered the huge foyer, Jack's annoyance over my insistence that Bun had been kidnapped was evident. He hadn't thought Bun was special, but Jack was unaware of Bun's brilliance, how shrewd and canny he could be.

My look centered on Jack, I said, "I have some business to attend, I'll see you later. Thanks again, Jack."

"You aren't going to search this entire arena for that rabbit, are you?"

My nerves tensed. In a snarky tone, I asked, "And if I am? What are you going to do about it?"

"Not a thing. Just watch your back, Jules, you might not be so lucky should there be a next time."

"I will. Do you plan to find the man who attacked me?"

"It's on my agenda. Right at the top of it."

"Know this, if I find who has taken Bun, and he's been harmed in any way, they will pay dearly for their mistake."

"I didn't hear that. Now get going."

CHAPTER ELEVEN

The crowd had thinned while awaiting the test results on Stephanie's rabbit to come in. Once they were known, arrangements were made to complete the games. The day would be longer than any one of us had anticipated.

A passing judge mentioned we would commence in a half hour. I nodded and kept on walking. With so much ground to cover, thirty minutes wasn't enough time. Booth attendants busily prepared their rabbits for the next attempt to win. Chances had increased due to the absence of Stephanie's rabbit.

I asked each attendant if they had seen Bun and measured their answer for the truth in it. No one had seen him. I was told a few of the owners had already left for the game room and I could catch up with them there. Walking on into the vendors area, I asked the same question again and again. I'd reached Jim's booth to find him unavailable, but asked the clerk instead. He hadn't seen any rabbit running around free. I kept going.

Concession stands had few customers and meant I had a chance to speak to each one without much of a wait. The clock ticked on, my time almost at an end while my nerves whined as would an unhappy violin. I'd reached the last stand, asked about Bun, and expected the same answer. I was told a man holding a crazy rabbit had crossed the foyer at a near run. My pulse zinged into overtime with excitement. I was on the right trail.

"What direction did he take?"

"I'm not sure. You lose track once they pass through the archway. He could have gone anywhere. Sorry, Miss."

"Thanks anyway."

The games were announced. I didn't waste time getting to the room and took my seat. I wiped sweat from my forehead and winced. The sheriff was right, I did have a whopping egg. Lucky for me I hadn't split the skin wide open. That would have created another problem I had no patience or time for. As much as I didn't want to see a doctor, I knew I should. Ever since my car accident a few years back, I've tried to avoid doctors and hospitals.

Focused on the animals, each contender did their best. They were praised and applauded for their hard work even if they hadn't won. A ribbon was awarded to the winner and I scanned the crowd directly across from me, noting a shift in a few onlookers. Money changed hands. I made sure

I could identify the bookmaker before I looked away.

A break was called to rest the rabbits before the last two contests. I sent a text to Jack asking for an update. A second later, my phone rang.

"I have men searching for the man who ambushed you and his cohort. I believe they took your rabbit because you asked one too many questions. What you've done since I cut you from the investigation wasn't as subtle as you thought. It's futile to deny it, Jules. I doubt the rabbit will come to harm. Back off and let me do my job, okay?"

"Okay." The line went dead. Under my breath I swore to keep an eye out for Bun and the two culprits. At least Jack had taken me seriously.

My mind flew in multiple directions when I considered why Bun was taken. Sure, the sheriff thought it was due to my nosiness, and he could be right. What if the attack and Bun-napping was a ploy to turn my focus away from Evelyn's death? If that were so, these guys wanted me to unravel and go nuts in search of Bun. Which I had done to a lesser degree than they hoped.

Could Evelyn's disagreements be the reason for their involvement? Why would they steal Bun? As though erasing a blackboard, I cleared my mind, and focused on the Bun-nappers. The only reasonable answer was to redirect my attention. That way, I wouldn't badger people over Evelyn. Why? Because Colin and his partner had their own agenda, that's why.

The room filled with onlookers, and rabbits were readied for the contest, which consisted of tunnel running, obstacle jumping, and included another test that I couldn't remember. By this time, I couldn't care less what went on, I simply wanted Bun back.

I'd resumed my position at the table, when my phone buzzed in my pocket. Startled by it, I peered at the screen. Anxious to not be heard by anyone nearby, I left the platform and stepped near the door to answer the call.

A deep voice said, "The rabbit is fine. If you want him back, do as I say. If you don't, the rabbit will pay the price for it."

Now angrier than ever, I agreed to do as asked. I could hear Bun, his voice desperate and afraid, yelling to me in the background. Aware that only I could hear him, relief flooded me as a sense of joy followed behind. He was okay, scared, but okay. He must have been a good distance away from me, or he'd have been able to contact me, I was certain of it.

"These guys mean business. I'm locked in a filthy cage with no comforts whatsoever. I'm exhausted and hungry, you've got to rescue me right away. Colin and Seamus are the guys you should be hunting down, I don't know how long I can survive in these circumstances."

Willing to give the Bun-nappers a birth certificate they firmly believed I stole from Evelyn's house, I gave in. Unwilling to argue that I didn't have it or knowledge of where Evelyn's house was, I agreed to make the switch-off the following day at ten in the morning here at the center.

The contest was half over when I returned to my job. A few glares came my way from other judges. I shrugged, lifted my cards, and gave the rabbit a ten for his efforts, whether the others liked it or not. I had bigger and far more urgent matters to deal with than who had performed the best. One of those was how I would find Evelyn's house, search for a birth certificate, and not get caught. All that without Bun's help. Crikey.

The best rabbit of the show was awarded the grand prize with much celebration of his beauty, and then the exhibition ended. Rabbits were packed and ready for travel, vendors made last-minute deals with customers, and Vera approached me with a smile on her face. For what? I couldn't begin to guess.

"Thank you so much for standing in as a judge at the last minute, Juliette. It was wonderful of you to help us out. Can I keep you in mind for next year?"

I shook her hand and said, "It was an honor for me. Thank you for the opportunity. I'm afraid I've fallen behind in the work at my farm by giving up the time to be here, and my own rabbits must come first. I'm sure you understand."

Her smile had somewhat faded. "I do, and thanks again."

That was one issue out of my hair and my life. Now to go home and address the Bun-napping. I prayed Jessica would have ideas on how I should proceed. She drew the line at breaking and entering, so it was out of the question to even ask her. I remembered Evelyn's address was on the application when I had entered Petra.

On my way to the farm, I stopped at a walk-in medical treatment center. The doctor looked over my injury, asked some questions, and then sent me for an X-ray. About thirty minutes later, he returned to say I would have a headache, but that my skull was fine.

Relieved at the news that my noggin was in good shape, I drove home. My brain was filled with what-ifs and how-tos. What if I convinced Jess to accompany me to Evelyn's home, at least as my wingman? Would she agree to that? What if I was arrested? What if we were arrested? Who would care for the rabbits and handle the clinic? Then there were the how-tos. How to break and enter without being obvious or seen. How to explain my actions to Jack if I was caught. How to not let him know of the upcoming meeting to retrieve Bun. There were lots of things to consider in this instance.

As if the car knew its way home, I found I'd reached the farm entrance and flipped the signal on to make the turn. Parked next to Jessica's car, I entered the clinic by way of the gift shop.

"Hello?" I called.

Jessica poked her head around the corner of an examination room doorway. "You're back. I thought you'd be later than this. How did it go?"

I took a deep breath and tried to hold tears at bay. "Bun has been Bun-napped." A tear trickled down my cheek. I swiped it from my face. "I have to meet two guys tomorrow to get him back."

Shocked, Jessica's mouth gaped open. She closed it, then opened it again. Questions flooded from her with no break between them. I raised my hand to halt her midstream.

"Stop talking for a minute. I'll tell you all about it. First, what can I do to help you finish for the day?"

"Nothing."

"Have the rabbits been seen to?"

"The kids took care of them. The rabbits have eaten and are set for now. All in here is ready for work tomorrow, let's go into the house. You must be a wreck."

That was the least of my problems. Angry, fearful, depressed, and angry again, that's what I was. I nodded and walked alongside her through the breezeway after giving the rabbits a quick look.

Meatloaf simmered in the Crock-Pot. A burst of goodness sprang into my nostrils when I lifted the lid. Carrots, potatoes, celery, onions, and spices blended with the ground beef and my mouth watered.

Jessica brewed individual cups of coffee and handed me one. "Tell me everything. I can't believe this happened in such a crowded place. Were there any witnesses?"

It was a long story, and as slowly as I told it, no new details came to mind. I lifted my bangs and showed her the bump on my forehead.

"Yikes. You're fortunate to not have broken the skin. Do you have any side effects? Like dizziness or nausea? You did lose consciousness, right?"

"Briefly. I'm okay, really, I am. I stopped to get checked out and was told I'll be fine. All I want is to save Bun. He's probably distraught to have had this happen. We had a run-in with Margery Shaw this week that left him rattled."

"That woman is a nuisance. She hasn't learned her lesson, has she? The court fined her heavily for animal abuse. You know Judge Forest is a stickler for that. He has two dogs, a duck, chickens, cows, you name it, and I tend to all of them. Brian's an animal lover. When Margery ended up in front of him in court, he told her he would jail her if he could, but the law didn't allow for that yet."

"Where did you hear that?"

"From him, of course. He asked how Bun had adapted to living here. Judge Forest was pleased when I said he had you wrapped around his foot. That's when he told me about Margery."

"A good man in my book, then. You call him Brian?"

"Well, yeah. He insisted on it. What's your plan for Bun? I know you have one. I certainly would."

"How willing would you be to help me out?"

"I'm not sure, why?"

"These guys want a birth certificate that's in Evelyn's house. I thought I might invade her residence tonight to find it. Are you in?"

Someone knocked on the door. We both started at the same time and gawked at Sheriff Carver, who waited for me to invite him in. "Oh please, I don't need this right now," I uttered.

I beckoned him in while Jessica made him a cup of coffee. He took it with murmured thanks and sat across from the two of us.

He took a swig of the brew and asked, "You've lost your rabbit and plan to get him back, don't you?"

Taken aback, I blurted, "How do you know what I'm going to do?"

"Have you heard from the kidnappers?"

I fiddled with my napkin.

He watched me for a second or two while I concocted a way to sidestep answering him.

"I'll take that as a yes."

"W-ell, uh, . . ."

"Don't lie to me." His words held an ominous tone that brought me upright in the chair.

"I was told not to contact you, or Bun would reap the consequences. I'm sorry, Jack, I won't let them harm him."

His attitude changed when tears sneaked from my eyes and paved their way to my chin.

"Jules, I know you're fond of Bun, but you can't break the law. What was the demand?"

"Evelyn has paperwork they want. I have no idea why."

He removed his elbows from the table and stared at me, his expression thoughtful. It was as if his internal wheels were moving at significant speed. His eyes had gleamed when I mentioned Evelyn's name. I glanced at Jess and saw the look of surprise on her face. This was a different Sheriff Carver than she had ever encountered.

"It's interesting that they're connected to or know a secret about Evelyn, don't you think?" Jack asked. "Does Carina Richland know what the secret is, or could she be in cahoots with them? Desperate people often make serious mistakes."

The furthest thing from my mind was the likelihood of Carina's involvement. Wait a minute, had I lost my capacity to connect the dots in this investigation? I hoped this was a mere loss of focus on the big picture.

"I wouldn't know and can't venture a guess. You

might talk to her about it." If I could point him in another direction, such as Carina, it would present an opportunity to break into Evelyn's home without his knowing it. Hmm.

"I will. In the meantime, stay away from Evelyn's house. I'll have a deputy watching you, should you disregard my order."

"Fine."

"I'm serious, Jules. Kidnappers play by a separate set of rules than most lawbreakers. Don't push your luck, you might find yourself in unfortunate circumstances." Jack rose from his chair, put his hat on his head, and gave us a nod before departing.

Silent the entire time Carver was present, Jessica now let out a long whistle. "He means business."

"As do I. If you can't bring yourself to help me, I'll go to Evelyn's on my own. I have to find that birth certificate."

"Why didn't you tell Jack what it was?"

"I didn't want him to know. He's been holding back information right along while expecting me to give him every bit of mine. Two can play that game."

"But, it isn't a game, is it?"

"You're right, it's a matter of life or death for Bun. I can feel it in my bones. Now, will you help me or not?"

"If a deputy has been assigned to watch you, things could get sticky if you leave the farm."

"You head out and pick me up down the road. I'll cut through the woods and meet you past the curve in the road."

"That's an idea. I'll be the driver, you be the one who enters Evelyn's house. I can't be arrested if things run amuck. Someone has to care for the rabbits."

"No problem. Let's have dinner and wait until after dark. I think Molly is teaching a class tonight, which means there will be a lot for the deputy to keep track of. I should be able to make my way to you without him noticing."

We set the table, ate a delightful dinner, and cleared up afterward. Twilight had set in as Molly, followed by the students, rolled into the yard and parked in front of the shop. Jessica and I walked out to greet them all and entered the shop behind them. We chatted with Molly while students settled in.

When the class began, I walked along the breezeway to enter the house. Jessica left the shop and drove off. Dressed in a dark coat with Evelyn's address inside a pocket, black jeans, a black jersey, and a black hat, I went out the back door and ran into the woods. In my haste, I stumbled once, then twice, fell to my knees the third time, and slowed my progress. It wouldn't do to injure myself in the woods as darkness was about to descend.

Her car idled on the side of the road. I rushed through underbrush, crossed behind the car, and slid into the passenger seat. Traffic was light, giving us a clear shot to find our way to Evelyn's. I entered the address into Jessica's Garmin while she drove. The directions were easier than I thought, but farther away, too. Fifteen minutes later, we reached her street. Homes were dark for the most part, a few had cars parked at the curb or in the driveways. Streetlights glowed as we searched for the house number.

I heaved a disgusted sigh. "Have I ever mentioned how difficult it is to find a house number these days?"

"Only you would know. I have no experience in this sort of thing."

I could hear the humor in her voice and grinned. It appeared Jessica was having fun.

"Maybe I should have asked you to accompany me on these jaunts before now."

"No, that's quite all right. I'm fine with being a law-abiding citizen, thank you."

I pointed to the house on our left. "That's it. Pull over and then park down the street, okay?"

"Sure. I'll be four houses down, in between streetlights. That way it won't look odd to be sitting in a car in the dark."

"You'd be great at this, you know."

"Not me, this is a one-time deal for the sake of Bun."

It took a few minutes to figure out how to access the house. Wishing all the while Bun was here to nose around, I entered the enormous Victorian by way of the basement. How could anyone as ruthless and nasty as Evelyn leave her bulkhead door unlocked? Or, had someone else entered the same way and waited for me inside?

My hand trembled as I closed the door behind me. I had tucked a tiny flashlight inside my pants pocket and now flashed the narrow beam of light across the floor. A set of steps were off to my right.

The flashlight showed me the way as I climbed the stairs on silent, soft-soled sneakered feet. I pushed the slightly ajar door wide open.

My heart pounded hard as if trying to escape my chest. Could anyone, other than me, hear the thumps? Was anyone else present? Hesitant, I walked into a clean home, empty of people, and seemingly unlived in. The furniture looked new with no signs of wear. It struck me as odd.

I glanced out the window at the house across the street. No cars in the yard, no lights on, and no garage. Did anyone live there? The neighborhood was strange, or was to me and for some reason I couldn't quite get a handle on why.

Wandering the rooms, I gave them a cursory look before I climbed to the second floor. It too was clean, neat, and appeared unlived in. Nothing was out of place, the closets were empty, except for one, which must have been Evelyn's room. I remembered Bun's remark about Evelyn's dowdy clothes and her terrible manicure. My own attire and horrendous manicure came to mind. I shook my head. Leave it to Bun to notice that sort of thing. Evelyn's bedroom yelled dowdy, right down to the ugliest coverlet I'd ever seen. I admit I was no interior designer. My taste was simply better.

I peered inside boxes, bins, and then rifled dresser drawers in each room. Nothing.

Like the first floor, the six second-floor rooms and furnishings had no personality and no secrets to reveal, at least that I could find. Plain, drab, and boring would be Bun's assessment. I stood still at the edge of the staircase. Not a sound filtered through the house. Creepy.

Sure-footed, I went to the first floor again. Not having searched it as well as I had the upstairs, I had no option but to do so. It was unlikely that I'd find what I needed but gave it a go anyway.

A door at the far end of Evelyn's office was closed. A key hanging at an angle from the lock begged to be opened. I swung the door wide, flashed light inside, and found three cardboard containers of documents. I shuffled through them like a madwoman in hope of finding the birth certificate. The worst part was I didn't know whose certificate I was supposed to hunt down.

The boxes didn't hold much of importance, not for me, anyway. My heart sank, and disappointment took over. I shoved it to the back of my mind and growled, "Focus, just focus. It's here, I know it is."

I had passed the desk to search the closet and turned to it now. It held an assortment of show applications and a small notebook filled with remarks written on each applicant. Fixated on what she'd learned or assumed about them, I read on. Halfway through the book, I found rows of figures and initials with dates listed beside each one. Was this blackmail money Evelyn had received? Astonished that Evelyn kept a running tab on people she blackmailed, along with their secrets, I snapped the book closed and stuck it into my jacket pocket.

The top drawer of the desk was locked. I grabbed the knifelike letter opener and made quick work of the lock. It was hard to believe no one else had tried to break into this house to do what I was doing now. Breaking the law, that's what I was doing now. Again, I banished the thought, just like my disappointment.

A thin file held a bunch of documents pertaining to the house, Evelyn's car, and an assortment of other things that didn't appear important yet might be. I folded them in half and checked the time on my watch. A half hour had flown by and to Jessica it would be seem like forever. She probably had the jitters by now.

I sneaked out of the house the way I had entered it and jogged along the sidewalk as if I belonged on this street. No cars passed me, no lights glowed in the homes, and no people walked the sidewalks. Weird, just weird. It was the kind of development built by developers but left empty to entice buyers. Yards were manicured to a fault, some of the homes would be furnished, yet not a sole resided there and the houses would be used as models.

Relieved when I got into the car, Jessica said, "It's about time, you were in there for hours."

"I was only gone for half an hour. I know you're nervous, don't be, please. I think I may have found what I was looking for. Drop me off at the same place and I'll find my way home. It shouldn't be a problem, all the interior and exterior lights are on in the house."

"Good idea. It would look weird if I arrived at your house this late."

CHAPTER TWELVE

Tripping and stumbling through the woods was prevented when I took to the edge of them instead of breaking my neck in the dark. Rather than call attention to my return, I kept the flashlight turned off. I'd lived in the area for so long, I knew my way.

The moon disappeared behind a cloud as I drew close to the house. The light from the rear windows welcomed me back. Dropping my coat and cap on a chair, I walked through the first floor to glance out the windows. I hadn't noticed a police car in the area, but it didn't mean I wasn't being watched. But then, the sheriff might have called it quits for the night if he thought I would go to bed early after the emotional day I'd had.

I looked in on the rabbits. They were calm and quiet, nestled in their hutches. In the shop, I found a note from Molly and a list of items to buy for the next class. The girl had a head for business, and I was grateful for that.

The house was quiet, too quiet. Bun would have talked nonstop after what we had done together, what I did alone tonight. His ability to tune in to his surroundings was a blessing when we engaged in breaking the law. I heaved a deep sigh as loneliness crept over me. The old saying that you don't know what you have until it's gone hit home.

Withdrawing the stolen folders from my coat pocket, I spread them across the table. By midnight I knew Evelyn's habits better than most. The picture drawn wasn't a pretty one, no matter how it was viewed. Opinions of her were on the mark, and this paperwork proved it. I sat back in the chair. I didn't have a clue as to what the Bun-nappers wanted in the way of a birth certificate. Three of them lay on the table in front of me. I rubbed my hands across my face, yawned, and then looked them over again. Selecting two of the three, I discarded one that belonged to a woman who had left earth in the early 1900s. I folded the other two, set them aside, and ruffled the rest of the papers into order. I put the file in my desk drawer, then stuck the certificates into my handbag.

A mist of rain fell into the light gray fog that covered the ground. As dreary as the weather, I did chores in soft conversation with the rabbits. Jessica arrived as I completed my workload.

"You look, well, uh, awful."

"Gee, thanks, I feel awful. The house is so empty without Bun, I can't stand it."

"Did you sleep well?"

"Fitfully." I hung the freshly scrubbed apron on

its hook and washed my hands. "Did you notice any police cars when you dropped me off last night? I didn't."

"Not a one. Maybe the officer assigned to you was in one of those unmarked vehicles." Jess shrugged. "Either way, we got away with what we did, don't you think?"

"If we hadn't, Carver would have been on the doorstep. Just be your usual self if he shows up today. I'm certain he will, he'll want to check in on me. Jack's not happy when I poke my nose where I shouldn't and he always suspects that's exactly what I'm doing."

Her chuckle was followed with, "I wonder how he's reached that conclusion."

I gave her a wry glance from the corner of my eye.

"You must admit he has reason to keep an eye on you. Consider what happened this summer. If he hadn't done so, you might not be here today. That woman had a deadly weapon and all you had was Bun."

"I should be grateful for Jack's behavior, it's just that it rankles me to know he's breathing down my neck."

Her first appointment arrived. I mentioned the list of things Molly asked for that I would pick up as Jess walked off and left me on my own. She was unaware I would soon drive to the exhibition center to meet with two very bad men. Though Jessica's schedule was likely filled with clinic appointments, she would want to accompany me. I purposely hadn't given the time of the meeting and wouldn't have told her if she had asked.

The clock ticked as I wended through traffic toward the center. Parked close to the rear of the building, I surveyed the area before locking the car. Unlike the past several days, the lot and grounds were deserted. In an instant, I crossed the parking lot and noticed the back door was open a mere crack.

I heard the faint squeak when I pulled the door open enough to slip inside in stealth mode. Every few steps, I stopped to listen. A sound echoed through the empty building. *"I know you're here. Be careful, these guys are rotten to the core. I'm in a curtained area in room four past the main lobby. Come and get me, please, Jules. I'm petrified they'll kill us."*

Fear fought for control of my body. I was already shaky and I advanced on tiptoe once again, then skirted the lobby, and followed Bun's directions. I'd left my handbag in the car along with my jacket to make our getaway easier. The folded papers were in the back pocket of my jeans.

Focused on the sound of Bun's voice, I wondered if he could read my mind, a mind filled with escape methods. At the closed door, I knocked and then backed away several feet. Not taking a chance of being hauled inside and pummeled, then searched and left for dead as I had been in the past, I stepped back when the door opened and stared at Seamus.

"You're alone?"

"I am."

"Got what we asked for?"

"I have it." I waved the folded wad at him.

"Then come closer and toss it to me."

"I want to see the rabbit first."

"That's not going to happen."

"That doesn't work for me."

"Too bad."

"Okay, keep the rabbit. We're done here." False bravado at its best, I quaked inside, fearful Seamus would call my bluff. I shook in my shoes at the probability of it, knowing that I could find myself in deep trouble here.

"Fine." He turned and looked over his shoulder, tipped his head in my direction, and moved aside.

Held in Colin's tight grip, Bun said, "*I'm fine, but they aren't going to give me back. We're doomed instead.*"

I gave him a slight nod, stared at him, and thought hard, hoping he knew what I wanted him to do. His ears flopped and then rose. I guessed he had gotten the message.

I turned to Seamus and said, "Let's do this then." I shifted my eyes to Bun. "Now."

Colin had loosened his grip on Bun and now held him in the crook of his arm. The young man didn't look mean and nasty, as did Seamus. Though, he had gone along with Bun-napping, and in my opinion, Colin was no better than his cohort.

In a flash, Bun leapt from him onto Seamus's neck. His claws extended, Bun clawed his face before he bounded toward me. At his scream of pain, agony, and astonishment, these two criminals were the last I saw as Bun and I hightailed it through the building toward the exit.

Hot on our heels, their footsteps pounded across the floors. Cursing, Seamus yelled as we reached the door. Like a wicked wind, Bun and I left them behind, fists pummeling the air in threat to our well-being.

"That was close. I wasn't sure you wanted me to try to escape, but when I saw your determination and false bravado, I knew what I had to do. Besides, you would never leave me with him. Would you?"

"Not ever. I've been so worried about you." I'd have reached out to pet him if I hadn't been driving fast and crazy. I peered into the rearview mirror to keep track of the cars behind us. So far, we weren't being chased, but a car I'd noticed in the past had joined the line behind us.

Three of the cars in line turned into various businesses, leaving a decent view of an unmarked police car when we stopped for the red light. From my rearview mirror, I recognized the driver as an officer from the station. We were safe, for the moment, at least.

Now that I had an escort, the rest of our ride home was slower. Adam parked his car next to mine. He came over to me and said, "Where did you get the rabbit?"

"From the animal rescue people. I thought you knew that."

"Don't be cute, Jules. You didn't have him when you left the house, so where did he come from?"

His no-nonsense attitude wouldn't bode well for me if I wasn't truthful. "Come into the house. Bun needs to eat and then I'll check him over. You know he was taken, and I was assaulted. I'll explain over coffee. How's that?"

He followed me indoors. I checked Bun from end to end and was satisfied he hadn't been harmed. I gave him an extra treat to go with his meal and filled his water container.

Jess had come into the house. Coffee perked,

she stood silent for a few minutes and then remarked, "You met them alone?"

"I did. I wasn't taking any chances of having Bun injured in any way. It wasn't long before I realized these guys are stupid, real stupid." I sighed and said, "I did what I thought best, take it or leave it."

I sounded rude, even to my own ears, but this was Bun, for crying out loud.

"I see, shrewd of you to keep me out of it. Thanks, Jules. I would have been in the way and could have caused more chaos than you probably did." Jessica poured three cups of coffee, passed sugar and cream around the table, and took a seat.

Adam had listened to our exchange without comment. He set his half-empty cup on the table and said, "Tell me."

I ran through what the men did, how the scene unfolded, and ended with our escape. I left out Bun's assault on one of the men, then thought better of it. I admitted that Bun had left minor scratch marks on the man's face in his effort to gain his freedom.

When Sheriff Carver stopped by, it occurred to me his visit wasn't a coincidence. Without his usual knock on the door, Jack walked in. I slid a glance toward Jessica, who got a cup of coffee and handed it to Jack. She refilled Adam's cup before going to her next appointment.

Carver slurped his coffee, sat back, and said, "I heard what happened."

Adam lifted his phone. He had dialed the sheriff and left the call open while I gave a rundown of my adventure, including descriptions of both men. "Sorry," he said.

I shrugged. "No, you're not, but I would expect that from any lawman."

Carver cut any further remarks short. "Now we have evidence to go on."

"That being?"

"The rabbit scratched the man, that's what."

"Oh, right. Glad *he* could be of help since there wasn't much forthcoming from you people." It was snarky and insolent of me, but once again, I'd taken action when no one else would. They didn't care about Bun the way I did.

On that note, Adam said he'd be on his way and asked Jack if surveillance was over.

"Not yet. Juliette isn't safe, though she thinks her issues with these guys are over." His expression stern when he turned to me, he remarked, "You won't be safe until we have them in custody. My advice, should you care to take it, would be to allow Adam to keep his eye on you."

"Does that mean he'll shadow me like a wraith for the time being?"

"It does."

I said it was fine by me. The idea of having this cop on my trail didn't thrill me in the least, but I was smart enough to let Jack think I agreed.

Before Jack closed the door on his way out, I asked, "Have you spoken to Carina as yet?"

"She's on my list. You don't make my job any easier by going off on these tangents. You could have found yourself in danger. Let me handle this, Jules. I have years of experience in the field of investigation."

"True, you do. Thanks for the reminder." I closed the door as he went down the front steps.

Bun hovered in the doorway.

"You certainly held your tongue while I was put through that. Thanks for not interrupting, it isn't always helpful. I like to answer you, but can't always."

"He wasn't happy with you, that's for sure. And how about the way Adam set you up? I would have been annoyed over that."

"Adam did his duty. It also saved me from having to repeat myself. How about a visit with your furry friends?"

Ears up, Bun hopped toward the front door. *"Let's go this way. I could use the fresh air."*

I pushed the screen door open. "You bet. Lead the way." I watched him race across the yard before he hopped onto the step at the shop door. Lightness filled my heart at the sight of his joy. Sooner or later he would tell me of being held against his will, but right now, he wasn't ready to share.

He joined the rabbits in the play area, said he was fine if I had other things to do, and turned to his friends. Brushed off so sweetly, I wandered into the shop, gazed at rows of colorful yarn and piled globs of roving that waited to be spun. Meredith opened the door and asked if she could come in.

"I saw you through the window. I hope I'm not interrupting you," Meredith said.

"Come on in, it's great to see you. How are your classes going?"

"Molly is patient with all of us. Worth her weight in gold." She held up a mass of yarn for my inspection.

"This is yours?" I asked, running my hands over the bundle.

"I couldn't have managed without help. It's one of the reasons I came to see you."

I handed her the yarn. "Great job, and Molly is a sweetheart. Now tell me why you're here."

She withdrew a folded envelope from her pocket, smoothed it, and handed it to me. I took it, saw the company name in the top corner, and looked at Meredith again.

"What's this?" Not waiting for an answer, I tore the envelope open and withdrew a letter.

"Jim asked if I would drop this off to you. I met him by chance today. Were you awarded grant money?"

I turned the letter toward her. "Jim's company has decided against my grant application. He doesn't give a reason."

She gave me a hug. "I'm sorry. I wanted you to get a grant from his company. The board is usually generous to those they feel have earned it, and I think you definitely have. The work you do here and the care you give your animals is well thought of in Windermere and beyond."

I held the letter up and said, "I guess they don't share that opinion."

The clinic door opened, and Jessica walked in. She greeted Meredith and reached for the letter in my hand.

"Wow, that's disappointing."

Meredith jumped into the conversation. "I agree. Jim said he'll call you this afternoon around four so make yourself available."

"I'm surprised at the refusal. He and his board members meet midweek and the show only ended yesterday. Maybe he thought better of it after what happened to me and Bun at the show. It wouldn't be good publicity for his company because I find myself in difficult positions with criminals and Jack."

With a pat on my shoulder, Jessica said, "That could be the reason. It makes sense."

Without a word, Meredith walked over to the yarn rack. She touched skein after skein, snuggled inside the diamond-shaped cubbyholes, as she always did. Meredith had once explained her method of choosing yarn when I had asked why she would shake or nod her head while she viewed and handled each type.

Jessica and I waited until she stepped back, shook her head, and said, "If I buy one more skein, I'll have the wrath of Jack upon my shoulders."

With a grin, I agreed. "I'm sure you will. No yarn for you today. If you have a favorite, let me know so I can hold it aside, in case you change your mind."

"I had better not. Nice of you to offer, though. I'll be on my way, oh wait, there's one more thing I wanted to say about Molly. Jim Brody supports kids in college. You might let her know she can apply for grant money to help with her studies. She's a top student, and an avid animal lover."

I walked her to the door. "I'll let her know. Thanks for coming by, Meredith."

When she'd gone, I sought out Bun. Jason arrived as we were leaving.

As another dog and its owner arrived, Bun and I went off to find the goods Molly had requested. I'd left a list of work for Jason and knew he was competent enough to get it done without me around.

Adam, in his unmarked car, followed us. It had finally sunk into my weary brain that Jack was right to assign an officer to me. Seamus and Colin had yet to be captured.

My phone rang while I waited at a red light.

"Hello?" I asked without giving the screen a look to see the caller's name.

"What you dropped in your rush to leave today wasn't the right certificate. It's stupid to play us for fools. We want the right one, and you're gonna give it to us."

I recognized the gruff voice. "Neither of them were what you wanted?"

"You know which one we meant."

"Fine." No sense insisting it wasn't in my possession, Seamus would think I lied. There was no reasoning with thugs like him.

His voice changed, became short and strained. "I'll be in touch." The line went dead, the traffic light turned green, and I went shopping.

Don't tell me, my fan club called.

"The certificates I took from Evelyn's were the wrong ones. I'll have to search again."

We can go together. My superpowers are functioning on high now that I'm free.

So be it. My partner in crime was back full tilt. I knew my way around Evelyn's home, which was a plus. Bun would be the lookout while I searched. What was so important about this birth certificate? What did it have to do with Evelyn's death? Something, for sure. Had she been murdered because of it? Was her death due to the secrets she kept?

Had Evelyn blackmailed the wrong person? So many questions with no concrete answers. Yet.

I kept an eye on Adam knowing he would do the same to us. When we parked at the police station, Bun edged into the sling buckled across my body.

In a spur of the moment decision, I had decided to ask Sheriff Carver a few questions. Adam didn't follow me in, but remained in his car at the curb.

"Do you plan to slay the dragon before he comes to visit you?"

"I want to know where he is in his quest to find our assailants."

"Good luck."

An officer at the front desk took down my name and asked my business. He knew who I was from previous visits but asked anyway. He rang the sheriff's office while I waited on a nearby bench. It wasn't long before I was told Jack was in his office and I could go in.

He teetered back and forth in his chair, a gleam in his eyes as I entered the room. Oh my, had I been foolish to come here? I sat in the seat across from him.

"What brings you by?"

"Have you come across those men?"

"Not yet. I got a lead this morning. A couple of my officers have gone to see if it will turn up something useful. Why?"

"I'm jittery over them being at large. They know where I live, Jack. I think Seamus is out for blood and won't stop until he gets it. What if Adam can't deal with them alone?"

"He knows what he's doing. I have you covered. Go about your work at the farm and leave this to me." He peered at Bun, who had stuck his head out of the sling. "How's the rabbit?"

"He seems okay. There were no injuries. The purpose of taking Bun was to prompt me to do what they couldn't. God knows why. I don't think they thought the whole thing through. If they had, Bun wouldn't have been a target." On the verge of asking if he'd spoken to Carina, I let the matter pass. I wouldn't push my luck since I was barred from looking into Evelyn's death.

A walk on the public park trail tempted me, but then I thought better of it. Adam wouldn't be able to follow us without looking conspicuous. From the police station, Bun and I went to pick up Molly's supplies and then returned to the farm.

I left Bun with the other rabbits just before the clock struck four. The phone rang and Jim Brody was on the line.

"Did Meredith stop by this morning?" he asked after a brief greeting.

"She did."

"You must be disappointed. I'm sorry to have built your hopes up, only to have them dashed, and quickly, too."

I'd nearly cried when I read the denial. I struggled to keep my voice neutral now. "Your letter didn't offer an explanation."

"I can't say, but I'm terribly sorry, Juliette."

"Thanks for calling." I hung up. Tears rolled down my cheeks, I blubbered for a few minutes, and then I straightened my backbone. My actions must have brought this on, and while I'd been given false hope, I had always managed the farm on my own and would continue to do so. This might have been a blessing in disguise. I would be able to follow through on my promise to Carina.

With Seamus and Colin at large, I put Evelyn's murder investigation on the front burner. The birth certificate was an important clue that could clear Carina of any wrongdoing. I worried Jack might arrest her using circumstantial evidence, if he had any, as his reason.

Chapter Thirteen

Dinner consisted of a light meal shared with Jessica. Her day had ended early when an appointment was rescheduled. Bun ate in his room, and the other rabbits were set for the evening.

"You're going to search Evelyn's again, aren't you?"

"Bun and I will go this time. Whenever he feels a change in the air, he grows frantic and I use it as a sign that it's time to leave. During our last adventure, it was clear that he wanted to tell me something. I paid him heed, and it saved us."

"He's an extraordinary animal. I watched him in the play area today. He doesn't appear to have any lingering fear from being snatched up and held like that."

"My thoughts, exactly. I wondered if you could help me out tonight."

"What do you need?"

"Adam is on me like a bee to honey. He's right behind me every time I go out, which makes it near to impossible to be sneaky. Would you mind switching clothes with me and lending me your car when it starts to get dark? That way Adam will think I'm home for the evening. Dim the interior lights and relax while we're gone."

"How long will you be?"

"An hour or so, not more than that. I don't want to put you in an awkward position. That's why I'll take Bun."

"Consider it done. I have an extra set of clothes in the clinic. I'll change into those and give you these." She plucked at her shirt. "They might not fit perfectly, but Adam won't see up close when you go to my car, so you needn't worry. I'll even give you the hat I wear." She went to the clinic.

The clothes she'd worn were snug on me. Jessica weighed less than I did, but I had more muscle. In my opinion, that is. I lifted and stacked bales of hay daily, which built strength, as did hefting rabbit cages for parties and such.

Jessica looked me over. "Thinking of cutting back on sweets?"

"Not at all."

Jessica changed the subject.

"Did you hear from Mr. Brody?"

"He called to offer an apology for the denial of the grant. I pressed him for a reason, which he said he couldn't give. It doesn't fly with me, but I can't worry about that, there are more pressing issues to deal with."

"What did he say, exactly?"

I stared at Jess and asked, "Why do you ask?"

She shrugged and was about to turn away. "There's a reason, spit it out."

"He said he couldn't say why. Nothing more."

"Your recent actions were the reason."

"I don't think so. Anyway, the grant was the last thing on my mind after Bun was snatched."

"You might be better off without a handout from someone."

"I came to that conclusion, too. Besides, I made Carina a promise and intend to keep it."

She slapped me on the back. "There's the Juliette I know. For a while I feared you'd be taken in by the likes of Brody. They're a big business, and not always friendly."

"What do you mean?"

"One of my clients came in with their cat the other day. Her husband manages Brody's publicity and buyouts. Jim has his fingers in lots of pies, Jules. She wouldn't be more specific but said the man has problems. She didn't enlarge upon them."

"Huh, I didn't sense that at all. My focus was on other things, so maybe that's why. Meredith spoke highly of him, why would she do that if he wasn't a good soul?"

"Weren't you charmed by him?"

"I guess."

"There's your answer. A man like that would make it his business to stay on the good side of the sheriff's wife, wouldn't he?"

"Mm." The clock struck seven, darkness had descended, and it was time to go. I grabbed Jessica's floppy hat, was certain it would hide my features, and called for Bun and tucked him under my arm inside the loose jacket Jess usually wore. I took her keys and my driver's license, and sauntered off by way of the barn. My back was to the outside lights, which gave me an advantage. With Adam parked down the road from the farm, he could see the comings and goings but without a clear view of who was in each car.

Bun left the confines of the jacket as I pulled the hat lower and we set off on our adventure. I kept a look out for Adam, or any other cars I'd noticed in the parking lot at the police station today. So far, so good.

I turned right onto Evelyn's street. The homes appeared much the same as they had the last time I'd seen them. No movements in homes, no people on the sidewalks or joggers who ran in the dark, as some do in other neighborhoods. Eerie and strange as it was, I parked a few houses down from the one I would again infiltrate. Was I crazy? What if Jack decided to stop by and take a look for himself? What if Adam was in a different car altogether? What if Adam wasn't the officer assigned to me? Surely Adam would have time off, at least to sleep.

Bun hopped alongside me on the sidewalk.

"This is a creepy place. Where is everyone? It isn't that late and there aren't any lights on in the houses. Is it one of those spec neighborhoods where Realtors and builders work together to get homes built and sold to unsuspecting fools?"

We went up the driveway of the Victorian. "Unsuspecting fools? Really?"

"Well, yeah, they don't know if the house they select is well built or not. Some builders skimp, don't they? I listen to the news, Jules. Make no mistake about that."

The rabbit made sense. We entered Evelyn's basement, me on tiptoe, and Bun on padded paws. I scanned the room with the beam of my tiny flash-light. Everything was the same as my last visit. We took to the stairs, reached the top, and walked into the living quarters. I stopped to listen.

"We're the only people here. Otherwise, I would know it. My superpowers are on high alert."

"Glad to hear it," I whispered. "You're the look-out, I'm the hunter."

"That's not fair. I can search and be a lookout at the same time. I do have amazing hearing, you know."

I pointed to my left. "Fine, you nose around in that room. Let me know if you find anything."

"Will do."

The first floor looked exactly the same as I had left it. No one had snooped around. If so, they'd left things the way they had found them. I delved into more papers in the library. There had been limited time when I'd come with Jessica. Bun and I could give this place a thorough search tonight.

From the other room, I heard Bun say, *"I've found nothing. How about you?"*

"Not yet. I searched the upstairs rooms the other night. There's nothing up there other than Evelyn's bedroom. All the guest rooms had furni-ture but nothing else."

Bun hopped into the library and watched me take a few dusty books from the top shelf of the built-in bookcase. I held the book by its binder and fluttered the pages. Nothing. With a grunt of impatience, I went down the short stepladder, then folded it and returned it to the corner.

"Let's check the cellar. There were plastic bins stacked under the stairs. It's the last place I can think of to look."

We'd started down the stairs when Bun stopped. His ears quivered as did his whiskers. *"We have company coming. I hear footsteps."*

"How many people?"

His head tipped to the side, and his attention rapt, Bun listened. *"Two, I think."*

"How close?" I said softly.

"In the bulkhead."

By this time, I'd scooped him into my arms. The sound of voices grew closer as I rushed down the last few steps. Crouched behind bins stacked under the stairs in darkness that surrounded us, I held Bun to my chest. "Relax," I whispered. He sagged against me as his released tension left him limp.

A beam of light streamed across the basement floor. "Let's go upstairs. I want that certificate. I think she told the truth when she said she didn't have it. That interferin' woman never had it and gave us what she thought we wanted. She's a nosy one. She's also friends with the sheriff." Spoken by Colin, who had set me up for the attack. He seemed the only intelligent one of the two, and he was no bright bulb, either.

I held my breath as they climbed the stairs. Seamus groused the entire time, insisting all he wanted was to get what was coming to them. "If that Juliette woman finds it first, she'll turn it over to the sheriff. Then we'll have to leave town before we get paid." His deep voice faded when they moved on into the house to begin their search.

"We won't stay here, will we?"

A tremor ran through Bun's small frame.

"No, we won't."

Bun scuttled inside my coat and snuggled up under my armpit, not a comfortable place for either of us. I crooked my elbow and tightened my hold on him. I cut across the basement floor on silent feet, then took the short flight of steps in two huge strides and went out the door.

Sneaking close to the side of the house, I broke into a dead run when we reached a group of shrubs located near the edge of the driveway. Jessica's car was where I had left it and we got in. I started the engine and slowly rolled away from the curb, the headlights off. Once again, I noticed there was no movement or lights on in other homes.

We passed the Victorian house. Inside, a beam of light from the flashlight bounced off the walls as Seamus and Colin moved from place to place.

"Not too obvious, are they?"

"Idiots. I told you, didn't I."

"You did." Bun turned his head, looked at me, his whiskers jittery, and asked, *"What are you doing?"*

"Reporting a robbery in progress."

"Oooh, do you think that's wise?"

I could hear the humor in his voice. I assured him that I did, and dialed the police station.

The dispatcher asked a bunch of questions, including my name. I disconnected the call, and turned the phone off. I parked on the side of the road, and we waited. In less than five minutes, two police cars sped past us in the direction of Evelyn's address. Once they were out of sight, I continued on home and parked on the other side of my own car. It was good to be back.

Jess was watching a TV program when we entered the house. She jumped from the chair and asked, "Did you find it?"

I shook my head and told her we were interrupted, and explained our escape. Bun went to his room and snuggled down in his new bed for the night. *"I'm tired, good night, Jules."*

I left him to it and joined Jessica in the living room. "Did you have visitors while I was gone?"

"If you mean the sheriff or his officers, no. You have a voice mail from Carina, though. She sounds kind of worried. I think Carver went to see her, I only heard half the message, so you'll need to listen to it." She shut the TV off and took her jacket and hat from me.

"Thanks, Jess, I appreciate your help. I don't think I'll be able to go back to Evelyn's again. Whether the police arrest those two guys or not, Jack is sure to have the house under surveillance from now on. I might have made things more difficult by reporting the break-in, but I needed Seamus and Colin out of my way and in a jail cell."

"I wonder what's so important that they'd go to such lengths? It makes no sense. Do you have any idea who wants the certificate? You did say you heard one of these guys say he only wanted what they had coming. Does it mean they'll receive compensation?"

"There has to be someone behind all this who's willing to pay them, but it's not Carina. I doubt she would jeopardize her daughter's safety by hiring those two bumbling fools. She knows she's still on Jack's list of suspects."

Buttoning her jacket, Jess put her hat on and

pulled it down tight. "I'll see you tomorrow. Get some rest, you look tired. You're sure you aren't having any residual effects from that bump on your head?"

"I'm fine, just beat. It's nice to be home and not have to go back to the rabbit show again."

We walked to the door. "Will you change your mind about doing that again next year?"

"I highly doubt it. Too much negativity behind the scenes for my liking. Have a good night, Jess. Drive carefully."

I watched from the doorway until her car disappeared from sight before I locked up for the night. While Bun slept, I wandered through the barn looking in on the rabbits. I yawned and went into the house, knowing all was well at the farm.

The message from Carina was brief and to the point. I leaned against the counter, arms folded, listening to her. She sounded paranoid, and who could blame her for that? I yawned again and worried over what Jack must have put her through when she said he had been to her house with questions about her relationship with Evelyn. Carina wanted an update.

Reluctant to tell her what had happened, I was glad it was too late to call her now. It would have to wait until morning. I shut the lights off and went upstairs.

My brain worked overtime while I lay in bed waiting for sleep. Questions swirled through my head. Would I ever get some rest? Determined to shut my thoughts off, I used the deep breathing exercises I'd learned a few years ago and hoped to relax.

* * *

Sunlight streamed across the bed into my eyes when I opened them. I shut the alarm clock off and flopped against the pillows. The exercises must have worked, I didn't remember falling asleep. With a busy day ahead, I tossed the bedcovers aside and got out of bed.

Bun sat in my bedroom doorway. His whiskers twitched. *"I've been waiting for you to wake up. The rabbits and I want breakfast."*

"I'll be downstairs after I get dressed."

He hopped away, mumbling down the stairs.

It wasn't as if I'd slept late, Bun was just being, well, Bun. I refused to rush and took time to get organized. When I was ready and had straightened up my bedroom, I joined Bun in the kitchen.

"Are we going to Carina's today? I heard the message you played last night. She sounds intimidated by your friend the sheriff."

Oh, so he was *my* friend, huh? Bun should have taken into account Jack's search for those who had taken him from me. I wouldn't rise to the bait, and prepared his breakfast while coffee perked.

Bun ate in silence while I drank coffee before I went into the barn to feed and clean up after the rabbits. Wide awake, they locked on to my movements in hope of receiving the feed I assembled and would deliver to each cage port. They were a ravenous bunch this morning, or maybe just happy to see me. They rushed about their hutches, then took to the food. I spoke to each rabbit as I moved from one cage to the next.

"Why do you talk to them? They can't talk back."

"It's good manners and lets them know I care about them."

Do you think they understand what you say?"

I shrugged. "Of course. You understand, so why wouldn't they?"

"Hmm, if you say so. You didn't answer my question about whether we were going to Carina's today."

"I have to call her first. Then I'll know what to do. You're quite interested."

"I'm bothered to think Carina might have been behind my abduction."

"I'm sure you're mistaken. We'll see what she has to say and then we'll form an opinion. How's that?"

"Doable."

Having served the rabbits, I proceeded to clean the interiors of each cage, and freshened the hutch end with bunches of fresh hay. While draped in my usual apron with gloves that went up to my elbows, I started to empty fecal pans. I'd nearly reached the end of one row when Jason came into the barn.

"I'll take over from here, Juliette. I have to say, you do a great job of taking care of these critters."

"They deserve it. After you're done, we'll put them in the exercise pens." I left him to his job, removed my work gear, and went into the shop. When Jess arrived, she came into the shop on her way to the clinic.

"I forgot my key to the clinic door." She sounded disgruntled. What caused it might be more from my escapades than having forgotten her key.

"Not a problem. You can always enter the barn this way."

She gave me a nod, crossed the room, and walked into the clinic. I watched her without asking questions. Sooner or later, she'd let me know why she was grumpy.

Chapter Fourteen

Dinner slowly cooked in the Crock-Pot. Bun accompanied me to the barn and I helped Jason release the rabbits into the exercise pen. The first group jumped and played with toys, while others zoomed through the rabbit tunnel that went outside into a larger, wire fenced area. I had opened that hatch to let them out.

Plexiglass covered the entire run, with a large window in the barn that overlooked the outside pen. It was an easy way to keep an eye on them. The only rabbit that was a cause for concern was Walkabout Willy. If he could find a way to wander freely about the farm, he did. Jess and I had secured the pen, the run, and the exterior playground to keep him from getting away.

A truck backed up to the open barn doors and the driver got out. Between the two of us, the supplies were unloaded and stacked on the barn floor. I checked off the list, and signed the bill of lading before he left. Included in the delivery were additional goods for the shop.

Bundles of roving, stuffed in plastic bags, were packed in a single box. When I lifted the first bag, the others puffed up and cascaded onto the floor.

With some rabbits in a different playground, Jason came indoors. They were older rabbits than the others and not as active. Petra was in the middle of the age groups and fit in either one, as did Bun. Through the window, I saw him sprawled in the sun.

"Can I put that away for you?" Jason asked.

"Sure, I'll take this part of the order into the shop. I know Molly has anxiously awaited its arrival."

Roving lay atop the counter, clusters of it filtered across the floor, soft to the touch. I knew where it was supposed to go, but wasn't sure it would fit within the confines of the shelves. I struggled to fit each clump and heard Jessica's snicker. She'd come into the room and watched me.

"Give me a hand, will you?"

Instructed on how to tightly bundle the roving into large diamond-shaped slots, I did so while Jess added the remainder to the cupboard under the counter. That job out of the way, I asked if she could take a break.

"I don't have an appointment for a half hour or so."

On our way through the barn, I told Jason where to find us. He nodded and kept working.

Tea brewed, Jessica set out cups, and I put a tin of shortbread on the table. While we sipped and snacked, I asked about her patients and listened to stories of their problems and their excitement at seeing her when they arrived. Jessica gave treats to the animals as they left, and not one of them forgot.

She fiddled with her napkin and said, "Colin and Seamus are free."

"Wh-what?"

"I was stopped on my way home last night. The cop wanted to know why I had come back here, and he asked a bunch of questions that didn't have anything to do with those men. I gave him a story about forgetting something important at the clinic and he seemed to believe me."

"How is that connected to the kidnappers?"

"I saw them in Windermere, at a gas station. I stopped to buy milk, and there they were filling their gas tank. They appeared nervous and left right away."

"Great, just great. Is that what was bothering you this morning?"

"Not just that. I didn't like lying to the policeman. He was watching the house. I didn't see his car, there isn't a streetlight in that section. He must have backed into the turnaround because when I went by, he pulled out right behind me. It gave me a start, that's for sure. Then I saw the men and that was all I needed to cap off the night. I slept fitfully all night. How do you deal with this?"

"No better than you do. Sorry, Jess, I shouldn't have asked for your help. I hope I haven't jeopardized your safety. Why didn't you call me?"

"I didn't want you to worry. Besides, you have a cop watching you. I don't think you have jeopardized anyone but yourself. Though, my credibility might come into question if the sheriff finds out about this. I wanted to call and report my sighting of these guys, but that would have been suspicious, don't you agree?"

"Sheriff Carver would have asked too many questions. You did the right thing."

"I guess we can't ask her to do anything else, can we?"

I glanced down and saw Bun sitting near the counter. Sneaky little bunny that he is, I was certain he had listened the entire time. "I promise not to ask you to get involved from now on. I'm truly sorry."

"Seamus and Colin gave me shivers that went straight down my spine and rattled me. When they headed east, I realized they weren't coming here."

"What's for dinner?"

"I made chili for dinner tonight. It always comes out so delicious cooked in the Crock Pot."

"Yum." With a half smile, Jess scooted through the breezeway to greet her next patient.

"Do you think those two left town or will they go into hiding until they get what they're after?"

"I'm not sure what they'll do. They aren't very smart, but desperation causes people to take chances they normally wouldn't. This might be one of those instances."

"Good thing we're being watched, then."

"They will be apprehended if they come here. Then again, they might try to search Evelyn's home again if they weren't successful last night. I hope Jack assigned an officer to watch the place. I know we can't go back there."

"Not without Jessica's help, we can't."

With a stern look in Bun's direction, I said, "I refuse to ask, so don't nag me, okay?"

"I hadn't planned to. I can't think of any other way for us to get back into the house unless someone assists us."

"Maybe Carver would allow me to go in." I wondered how I could get him to agree to it.

"Sometimes you're so funny."

"I'm serious, Bun. If I can come up with a good reason, Jack might say yes. I just need a good reason, is all."

"I'll think on that for a while. Together, we might come up with a plan."

"Do that, I have to give Jason a hand with the remaining chores. He and Molly have had their hands full for the past several days."

He hopped alongside me as I went into the barn. Jason sat on a bale of hay and jumped up when he saw me. I brushed off his actions. "Don't get up, you've been working alone most of the morning. I should have asked if you wanted to take a break and have some refreshments."

"I brought something to eat, but Molly says you make lunch for us when you are here."

"I do, and you can join Jessica and me, if you'd like. We take lunch between twelve and one-thirty. Jess tries to be done with her morning patients by noon." I lifted the schedule list off the wall to see when Molly would be in and then hung it up again. She was due at six o'clock tonight to teach for two hours.

We gathered the rabbits as dark clouds moved in with a promise of rain. Before we got the last few critters inside, large raindrops spattered the ground. In its hutch, the last rabbit settled down.

It had been a busy morning for them and they earned a molded treat of fruits and veggies. I hung one on the inside of each hutch, while Jason topped off their water bins.

"Where is Walkabout Willy?"

"He's here. I think he's sleeping way back in the hutch."

I peered into the roomed-off portion of it and saw Willy cuddled up and asleep. "He must have had a fun-filled time outside."

"I can't get over how he searches for ways to get out. Was he rescued from the woods?"

"Not that I know of. He was rescued from a man who lived there, though. He wasn't in good health upon his arrival, but I took care of that in no time flat."

"You know, I asked around when I was looking to work here. I wanted to work in a good place. You have a terrific reputation, Juliette. The good care you give the rabbits and the way you treat us workers is well known by everyone."

"Gee, thanks. That's not the first time I've been told, and it's nice to hear it. I adore these rabbits. It makes me angry when they have been abused. There's no need for it, ever."

"Molly mentioned you had an episode this past summer where you and they were in danger."

"Yes, but it's over now."

He must have taken my remark as the end of that particular conversation. He busied himself by cleaning the floors. I left him to it. In the house, Bun went to his room and had the treat I brought him.

The accounts, set up in a computer program,

needed attention. It didn't take long to see that I had neglected them. I spent two hours catching up with payments to vendors, payroll for employ- ees, and making certain taxes were paid. None of these jobs thrilled me, especially when I couldn't offer the kids a raise. How could I increase their compensation? A half an hour later, I still hadn't come up with an idea. I closed the accounts pro- gram, turned off the computer, and prepared to take a walk.

Bun and I had nearly reached the road when Sheriff Carver drove in. He stopped next to us and motioned toward the house. Oh dear.

I nodded, all the while curious about what he wanted this time around. I didn't drag my feet, but close to it as I returned to the house.

He waited on the porch while I climbed the steps and entered the kitchen. Jack took his usual seat at the table.

"Coffee?"

"Please."

"Is this a professional visit?"

"Yes and no. Our dispatcher received a call con- cerning intruders at Evelyn Montgomery's home last night. Two suspicious-looking men were seen loitering near the house. Officers dispatched to that location were unable to apprehend them." He dipped his head toward Bun, who sat in front of the sink. Intent on Jack, Bun didn't move a whisker.

"It could have been Seamus and his partner. The rabbit has been okay since his episode with them?"

"Ask if he would let you into that house. Say you have

to pick up paperwork for that woman, uh, Vera. She has to finish the show stuff and needs Evelyn's files."

"I see, yes, Bun has been fine. How did they get away?"

"The officers themselves were seen by them." He sounded more angry than disgusted. I thought it could be a mixture of both.

"Rookies, I take it."

With a sigh, he nodded. "You'll continue to have a police presence. I know you don't like it, but your safety is at risk."

"Okay. Vera Benedict called me to find out about Evelyn's estate. I said I didn't know, and she asked if I could get access to the house. Vera's in the process of reviewing the rabbit show information. She wants all the applications that were submitted, but Evelyn handled all that. Vera said it's important, because she has to review the rejected applications to see why that happened. I said I'd ask if you'd let me go there."

"Well said."

Jack looked at me, long and hard, before he said, "Adam will accompany you."

Thrilled to think I'd get into the house without once again breaking the law, I agreed. Adam would be there to deal with intruders, should that occur. "Great, and I do feel better with protection. Thanks, Jack. Are you still searching for those two men?"

"We are. You won't go anywhere without protection, is that understood? I'd never hear the end of it from Meredith if anything happened to you. She's quite a fan of yours."

We made arrangements for Adam to go with me to Evelyn's house. Watching Jack leave, I called Vera.

"Juliette Bridge here. I've been given access to Evelyn's house and wondered if you want the applications for the rabbit show or any other documents Evelyn had?"

"Oh, thank you, I do need that information. Would you like me to go with you?"

"That's not necessary. Just tell me what you require, and I'll find it for you."

After jotting down a list, I hung up. Certain Evelyn had everything in a computer program, I knew access was out of the question without a password. I had seen a file for the rabbit show in her desk and hoped most of what Vera lacked would be in there. I'd also search the desk drawer for flash drives.

"Did Jack agree too easily?"

"Maybe, he does seem worried. I'll tread carefully. My familiarity with the house would seem odd. You'll have to stay here while I'm gone. I hope you don't mind."

"I wouldn't want to make this hard for you."

While I thought that was unlikely, I took his consent as a good sign and breathed a sigh of relief over not having to argue with him. Bun liked to be in the know.

We went into the shop where Jason and Jessica were discussing the pros and cons of rabbit training. I listened for a few minutes. When they noticed me, the conversation ended. I mention I'd be away for an hour or two, but would be back in time for dinner.

"I'll feed the rabbits, then?" Jason asked.

"Please do. Just put together the ingredients I have lined up and labeled on the second shelf of the rack in the barn. Bundle it and put it, well, you know what to do."

"Yes, ma'am."

Jess waited until Jason was out of earshot. "I have a patient due any moment. Come into the clinic."

With Bun at my heels, I went with her, whispering what Jack had said during his visit.

"Adam will go with you this afternoon?"

"He will. It shouldn't take me long to get what I need."

"I'm glad you'll have someone there to make sure you're safe." She gave Bun a glance and said, "Besides Bun, that is. He can be quite ferocious."

"Bun won't be going. He'll be here with you two."

Hearing that he'd be left behind, Jess knelt beside Bun and stroked his ears and scratched his nose.

"Aah, that feels so good. Jessica loves me."

I gave him a wink. Jess said they would take good care of Bun and the other rabbits. "Don't worry, he'll be fine."

Adam arrived as I walked through the breezeway. He knocked on the door while giving the area a quick study.

"Sheriff Carver instructed me to accompany you to Evelyn Montgomery's house. Are you ready to leave?"

I donned my jacket and we set off to Evelyn's. "Do you know how to get there?" he asked.

"No, I've never been to her home. We always

spoke on the phone, although we chatted the day she was killed." I nearly clapped my hand over my big mouth. I knew he'd question me over my slip of the tongue. I become annoyed when I can't keep my mouth shut.

"Oh?"

"She commented on the beauty of the rabbits."

"Is that all?"

"Yes, why?"

"I remember this past summer when you said I was a poor liar. Well, so are you."

I looked at him with surprise. "I'm not lying. That's all she said."

"I'm sorry, Juliette, I don't believe you. Tell me what she said."

"She was a cranky person. When she passed by the rabbits, she said nice things about them, but said she wasn't sure Petra would be entered into the show after all."

"What was her reason?"

I shrugged and said I had no idea. "The children were crowded around the rabbit pen, so I couldn't ask. She had a mean look on her face when she walked away."

"You're sure you don't know why?"

"I don't know what her problem was, maybe she was having a bad day."

He glanced at me, then turned onto Evelyn's street. We slowed while I looked for the house number he'd given me. I saw her house, but said nothing until we were opposite from it. "That's the house. The number is on the mailbox." I pointed to the mailbox. It was black like all the others in the neighborhood. Weird, I know, but not uncommon in some developments.

Adam parked the unmarked car three houses away. Casually, we went to the front entrance. Since I never entered this way, it was a unique experience. Adam unlocked the door, opened it, and took the lead. "Wait here while I look around. I don't want any surprises."

Smart man. I was in good hands. He crooked a finger to let me know I could enter. This was much better than fumbling around in the dark.

"What are you supposed to get?"

"Information for Vera Benedict, the chairwoman of the rabbit shows. Evelyn handled applicants and such."

"Was Petra allowed to compete?"

Certain he already knew, I answered him. "She fell ill before the show began."

It took some doing not to head into the office straightaway. I wandered the first floor, peered into rooms that led off the living room. "The furniture is nice, isn't it?" I mused aloud, and ran my hand across the top of the sofa. "That must be her office." I went in, peeked at papers strewn across the floor, and motioned Adam to join me.

"Would you open those doors?" I pointed to the closets.

He did as I asked and left them wide open. "Nervous?"

"A bit. I don't know what to expect now that the sheriff has said Colin and Seamus are still on the loose."

I knelt on the floor to scan the documents, I already knew they were of no use. I had shuffled bunches into a pile, when an official-looking piece of folded parchment caught my eye. Wary of snatching it up, I put it on top of the pile and set it on the desk.

"Nothing there pertaining to the show. Would you look at the file folders on those shelves for me? Otherwise, we might be here for hours. The file should be labeled for show entrants or something similar."

"Sure." Adam got to work.

I tucked the sheet of parchment into my jacket pocket and searched the desk drawers. Several flash drives sat in a divider in the back of the drawer. I added them to my pocket before I moved on to the file drawer below.

Files, still neatly arranged, gave the impression the two thieves hadn't had time to touch them before the police arrived. I fingered each one, read the headings, and found two files for Vera. Both were labeled with large letters. The first was show acceptances and the second was filled with rejections. I set them on the desk chair.

"Any luck?" I asked.

"Not yet."

A few minutes later, I said, "I think I found what Vera's looking for."

In one quick stride, Adam was at my side. His hand out, I gave him the files and watched him look through each one. He whistled over the file of rejections.

"What?" I asked, and peered past him to see what had caused his reaction.

Good grief, she had used a broad nib marker

on those who, in her opinion, were unacceptable. That wasn't the worst of it, her remarks were cruel. Words like *poor, no money, destitute, stupid idiots, no secrets found,* and other uncomplimentary remarks. It didn't matter that the rabbit met the requirements.

"She was a piece of work," Adam remarked when I sucked in a breath of air after reading the last remark scrawled across the page: *Dead in the water.*

It was Petra's application. I closed my eyes for a second and gathered strength to face Adam. He'd question why she'd written such a thing and would know if I lied. A tight spot to be in, no matter how I viewed it.

His brows arched, Adam pointed to the words. "And this is because?"

I flounced into the desk chair, hugged my folded legs to my chest, rested my chin on my knees, and groaned. "If I say I don't know?"

"Not acceptable, sorry."

"Hmm."

"Try again."

By this time his arms were folded across his chest as he leaned against the edge of the desk focused on me. Her harsh words, boldly scrawled across the application, glared at me.

"Fine." With what pluck I could manage, I said, "Carina and Evelyn had a brief disagreement. I didn't hear what was said, but their body language showed they were upset. When it was over, Evelyn stopped by my rabbit pen and cooed over the rabbits. Before she walked away, she told me to keep my mouth shut or Petra wouldn't be in the show." I jutted my chin toward the folder. "It seems she had already decided before that incident. I haven't a clue why, so don't ask. A short time before the party ended, Carina and I found her body."

"Was that so hard?"

I gulped, took my time answering him, and then said, "Not really."

"Why would she discard your application?"

"How would I know?"

"You must have some idea."

"The one thing I heard over and over from those in the show concerned Evelyn's malicious behavior. She harbored secrets about others and used them for her own gain. Quite an unprincipled woman. I don't have secrets, which meant I was no use to her. Maybe that's why she wouldn't consider Petra's application. Evelyn might have thought I heard what she and Carina argued over and that I'd use it to my benefit. Which, by the way, would never happen."

"Carina didn't hint at what they argued about?"

I shook my head. "I was too busy with the rabbits to pay attention. Besides, I wasn't close enough to hear more than a few words."

He stood up, seemed satisfied, and asked if I was ready to leave.

"Sure am, let's get out of here."

CHAPTER FIFTEEN

I flipped through other applications while I trailed a short distance behind Adam. He had passed the basement door when it swung open. Seamus charged off the first step. Shocked, I slid to a halt, crushed the file in my hands, and watched in horror as Adam was struck with a piece of wood. Seamus hadn't aimed high enough to strike Adam's head, but had caught his shoulder, throwing him off balance.

Slow to recover, Adam gave him the advantage. The files hit the floor and I jumped on the beastly man's back as he continued to attack Adam. With my arms wrapped tightly around his neck, I leaned backward to choke him. Garbled words came from him as he struggled against my hold. Having done heavy lifting at the farm gave me added strength.

As he weaved and shook his body to free himself, Adam tackled him. Seamus and I fell backward. I slid sideways as Adam crashed on top of

Seamus. Grasping the collar of the man's jacket, Adam hauled Seamus to his feet.

I'd risen from the floor, looked past them toward the basement, and glimpsed Colin. He saw me and took off. On my way to catch him, I heard Adam yell, "Stay where you are, Juliette."

I stopped mid-stride. He was right, it wouldn't be in my best interests to take on someone who might have a weapon. What would I do with Colin if I did catch him?

I said, "I'll call the station."

He nodded while he handcuffed Seamus. Moments later sirens blared, and the police arrived. They entered the house with guns drawn, which scared the daylights out of me. They took Seamus into custody as I sank onto a nearby chair, wiped sweat from my face, and thanked my lucky stars.

If I had come here on my own, I'd have walked into a deadly situation. In the future, I'd do well to think first and act later. But then . . .

"Are you okay?"

"Are you?" I asked in return.

"He caught me off guard. I didn't hear them enter the house."

"Me either. If you hadn't recovered so quickly, I think we might have been in big trouble." I wiped dribbles of perspiration from my face with the sleeve of my jacket.

"Is anyone looking for Colin?"

Adam nodded. "He's probably long gone, but a search is underway, regardless. What possessed you to chase him?"

I shrugged. "Anger, maybe. Who knows?"

We gathered papers from the floor. They had flown willy-nilly across the room. Gathered into the folder once more, I straightened up. "We'd better leave now."

Our return trip to the farm was quiet for the most part. Every now and then, Adam would ask a question.

"Why did you jump Seamus?"

"He's dangerous. I was afraid he'd harm us both."

"It was foolish."

"Really? You think I was foolish to help you? I lift bales of hay and deal with heavy rabbit hutches for a living. Besides, I was strong enough to choke him while you got your act together. You might be a little more thankful," I complained.

His silence lasted for a moment or two, yet felt like forever, before Adam said, "Thank you." He turned into my driveway and parked next to Sheriff Carver's car.

Unsettled over what would happen next, I walked into the shop. Jessica and Jack were deep in conversation. I hung my jacket on a hook and set the crumpled file folder on the counter.

The conversation had come to a sudden end when we had entered the room. They looked us over, Jess with a worried expression on her face, the sheriff glaring. "You're both fine, then?" His look directed at Adam, I kept my mouth shut.

"No injuries, except to the intruder, sir."

"I heard." Jack turned to me. "You were lucky Adam went with you."

"We worked as a team to take Seamus down," Adam admitted.

"Did you? I'll expect a report on my desk by the end of your shift." His cool attitude toward Adam surprised me. If he was upset with Adam, I could only imagine how he felt toward me.

When his silence lengthened, Jessica blurted, "I think dinner is done. I turned off the Crock-Pot a while ago. Would you like me to set the table?"

"No, I'll do it, thanks." I left them in the shop.

Bun waited at the kitchen door, so still he reminded me of a garden decoration.

I knelt in front of him and stroked his fur. "I'm so glad you didn't come with us. I was scared when Seamus McKenna entered the living room and attacked Adam."

"I would have taken him down in a heartbeat. You and I know how ferocious I can be."

It was true, he could be quite wild at times and protective to a fault. "You sure can. I feared for both of us, and jumped on his back to help Adam, who wasn't pleased by my actions. It all happened so fast, I reacted the way I was taught."

"Let's face it, we aren't always appreciated for our fearlessness."

"True. Have you and the others been fed?"

"Jason and Jessica took care of us. We're all fine. Jess also made lunch for her and Jason while you were out."

"Then I'll set the table for dinner."

"I listened to the sheriff and Jess talking before you arrived. He questioned her on what you were up to. She handled herself well, and didn't give you up. Proud of that girl, really proud."

Footsteps sounded in the breezeway. I murmured that we'd talk when Jessica left for the day. Bun hopped into his room and munched his leftover veggies.

Once I set the table for two, I noticed Sheriff Carver was still with Jessica.

"Sheriff Carver is working tonight," Jessica said.

I set another place. "You may as well have dinner with us, I know you want to talk about today's incident."

He tried to deny he was hungry.

"You're nearly drooling over what's for dinner, so take a seat and get it over with."

We ate and spoke of mundane topics at the farm and clinic. Near to the bursting point, my anxiety over his avoidance of the inevitable ran rampant. I put my fork down and looked him in the eye.

"You might as well ask your questions, Jack. Let's discuss what's on your mind and then have dessert."

He studied me, and then asked, "Why would you interfere with an arrest in progress?"

I handed a plate to Jack. "The problem being that it wasn't in progress until I got involved." I explained how Adam had been taken by surprise, struck hard with the wood and thrown off balance. He'd have been in serious trouble if I hadn't interfered.

"I suppose you'll tell me I was foolish, but I knew what I was doing, Jack. My actions increased Adam's chances of making an arrest."

"Okay, enough said about it. We haven't apprehended Colin yet, but we will. Every officer in the area, and the towns surrounding Windermere, has been alerted."

I set a piece of apple pie in front of Jessica and said, "He might not be as dangerous, but desperation changes people."

His dessert plate empty of pie, Jack nodded and rose from his chair. "Thank you for dinner and that pie was tasty. I'll be in touch."

After he'd gone out the door, Jessica leaned across the table and whispered, "He had a fit when he found out you two were attacked. When he learned of your part in the event, he began to rant about it. Gosh, I thought he'd never stop. He worries about you, I don't know how he'd deal with you being seriously injured."

"Not well, I'm sure. He knows Meredith would take him to task over it. Did Jack ask you anything specific? Your conversation appeared intense when we arrived."

"His nose is out of joint because you won't leave the investigating up to him. How he knows that is beyond me." Perplexed by Jack's knowledge, Jess said, "I was careful with my answers. I told him I thought you were concerned about Carina and her daughter. Other than that, I didn't share anything."

"Thanks. I think he was bluffing when he said I wasn't leaving his business alone. We've been very careful to not draw attention to what we're doing. I certainly don't want him to know what I've been up to. I also don't like lying to him."

"I know." Jessica set the dishwasher to run. "I have to leave. See you tomorrow."

I waved as she walked out the front door.

"I knew she wouldn't tell the sheriff about our actions."

I looked at Bun and sat on the floor next to him. "She's a good friend to us, Bun."

I answered the phone on the second ring.

"Hello."

"You found it, didn't you?" Colin wanted to know.

Why would I tell him? If I said yes, he'd try to take the certificate from me, by force if necessary.

"Why would you think that? I was at the house to look for files Ms. Benedict asked for."

"You're a liar. I know you have it, and I want you to give it to me."

His voice tense, I was sure he knew he was hunted by law enforcement. I took a deep breath. "Well, good luck with that. I don't have it and if I did, I wouldn't give it to you."

"I didn't mean for you to get hurt, you know. When Seamus shoved you at the show, I was afraid for you. Then Seamus took your rabbit. I couldn't let him be harmed and protected him for you. I'm sorry about all that's happened."

Was he trying to convince me that he'd been an unwilling participant? Colin was the liar, not me.

"It doesn't matter now. You're being hunted across several towns and cities. Do yourself a favor, and turn yourself in. You wouldn't want to be shot on sight, would you?"

"N-no. I don't want to go to jail, either."

"I can't help you there. I'm afraid jail will be the

end result for you and Seamus." I heard what sounded like a train running in the background and used my cell phone to text Sheriff Carver. He texted an *okay*.

"Would you put in a good word for me?"

"Since you protected my rabbit, I will do so, but it's important that you surrender."

"I don't believe you."

Cripes, we were back to square one with the *liar, liar* thing. I held back a snappy retort and sat down. "Tell me where you are. I'll come and talk with you in person. I don't think you're the violent type, I really don't."

"I need money to get away. Do you know what that certificate is worth?"

"No, and I don't know what's so important about it, either. Why do you want it so badly?"

He hesitated, then blurted, "Because she's rich and will pay to get her hands on it." The line went dead. I'd lost any hope of saving this young man from being wounded or worse.

The entire day had been busy from start to finish, and I hadn't taken a minute to look the certificate over. I searched through the pockets of my jacket to see if it was what he wanted. Empty. Panic surged through me as I searched a second time.

I paced the floor and considered the possibilities. How had I lost it? During the scuffle maybe? Surely, I'd have seen it when Adam and I had gathered the papers from the folder. The truth slammed me with a jarring effect. Adam had found it. He and I weren't always within each other's sight as we picked the papers up.

Why didn't he offer to put it in the file? Had he realized it wasn't what Vera had asked for? I remembered saying she only needed the applications. I growled at my stupidity, before I pounded my fist on the table in frustration.

From his bedroom doorway, Bun asked, *"Are you okay? You're awfully upset. What can I do to help?"*

I sat on the floor as he came up to me. Running my hands through my hair, I swept it back from my face and told him my suspicions. Disappointment gnawed at me. I'd been deceitful in my efforts to find the certificate, with no idea of its importance. Ashamed of my actions, and fearful that I'd be in more trouble than ever, I called Jack to ask if I could come by his office.

"I'll be here. There's a different officer watching over you tonight. Don't be nervous if you don't recognize the car, Adam is off duty."

"Okay. I'll see you soon, then."

"Can I go? I'm sort of feeling left out of what's going on."

"Sure, I'll get your sling."

Ready to travel, I set Bun on the passenger seat before we set off. Now and then I looked in the rearview mirror. A single car was behind us, closer than Adam had ever been. Anxious, I sped into the back lot of the police station and parked as close to the door as I could. The other car had kept going. Maybe it hadn't been my protector, after all.

With Bun in his leather sling, we entered the station. The officer at the front desk motioned me toward Jack's office. I reached his door, knocked once, and entered on command.

The certificate sat on the desk in front of Jack, who had a smug look on his face. Why? I wouldn't ask. All I knew was that I had been doing the dirty work to find out who was to blame for what had happened to Evelyn, and why. The birth certificate held the key to the answers. I was certain of it.

Indicating a chair in front of his desk, Jack asked, "What can I do for you, Juliette?"

I took a seat. Eyeing the folded parchment paper, I dragged my gaze from it and asked if Colin had been found.

"Not yet. I sent a team to scour the railroad tracks, but he wasn't there. Are you sure you heard a train? There isn't one scheduled until midnight."

"I swear it sounded like a train in the distance."

"Hmm, well, it was worth a look. You could have asked me that question over the phone. What else is on your mind?"

"I wondered how your investigation is going."

"Don't play games, can't you tell he knows something? Whatever you do, don't walk into a trap. Carver can be wily."

His hands posed as a church steeple, Jack tapped two fingers against each other.

"It's going quite well. As a matter of fact, this is what you have been in search of. It's most interesting." He leaned forward to tap the parchment with a fingertip.

I eyed the certificate and asked, "May I see it?"

He handed it to me, then leaned back and rocked in his squeaky chair. Carefully, I unfolded the parchment and began to read. My mouth must have hung open, because drool ran down my chin. I wiped it away and gawked at Jack.

"Am I right? This is what you had to find?"

"Y-yes. I had no idea what it contained, though."

"Do you know now?"

"I-I think so." My heart sank into my shoes at the significance this information had. "Seamus and Colin were hired to get it. By whom, I can only guess. When Colin called me tonight, he insisted I had it in my possession and said it is worth a lot of money, that someone would pay a huge sum for it."

"Did you say you had it?"

"I denied it while trying to get him to turn himself in. He's very scared and will continue to act rashly. He might even come to the farm to force me to give it to him. He never believed a word I said about not having it."

"Who asked you to retrieve that?" He pointed to the paper.

"Seamus wanted a birth certificate from Evelyn's files. He never named anyone." I stared at him as a look of disbelief spread across his face. "Honest, Jack. I only looked because these two guys were obsessed with it, and they had Bun. I figured that document and Evelyn's death were somehow connected, and would produce her killer."

With a snort, Jack remarked, "With those instincts, you should give up rabbit farming."

I gave him a slanted look, and said drily, "Really?"

"Just joking. Don't get any ideas of joining the force."

"You have nothing to worry about."

"I wouldn't say that. Due to your antics, I have more gray hair than ever from pure worry alone. Tell me every detail of what you've been up to. All of it."

Other than Carina's argument with Evelyn, Carina's request to clear her as a suspect, and Evelyn's murder, I gave Jack a full picture of what took place from the moment I had entered the rabbit show. He listened with rapt attention, didn't comment or interject his personal views, nor did he ask a single question. Until I stopped talking.

Bun peeked out at Jack, got more comfortable in the sling, and said, *"That ought to give him something to chew on."*

"You actually went into the Montgomery home for this?" He held the paper up, waved it a bit, and slapped it back on his desk. Oh, boy.

In my own defense, I said, "I didn't break in, the basement door was unlocked. It was quite unsettling to think I might come across Seamus McKenna and Colin Bedford. Seamus is mean and nasty."

"Nasty? He's an outright criminal. He's been jailed a few times. Mean, yes, but nasty doesn't come close to what he is." Jack's voice had risen quite a bit.

To quell his anger, I spoke softly. "I would appreciate it if you didn't yell at me."

His eyes narrowed to a near squint and then he did as I asked.

"It's clear you have a mind of your own, which has placed you in an untenable situation in the past. My goal is to keep that from happening again. You might not be so lucky this time."

"I appreciate that you look out for me, and I thank you for doing so. My curiosity does get the better of my common sense, which leads to involvements I should, but can't, refrain from. That said, I don't believe Colin would harm me. He was horrified when Seamus attacked me at the show. He might not have considered what the consequences of all this would be, mainly because Seamus could have made it seem like an easy job. They hadn't expected me to ask questions at the show, or nose my way into Evelyn's background and her business." I stuffed my hands in the pockets of my jacket and touched the notebook.

I took it out and held it out to him. "I found this at Evelyn's. I wasn't sure what use you'd have for it, but thought I should give it to you." I watched as he skimmed the pages. When he reached the numbers noted with initials, his eyes widened. "Have you seen this?"

"Just before I came here. Evelyn had dirt on every person she allowed into the show. Adam must have told you what was written across many of the show applications. Do you think those figures are payments she received from blackmail?" I waved my hands a bit before he could speak and said, "Just a thought. If anyone was going to kill her for something, other than the birth certificate, one of those people on that list might have performed that task. If so, the certificate would then be irrelevant, don't you think?"

He examined the book more thoroughly and fingered the first page of sums. "I'll look into it. Thanks for this." He held the small book in his hand and waggled it. "Evelyn wasn't quite the up-standing citizen she wanted everyone to think she was."

"I guess not." Unwilling to offer my opinion of her beyond what I had already said, I left it at that. No need to generate questions I didn't want to answer. Jack, being a keen cop, was likely to jump to the conclusion that I held back on him and that was the last thing I needed.

"Are we done here? I'd like to go home now. We have a lot to talk about, and you can't say a word now without Sheriff Carver thinking you've lost your marbles."

I cleared my throat and started to rise. Jack motioned for me to remain seated. "We have some other things to clear up before you leave."

"Oh."

"If you hear from Colin, let me know. Tell him you've decided to give him the certificate because you have no use for it. Officers will be in place, and you have to give this to him before he's taken into custody." He offered me the folded paper.

With a sense of dread, I took it. This was way more than I had bargained for and knew I had passed the point of no return.

"This isn't going to be healthy for us, Jules. What if Colin has a weapon? What then? This could go terribly wrong, you know that, don't you?"

I tweaked Bun's ears and gently patted his head to let him know I agreed. "Jack, what am I supposed to do if Colin is armed?"

"You're not to concern yourself with that. Like you said, he doesn't seem to be willing to harm you, so just give him what he wants."

"What if he thinks I shouldn't be left alive as a witness? Colin will get paid for his efforts, but he has broken the law and is being sought by the police. He may not want me to testify against him."

"You're going to be fine. Nothing will go wrong if you do as I say. Let me do my job."

I rose from the chair, took the birth certificate from him, and remarked, "Easy for you to say." With that, I left the station.

CHAPTER SIXTEEN

The idea of dealing with Colin, face-to-face, gave me the jitters. Bun and I were on our way home, when he said, *"This will work, I will be there to protect you. Don't you worry for a minute. My superpowers are working perfectly."*

Right about now, I wanted some superpowers of my own. If I offered the document to Colin, he could very well take it and just walk away. I hoped that would be the case, because he was apt to show up unannounced at my house anytime now. His desperation was out of control, I'd heard it in his voice when we'd spoken earlier. The money he'd be paid was his ticket out of town, or so he thought. Life isn't that easy, nor would it ever work out the way we wanted it to.

Who was the buyer? The name on the certificate was a shock when I had read it. I'd never have guessed, and was curious over the importance put on acquiring it. We arrived home, I took Bun into the house, and left him while I took time to check on the rabbits. Finished with the job, I returned to the kitchen.

"Whose name surprised you so much?" Bun asked as the phone rang.

The caller ID said the caller was unknown. I dialed Jack's cell phone and said Colin was calling me. I left both my cell phone and the house phone on speaker mode when I answered Colin's call.

"Hello."

Colin sounded breathless. "This is the last time I will ask nicely, Juliette. I want that document."

"Okay, okay, I have it, come and pick it up. I'm here alone with the rabbits. Be careful, I don't want you to be seen. Sneak along the edge of the woods near the rear of the house if you have to."

"This better not be a trick."

"It isn't. I just want this nonsense to stop. I'm a wreck for fear you'll hurt me."

His voice was soft as he said, "I would never do that, you have to believe me."

"I do. I'll be on the lookout, then. How long before you get here?"

He hesitated a fraction of a second, before he said, "I'm outside your back door."

Bun sprang forward. His ears vibrating as fast as my nerves were. Frantic, I closed my eyes, took a deep breath, and stilled my body. Another breath and then a third brought a reasonable level of calm.

"Will the sheriff be on his way or what?"

I leaned toward him and whispered, "We can only hope so."

I'd never have guessed Colin would show up so soon. He had been awaiting my return. Dang, that was annoying. I left the cell phone call open on the desk, behind my handbag. Hopefully, Carver would have sent a slew of cops my way by now, but who knew what was taking place on his end of things?

I sent Bun to his room and walked through the hallway to the back door, which was bolted, and the door handle locked. I undid the locks and opened the door, and there stood Colin on the doorstep, nerves frayed. He kept glancing over each of his shoulders, his angst showing on his face.

I moved aside to let him in and led the way to the kitchen, where he looked around and peered into the rooms that led off it. His gaze went to the stairs. "Anybody up there?"

"Not a soul. Sit down, you're a mess. Would you like something to eat or drink?"

"Stop with the niceties, but yeah, give me whatever you have to drink that's handy."

There was hope for me yet. I handed him a tall glass of iced tea and watched him gulp it down. He set the empty glass on the table. His clothes dirty and disheveled, Colin was in need of a shower. I could smell his body odor from where I stood, next to the sink.

"Where's the document?"

"I have it right here. Before I give it to you, will you tell me why you were asked to fetch it?"

"Seamus got asked. He convinced me that the job was easy, but he was wrong. He said we'd be paid a huge amount of cash. He never mentioned why, or who would do that, he just said this was a chance of a lifetime for us. Seamus woulda worked

alone, but needed a lookout while he hunted for
it. Do you know what's so important about this
piece of paper?"

"Not a clue, I'm afraid." I was baffled. As surprised as I was when I'd read Bailey Kimball's
name on it, I was unsure what she had to do with
Evelyn's death, if anything at all. She'd left the
birthday party before I had finished packing up
the rabbits and their paraphernalia. We hadn't
had a minute to talk. Bailey entertained throughout the day, then showed the children the puppets
and how things worked behind the scenes before a
puppet show started.

Busy as I was, I hadn't noticed if Bailey left her
station at all. I'd think about the day when my present circumstances ended with Colin's arrest. Was
Bailey behind all this? Or was someone else pulling
the strings?

"You wouldn't be lyin' to me, would ya? I don't
take kindly to liars."

I crossed my heart with two fingers. "I promise,
I'm not lying. The only reason I lied before was because I hoped you would go to the police and tell
them the entire story."

"I'm no snitch, but this is all Seamus's fault.
He's a cruel man, he threatened to kill me when I
wanted to get out of our agreement."

"I see. Well, here's the document you were in
need of. I'm sorry you went through such a difficult time these past weeks. At heart, you're a good
person, Colin, and Seamus led you astray."

Good golly, I was full of crap. The young man
might have been fooled by the idea of easy money,

but that's where it ended. We both knew it, too. His eyes took on a slyness that gave me a sudden case of the chills.

"I'm listening and ready to go when you need me to."

I held the paper out to Colin, who snatched it from my hand as fast as a bolt of lightning cuts into the night sky. Greed covered his features, I'd seen it in the past when I'd found myself in dire straits.

"You talk a good line of crap, Juliette, but I don't believe a word of it." He shoved the paper into a pocket of his filthy jeans and started for the back door. "I said I wouldn't harm you and I meant it unless you tell anyone about me being here. Then I'll have to come back, understand?"

I nodded, my stomach doing flip-flops, and watched, with Bun at my side, as he opened the back door. In an instant, armed men pushed their way in the front and rear doors. I scooped Bun and ran into his room. We peeked around the edge of the door casing to see what happened.

Sheriff Carver entered last. A scuffle had taken place in the hallway and all I could hear was Colin yelling threats on how he'd get even with me. The words sank into the core of my bones. I breathed a sigh and waited until the officers manhandled him out the front door.

"Let's hope he doesn't escape."

"Mm."

"You can come out now, Juliette."

Sheriff Carver held the birth certificate in his hand and then tossed it onto the table. "Sit, I'll get you something to drink. You've had a harrowing experience."

Bun and I sat at the table, where he nestled into my lap while Jack brought me a shot of whiskey. How he knew where I kept it, I didn't know, but was glad he'd found it. I wasn't a heavy drinker, in fact, I rarely drank hard liquor, but downed this as if it were my last drink. My innards instantly warmed, then burned, and I nearly choked. Maybe that was why I didn't care for it, but stuck to an occasional glass of wine.

"Thanks for coming to the rescue. I kept him talking as long as I could."

"You did well. It was surprising to all of us that he was on your doorstep. My team was in place, but hadn't seen him until I gave them a heads-up that he had arrived. When you turned on the outside light, Adam saw him plain as day. He notified the others and we waited until you had done what I asked of you."

"I didn't know if you had things under control or what. If Colin had tried anything, I would have fought him tooth and nail. He's a wiry guy and they tend to be strong."

"From what Adam told me, you don't do too badly yourself in the way of self-defense." He smirked and shook his head as he sat across from me. "What do you think about this?"

"I tried to remember if Bailey left her puppet station during the day. I didn't see her do so, but that doesn't mean she didn't. I was busy with the rabbits and the partygoers. Even the mothers came by to visit. Sorry, Jack, I just didn't notice what Bailey was doing all day. The one question I do have is, why would she kill her own mother, if Evelyn was indeed her mother?"

"I can't say. I don't know Bailey like you do, and it would be useless to guess. By the way, does Bailey have loads of money?"

"Not that I'm aware of. If she did, why would she perform puppet shows? Her business has taken off and we even have a gig together this coming weekend. We usually chat or get together to discuss our strategy for the day."

"Why a strategy?"

"Have you ever had to handle ten to twenty children all at once?"

"No."

"Then think of them as loose rabbits, scrambling everywhere, getting into everything they shouldn't. Top that with them being as loud as possible without listening to what their mothers say, and you'll have a fair idea of what I go through at every party."

"I see. You haven't heard from Bailey?"

"No, she is on my call list, along with Carina Richland. Have you taken her off your suspect list?"

"Not yet. There's something about her that bothers me."

"Like what?"

"I can't figure it out. Something doesn't sit right with me when I talk to her. It feels like she's hiding something from me."

Was this a gambit or should I come clean and tell Carver what Carina was worried about? Gambit or not, I said, "She and Evelyn had one heck of an argument. Neither woman wanted me to tell anyone what I heard, which was nothing that made sense, anyway."

"What do you mean?"

"I heard a few words. Evelyn said she had rights. Carina was distraught at the time. A few minutes later, Carina remarked Evelyn was nothing, then mumbled a few words and said loudly Evelyn would remain that way. Like I said, it made no sense to me. I wasn't even aware they knew each other. Not that I would know, but to see her at Adrian's party seemed odd. Everyone else had a child or two with them."

"Adam filled me in on what you told him. You should have come to me with any information you had. You realize that, don't you? All of this might have been avoided if I'd been made aware sooner of all you knew. I'm disappointed in you, Juliette."

My heart plummeted. This man and his wife cared about me and my life, my safety, and the farm. Guilt rolled over me, then settled like a mantle on my shoulders, weighing me down.

I stared at the floor, and said, "I'm sorry. I should have been honest with you. I'll try harder in the future."

"Keep that in mind the next time you go on a tangent. I have to get to the station and interrogate Colin. I'm glad you're safe. Really glad."

"Thank you."

After he'd gone, Bun leapt off my lap and sat in front of me. His whiskers jittered, and his nose worked overtime. *You shouldn't feel guilty. We've assisted Sheriff Carver in furthering his investigation. Imagine where he'd be if we hadn't nosed around the way we have? So what if I was used as a pawn, no big deal. We do what is necessary, you and I, we're a great team. Don't let the sheriff drag you down, it isn't good for you.*

"I've been reckless, again. You'd think I would

learn from past mistakes, right? I'll do better from now on to keep us both out of danger. When you were in their hands and I couldn't find you, I nearly lost my mind. Instead, I got angry and walked into a possible trap. If I'd notified Jack, he would have caught Seamus and Colin then."

"Maybe."

"No maybe about it, Bun. It's true. I should have been forthcoming and because of it, we ended up in tonight's situation."

"You were only trying to help Carina. Let's look forward instead of thinking about what's happened in the past. Isn't that what you always say to me?"

"I guess." This four-legged character always made me feel better. While my guilt lingered, there was nothing I could do to change what had happened, but I could move forward and let Jack know my plans.

"I can tell you're starting to feel better. Can I have a snack? All this action has made me hungry."

I went to the fridge and took a couple of nibbles of fruit and ripped some greens from a bunch. I put it in his dish and let him have at it. My cell phone jingled. Carina's name appeared on the screen.

"Hi, Carina."

"I just heard the news. Sheriff Carver has caught Evelyn's killer?"

"Not that I know of, though it's a possibility. He has arrested two men who broke into her house in search of some documents."

"Uh-oh, the newscaster must have gotten the story wrong. Fake news, and all that."

"That must be it, more fake news."

"You and Bailey Kimball are scheduled for Adelle Philby's kid's party this weekend, aren't you?"

"We are. Will you and Adrian attend?"

"Adelle's daughter, Tricia, is one of Adrian's closest friends. I think it will do us some good to join the festivities."

"I will see you there, I'm sure. As for who killed Evelyn, it might not be the two men who were arrested. The sheriff mentioned he's on the trail of another suspect. I apologize for not staying in touch, I hadn't learned anything of use to tell you."

"I understand. You are busy with your farm and judged the rabbit show, too, which must have kept you on the run."

"It sure did. I'll see you Saturday afternoon. Oh, before I let you go, have you seen Bailey at all?"

"No, why would I?"

"I don't know, I thought you might have run into her in town, is all."

"No, I haven't seen or heard from her."

"Okay, thanks."

The call ended, I tapped my lips with my fingertip while considering what connection existed, if any, between Bailey, Evelyn, and Carina. As I paced the floor, Bun hopped into the room and said, *"Carina will be at the party?"*

"She and Adrian. She sounded strange when I mentioned Bailey. I can't figure out what the commonality is between those three women."

"In my most humble opinion, it would make sense to think Evelyn held a threat over Carina's head. Bailey

could be in the mix by being Evelyn's daughter, but begs the question of what her relationship to Carina could be. You should have asked her."

"Not without tangible evidence. We can't burn our bridge of communication with either woman, especially now that we know about Bailey. I have to reach out to Bailey tomorrow to coordinate our arrangements as we usually do before a party. I wouldn't want to raise her suspicions at this point."

"Sounds like a plan. The snack was tasty, thanks."

"My pleasure."

Bun sprawled on the floor next to my desk, and I hauled out paperwork that I had ignored while poking my nose into other people's business. Time had flown, or so it appeared, and more tax bills waited to be paid. My funds weren't seriously low, but low enough for concern.

As much as I loathed taking funds from my private bank account, it looked like I had no choice. I leaned back, heaved a sigh, mentally calculated how much cash to withdraw, and muttered, "Jim Brody's money sure would have come in handy." I wrote the checks, made a call to my bank, and deposited money from one account to another through the automated teller. Solvent again, I closed the computer ledger.

Out of boredom and curious over his death two years ago, I Googled Paul Richland's name and let the program search him out. Seconds later, his obituary and other articles about his standing in the community appeared. I read all that was available. Paul had supported several foundations, and he had donated to a surrogate clinic. With a start, I gawked at the information, my brain on high speed, as it jumped from one possibility to another. I considered whether or not Adrian might have been carried to term by a surrogate. I searched for pictures or newspaper articles that might have covered Paul's funeral. One appeared in the *Windermere Gazette*. The only photo of Carina was blocked by a heavyset woman as Paul's closed coffin was prayed over. I scanned articles about Paul and Carina. Most of them featured the couple standing together and smiling at the camera. None showed Carina while she was pregnant. Hmm.

I had to know what caused his death. Paul's car had crashed into a tree; his seat belt hadn't been buckled, and he had died upon impact. Was it accidental, suicide, or murder? With no other information on Paul or his family, I ended the search and shut off the computer.

CHAPTER SEVENTEEN

The following morning passed with hard work. My mind never rested for a minute as I went about daily chores. When Jessica entered the barn, she asked why I was working with a vengeance.

I looked around and found she was right. I'd accomplished the chores in half the usual time it took. "I didn't realize I was."

"I'm between patients and thought we could take a break."

The day, warm and sunny, beckoned us to sit on the porch. Not one to let enjoyable weather pass, I promised myself to take Bun to the lake after lunch. Molly would arrive before then, as would Jason, and I wanted to chat with them before I got involved in other things.

"Have you heard the sheriff has arrested Colin?"

"It happened here, last night. I'm so glad he kept the farm out of the story. Reporters would be camped at the edge of the property, news-hungry beggars that they are. The last thing I need is negativity from the media and the public. There's enough of that going around as it is."

"What happened?"

Keeping the story short, I gave her the basics. She rolled her eyes a few times, exclaimed a couple more, and then added a string of questions at the end. I answered as best I could, knowing Bun was listening at my feet. Unwilling to share what Jack said to me and how guilty I'd felt, I left out that whole discussion.

"I guess you never can guess what people will do, especially when they're in a tight spot."

"You've got that right. I wasn't afraid of Colin, but I would have shaken in my shoes if Seamus had been present. He gives me the willies." I shuddered and added, "Carina called me last night. She asked about the arrest. I kind of thought she was looking for information, but can't figure what exactly she wanted to know. We talked of the party this Saturday. She and Adrian will be in attendance, along with Bailey. I'll be on alert for sure. So much has come to light, it's got to connect somewhere, I simply can't see the whole picture yet."

"You're thorough, smart, and can make it fit together like puzzle pieces, so don't overthink it. Let it happen on its own."

"You're right. Here comes Mrs. Mallory. You'll have your hands full with her cat. She's a crazy critter."

"Wasn't she rescued from the same home as Willy?"

"Yeah, their circumstances were terrible." I gathered our cups from the small table between us and wished her luck as I entered the house. From behind the screen door, I watched Jessica cross the lawn and greet Mrs. Mallory with a smile. Jess had a way with people and animals.

I set about cleaning the house, organizing Bun's room, and then put together ingredients for dinner. A car drew to a stop in front of the barn. I glanced out the window and saw Jason and Molly enter the shop. I tossed dinner into a covered pot and slid it into the oven. I washed my hands before heading into the barn, with Bun at my ankles.

The two kids greeted me happily. I handed their paychecks to them and gave Jason a list of chores for the day. He went off to get started while I stayed behind to speak with Molly.

"How are your college classes going?"

"They could be better. Honestly speaking, I'd rather be here with the students, teaching them fiber arts."

I could feel my eyes widen in wonder. "I would like that, but at the moment, I can't afford to pay you for full-time work. Sorry."

"What if we had a full schedule?"

We were on opposite sides of the counter, facing each other, and her face was alight with excitement. Oh, my.

"You aren't leaving college, are you?"

"It would be possible to transfer my credits to a local college where I can enter a fiber arts program. I'd take a certificate course first to see if it's what I'd like to do for the rest of my life, and if it is then I would become a full-time student."

"Have you discussed this with your family?"

She nodded and grinned impishly. "My mother is very supportive, but then she's a crafter at heart. My father, well, he wants me to finish this semester before I make a change."

Wow, I'd never been that lucky. Dad had always insisted I did this or that, while Mom went along for the ride, never protesting in front of him. When she and I were alone, she'd tell me to follow my heart, no matter what Dad said.

"If you're sure this is what you want. It will take hours of hard work to pull this off, and I can't make a change here without knowing it will pay for itself. I'd like to have you teach here. You do such a fine job, the students adore you."

She raced around the counter and hugged me hard. Having won the day, Molly had complicated mine. Expanding the classes with a fuller schedule might increase income, which would be helpful. Some time ago, I had tossed the idea around without purposeful consideration, until now.

"We could host an open studio to generate publicity for class enrollment and allow the present students to show their work, what do you think?"

With a broad grin, I said, "I'd say you have it all worked out in your mind. Does Jessica know?"

She nodded. "I mentioned it to her in passing and she thought it a worthwhile idea. Will you give it some thought? I know how much responsibility the farm and rabbits are, and I wouldn't want to make your load any heavier."

"You, Jessica, and I can get together next week to talk it over, how's that?" Watching her excitement grow, I raised a hand. "No promises, it's quite an undertaking and like Jessica's clinic, it won't happen overnight. Financing must be sound, before we start. Okay?"

She nodded like a bobble doll on a bumpy ride. It was clear that Molly was thrilled to her core. Now, to make this work.

One after another, Molly's students arrived. I left her to set them up for their class and looked down at Bun.

"Come on, let's go walking," I said.

"Does he understand you, Jules?"

"I think so. He's intuitive, at least." I waved good-bye as we left the shop and walked through the barn on our way to the house.

In the breezeway, Bun said, *"I didn't know you thought I was intuitive. Thanks."*

"Well, aren't you?"

"It's mainly due to my superpowers."

"I see. Good thing you have them then." I slipped a lightweight sling onto my body and leaned over for Bun to climb inside. "One of these days, you'll have to walk beside me rather than ride all the time."

"I can't, don't make me. My feet will get filthy, and I don't like it when cars go by. What if I got run over, huh, what would you do then?"

We went down the front steps. "Okay, okay. No need to get jumpy."

"Whew, I thought you meant it. I should have known better. You always take good care of us rabbits. Especially me."

He had a point. I started to jog, thought the better of it, and slowed to a fast walk instead. Bun would only complain about the jostling as I ran.

We had reached Lake Plantain when Bun asked me to let him out. "Why?"

I want a drink of water. The lake is calm, like glass today. I won't get my feet wet, I can balance on that stone over there to drink.

I set him on the ground knowing he'd checked to see if the beach was dry. I sat on the sand, enjoying the light breeze coming in off the water while Bun drank from the lake.

This is a very nice place. Isn't there a house of sorts down the road? A place where summer activities are held for old folks?

"There is. Why don't we take a look?"

He climbed back into the sling. I adjusted the straps and set off down past the gate, listening to Bun's point of view on the area.

He stretched his neck out as far as he could and stared into the trees on our right. *There might be bears in the woods, you know.*

"Maybe, you never know. Let's not worry about that, shall we?"

If you say so. I'll keep an eye out, just in case. His ears and whiskers quivered slightly before his attention wandered elsewhere.

About a half mile down the road, we arrived at a spacious clearing where a large log building squatted. It spread out into a square, with long windows spaced evenly apart, except for the solid log wall at the rear, which had a door with a window in it. A wide porch spread across the front and along one side of the structure.

On the porch, Bun and I peered through the windows. Other than a counter in front of the galley-style kitchen and a couple of restrooms, the interior had an open floor plan. Folding tables and chairs lay stacked against one wall. Weathered rocking chairs lined the wall opposite the one of tables and chairs. All was neat and clean, awaiting another event for the elderly to enjoy.

As we turned away, I noticed a small plaque on the wall. Jim Brody's company name was printed on the front as sole sponsor for this place. The man's good deeds popped up everywhere I looked. Hmm.

I checked the time, our outing was near an end. Bun and I turned toward home at a trot.

"We've been to one of those places where old people live, maybe we could come here and entertain more old folks sometime."

"Funny, I was thinking the same thing. I'll call Mora Lindsey to see what she says about that. Good thinking."

As we approached the farm I noticed Bailey's light blue van parked next to my car. Why had she come by? Though I would have called her to confirm our arrangements for the Philbys's party, multiple other reasons popped into my mind for this visit. One of them was about her birth certificate. Ready to ask a load of questions, I went toward the studio to greet her.

"Is that Bailey's van?"

"Mmm."

"I wonder why she's here."

Me too. I greeted the students, including Bailey. She stepped next to me and whispered, "We need to talk."

I responded softly, "Come into the house."

We set off for the kitchen. Settled at the table, Bailey looked around. "Nice place you've got here."

"I like it." I stirred the contents of the pot in the oven, replaced the lid and asked if she wanted a cup of tea.

"That would be great, thank you."

"I intended to call you today to arrange our day at the party. Is that why you stopped by?"

"Partly. We can discuss the party later, I was wondering if you had heard from Carina?"

"We spoke last night, why?"

"She left an odd voice message on my phone and mentioned you."

I set the teapot on a tray, added teacups, milk, and sugar, and carried it to the table. "Oh?"

"What's going on with her?"

I shifted in my chair and reached for the teapot. "Carina was upset when we found Evelyn on the path between her and her next-door neighbor's land. She and Adrian are still recovering from her husband's death. What did she say?"

"That you and I better talk."

Thoughtful, I leaned back. "Did she say what we should talk about?"

Silent for a minute, she suddenly blurted, "I can tell you know that Evelyn was related to me."

"You're right, I found your birth certificate among her papers, but it has been crazy here these last few days and I didn't know if she was a surrogate for your real mother, or if she was the real thing. I was asked to pick up rabbit show applications for Vera Benedict, who runs the rabbit shows. I came across the document then."

"Evelyn gave me up for adoption when I was born. I think she might have been a surrogate or something. In high school, I had an accident. When I needed a blood transfusion, the doctors found I have a rare blood type. My family admitted I was adopted, which made sense after all the years of trying to figure why I didn't resemble either parent, or anyone else in our family. Anyway, my parents were wonderful, but I wondered, you know, like most adoptees do."

"How did you find out Evelyn was your birth mother?"

"After my mother passed away, my father left for a business trip. I searched everywhere I could think of for information about my birth parents. I finally found a sealed envelope. It wasn't my birth record or anything like that, it was the agreement of funds paid to Evelyn Montgomery. It mentioned a man as well, but all I was concerned with was knowing Evelyn was my birth mother."

"I assume you approached her."

Bailey nodded. "It didn't go well. She wanted nothing to do with me, not ever. I was fine with that, but had questions. She refused to tell me anything at all and was unpleasant, extremely unpleasant. It wasn't until Adrian's birthday party that I saw Evelyn again. She was an unhappy woman."

"That's putting it mildly," I said drily. "What was the man's name? I didn't see it on the birth certificate I got from Evelyn's house."

Her teacup empty, I watched her pour more into it. "I don't remember, I was more interested in finding out who my mother was. I could tell you knew about my link to Evelyn by the expression on your face. You should never play cards, Jules."

"So I've been told. I'm glad you've been forthcoming about this. The sheriff was interested and will probably talk to you. Just answer his questions, I'm sure you'll be fine."

"I never left my section at the party. I fear curious children will mess around with my puppets or harm themselves by getting into the workings of the stage set if I did step away."

"Good to know. Share that with Sheriff Carver, too. If there's nothing more you want to say, let's talk about the party."

An hour later, we had set our plans from a sketch of Adelle's backyard. We would arrive and set up well before the children came to enjoy yet another birthday party. "What bothers me is why Carina called you. It is strange," I remarked.

"Her voice sounded strained. Like she was under pressure of some kind."

"She tends to be high-strung, but it's still . . ."

"Mm, she might be hiding something. Had you thought of that? I only ask because I know you're always poking around for information to help the police do their job."

"Right, much to Sheriff Carver's dismay. He suspects everyone in the beginning of an investigation. When Carina started to fall apart after he questioned her, she asked if I'd try to find who killed Evelyn. I agreed, and here we are."

"You're amazing." Bailey's eyes held a humorous twinkle.

"Not according to Sheriff Carver, or his officers."

We rose from the table, and I walked her to the front door. "I'm glad you came by, Bailey."

"I think it was a good thing. You might visit Carina to see for yourself how she's reacted to all this. In person is always better."

"She and Adrian will be at the party this weekend. I may be able to speak with her then. Before you go, Bun and I went by the lake today and ventured onto the lodge grounds. I'd like to get together sometime and toss around ideas for entertaining the elderly people who go there in the summer."

"Love to. I've entertained at a residential senior living complex in Windermere. The residents enjoyed my puppet show, and got a chuckle out of the puppets antics."

"Then I'll give Mora Lindsey a call and set something up if she agrees to let us do a stint."

"Let me know what she says. I'll see you then." Bailey went down the steps.

While she drove away from the farm, I pondered what she'd revealed. If what she said was true, then Bailey couldn't have killed Evelyn.

In the kitchen, I reached for the phone and called Jack Carver.

CHAPTER EIGHTEEN

A conversation with Sheriff Carver didn't always turn out as I hoped. This was one of those times. Short when speaking to me, I guess his day hadn't been filled with fun and games, but had taken a downturn. He thanked me for sharing the information Bailey had given me and said good-bye after warning me to stay out of police business.

Annoyed by Carver's attitude, Bun and I went into the barn. I assisted Jason in settling several rabbits into their hutches and then gave them all fruit, greens, and timothy hay. Bun ate his in the playpen with Walkabout Willy. I left Jason to refill water bins and entered the shop.

Students straggled out the door, thrilled with the work they had accomplished in their lesson with Molly. It didn't take long to straighten up the room, to tidy odd bits of roving that had gone astray, and organize what was left. Students took their work home with them after every spinning and weaving class. Glad they did, I remarked on it.

Molly finished storing supplies, and said, "If they didn't, there wouldn't be enough room for other students to work. Whew, what a day."

"Challenging, was it?"

"To say the least. One of the women had a granddaughter who has asked to learn to spin. Could I set up a day for children to come and get acquainted with spinning and weaving?"

"What are the ages you're looking at?"

Molly had thought it over before she had asked. She offered her thoughts, and I decided she could give it a try, considering myself lucky to have such an enthusiastic employee.

After she packed her supply bag, she went in search of Jason to let him know it was time to leave. I waited until they were gone before I entered the clinic. Jessica put items in a bag for the dog's owner, accepted payment, and handed the man a card for a follow-up appointment.

She petted Arly's ears, ruffled his curly coat, and handed him a treat before he and his owner left. I'd seen Arly on various occasions at the park, in town, and here at the clinic. A friendly dog and owner, it was clear they were a perfect match.

They had reached the door when Mr. Fisher turned and asked, "You still doing those birthday party events?"

"I am."

"Good, 'cause my daughter-in-law wants you to entertain at her daughter's party next month. I'll have her call you."

"Thanks, Mr. Fisher. I appreciate that."

Jess and I waited until they were gone before Jess said, "Things are looking up for you."

"I can't begin to say how good that feels. The party engagements seemed to drop off a bit. I make a good income from them and always try to book as many as I can."

"I know how disappointed you were over Mr. Brody's grant rejection, but sometimes things work out for the better. Would supper be ready? I'm hungry."

"Then, let's eat." We closed the clinic for the day, locked the shop door, put the CLOSED sign in the window, and collected Bun from the pen.

"Jason put Willy in his hutch. I've been waiting here, alone, for you forever."

I set him on the floor and followed him into the house. Jessica set the table, I made sure Bun was settled, and then we ate our own meal of roasted pork, veggies, and salad.

Our meal finished, we set about clearing the leftovers away. The phone rang. I rolled my eyes and sighed before taking the call.

"You have to come over straightaway. I have to discuss a few things with you."

Her voice stretched as thin as wire, Carina sounded more desperate than I'd ever heard her before. Was she unraveling? Would I be in danger if she lost her marbles? Had she become totally unhinged? I didn't know, wasn't sure I wanted to, but there was my curiosity, mounting again, so I agreed to visit her.

"Who was that?" Jessica wanted to know.

"Carina. I think she's having a mental break or something. She's not the coolheaded woman I first met, that's for sure. Since Evelyn's death, she's been a complete wreck. Now she's insisting I go to her house for a chat." I reached for my coat and purse and asked, "Can you finish loading the dishwasher before you leave?"

"Certainly, are you going alone? You might want to call Jack Carver," she advised.

"I spoke to him earlier today. He wasn't having a stellar day and snapped at me. I have enough to worry about with Carina. I don't need to add Jack to the mix."

"Do you have a policeman watching you any longer?"

"I don't think so. With Seamus and Colin in custody, I'm safe."

"Be careful, Jules. Don't take any chances."

"I won't, I promise."

My coat buttoned, I was about to leave when Bun came out of his room.

"You aren't going without me to back you up, are you?"

I glanced at Jessica, whose back was to me while she loaded the dishwasher. I nodded my head.

"I won't allow it. Get the sling, I insist on going with you." He tapped his foot.

I took the sling off the hook, slipped it onto my body, and picked him up. Once he was settled, I walked toward the door.

"You're taking Bun?"

"Just for company. He can stay in the car while I'm with Carina."

Her brows drawn together in a unibrow line, a look of confusion settled on Jessica's face. "Okay. I'll be leaving shortly. If you need to, feel free to call me."

I agreed and went out to the car. "I don't know why you think you need to come along."

"Somebody has to watch out for you and that would be me. We are partners, right?"

"Right." I started the car and drove away from Fur Bridge Farm. In no rush to get to Carina's, I drove at an even pace, staying within the speed limit. I checked the rearview mirror once or twice, couldn't tell if a policeman was behind me in an unmarked vehicle, and not caring whether I had an escort or not, I shrugged.

I took a right turn onto Carina's street and parked at the curb behind a sportscar outside her home. Unlike Evelyn's neighborhood, homes near Carina's were well lit, with people busily walking or jogging along the sidewalks.

"Stay in the car. You have your blanket and should be fine. I'll leave the window open for fresh air."

"I think I should go inside with you."

"That's not a good idea. I don't think Carina would be happy about that. Just stay put. I shouldn't be long."

"Fine. Just give a yell if things go bad. I'll rescue you."

As if. I left Bun to think he was my savior, and frankly, he had assisted me on other occasions when I had been in a tight spot. I looked at my furry friend and tweaked one of his ears. "Great. Thanks."

I heard the doorbell chime when I tapped the button. Adrian opened the door and welcomed me in. She peered past me. "Did you bring Bun?"

"I left him in the car. I didn't think your mom would like it if he came in with me."

She considered the reason for a second and nodded. "Mom's in the living room." She crooked her finger and I leaned forward. She whispered, "She's ever so upset. Maybe you can get her to be happy again."

"I'll try."

I found Carina pacing the floor in front of a marble-fronted fireplace three times the size of mine. Certain it was for show more than for heat, I marveled at its beauty. This woman had a lovely home, in a high-end neighborhood, with friends as wealthy as she was. When I caught sight of her, I paused, taken aback by her apparent unhappiness.

I guessed all the riches in the world couldn't soothe her. I pointed to the sofa. "Sit and tell me why you're so upset and how I can help you."

She flopped onto the sofa while I sat opposite her and well out of reach. Carina was on her way downhill, fast, real fast. Worried over her disheveled appearance, her makeup-free face, and her overall mental state, I sat silently, waiting for her to begin.

Carina sent Adrian to practice her new dance steps in her dance room. After Adrian scooted away, I leaned forward and asked softly, "What was your relationship with Evelyn Montgomery?"

Upset by the question, tears rolled down her face. Wishing I could take the question back, I apologized and rose to leave.

"No, please, don't go. Come into the kitchen, I'll make coffee, I have to tell you something."

I followed her and stood near the island opposite the counters, waiting until Carina gathered her thoughts. She put a coffee pod and a cup into her Cuisinart coffeemaker and pushed the start button.

A knock sounded on the glass door that led to the deck at the rear of the house. Startled, I put my shaking hands into the pockets of my jeans. Carina motioned Adelle to come in.

Adelle and her daughter had attended Adrian's party. She hadn't said a word since entering, but studied Carina instead. When she did look my way, her face was filled with dismay.

"You should leave. Right now."

Interested in their relationship, I said I had been invited and was about to inquire why she was present when Adelle stepped forward and took hold of my arm. She tried to lead me to the door.

"What are you doing? Let go of me this instant." I withdrew my arm from Adelle's grasp.

Carina insisted, "I did invite Juliette to come here."

That's when I heard Bun say, *"This is interesting. Are you okay?"*

I dipped my head and peered through the glass into the pool of light that ended just past the deck. I could see Bun just inside the edge of the light, his ears tipped forward.

I stepped back from the glass doors, but remained in his sight. The last thing I wanted was Bun's involvement. I knew he'd continue to watch and was comforted by it.

"If it's not too much to ask, I would like an explanation." I directed the words at Carina, then gave Adelle a glance.

Adelle swept the hair back from her forehead as she watched Carina.

The doorbell chimed again and again as Carina rushed to answer the summons. Without a word, Adelle took the cup of coffee from the machine and plopped the cup on the counter in front of me. Then she made one for herself and sat in a tall chair to drink the hot brew.

"What is this about?" I asked.

"I'm sorry, I didn't mean to be rude, Jules. Carina's on her last nerve and frankly, I don't know how to help her. I assumed you were here to ask questions, which would only increase her stress level."

"She was frantic when she called me. At least that's the impression I got when we spoke on the phone. I'm only trying to help her, Adelle." In silence I gazed at the woman across from me. Bailey and I were scheduled to entertain the children at her daughter's birthday celebration on the weekend. Other than that, I had seen her around town and at Adrian's party. As Bun had said, this was an interesting turn of events. Adelle lived across town. She didn't fit into the financial bracket of this neighborhood, and I wondered how the two women were connected.

"Have you known Carina very long? I noticed you were at Adrian's party."

"We've been friends a long time. Our daughters

go to the same school and are in dance class to-gether."

Before I could ask anything else, I heard Jack's voice echo through the enormous house.

"I would like to speak to Juliette," Sheriff Carver demanded.

I went into the foyer. Carina left me alone with Jack and returned to the kitchen where Adelle waited for her.

His gaze cool, Jack asked in a soft tone, "Why are you here, and what has Carina so upset? I can see she's been crying. Who else is here?"

With a glance over my shoulder, I motioned to the front door and we stepped outside.

Aware I had been followed to Carina's, it occurred to me that Jack might think I was still in some sort of danger.

"Carina invited me. I don't know why, but after seeing the state she's in, I think she's lost control of her emotions. Adrian answered the door when I arrived and told me to make her mom happy again. When I saw Bailey today, she also commented on Carina's frame of mind. We were about to discuss what was going on, when Adelle Philby popped up out of nowhere. She wasn't friendly, either."

"Tell Carina you have to leave, and I'll meet you at the farm. We can speak frankly there." Jack turned and left me on the doorstep.

Frustrated by the events, I did as Jack asked and told Carina I would be in touch. Adelle watched as I explained and didn't say a word until I crossed the room to leave. Apologizing again, Adelle said she looked forward to the party.

I nodded. Carina escorted me to the door. I murmured, "Will you be all right?"

"Yes, thanks." Carina stepped back and closed the door.

Hesitant to leave her with Adelle, I went to my car, got in, and remarked, "What possessed you to watch the house?"

"I had to relieve myself. Rabbits do, you know. I hopped behind the bushes, heard that woman enter Carina's grounds, and followed her. Good thing I did, too. She might have harmed you."

"There was no chance of that, she was worried about Carina. I didn't learn a thing before she arrived. Carina's a mess, the sheriff arrived and demanded I leave, and I'm no further now than I was at suppertime."

"I can understand how annoying that can be, after all, you've left me out of this more often than not. Which, by the way, I don't appreciate at all."

"I have already apologized, so don't try to guilt me for it."

"I think we should see what Sheriff Carver has to say. The evening might not end up a total loss."

"One can only hope. He'd better not badger me, I'm in no mood for it. Adelle and Carina have been friends for a long time. At least, that's what Adelle told me. What do you think?"

Bun considered the information while he nestled into the soft blanket on the seat. *"You should look into their friendship further. Don't you think they look similar?"*

With a grimace, I started the car. "I never gave it any consideration. I think your imagination is at work again, Bun. Don't look for things that aren't there."

With a slight sigh Bun remarked, *"If you say so. I had the opportunity to watch the two women while you were in the mix of things."*

CHAPTER NINETEEN

"What was your purpose in going to Carina's house?" Jack demanded when he'd taken a seat in the living room.

"None. Like I explained before, Carina asked me to stop by."

"Did she offer anything at all that could be useful to my investigation?"

"Not a thing. I assumed Seamus and Colin's activities would do that for you."

"Between the two of them, Seamus is more likely to commit crimes, though his rap sheet doesn't indicate murderous behavior. I hate to say it, but they might not have killed her. They were after easy money, that's all. They refuse to tell me who hired them. Have you any idea who would pay them?"

"Colin said they would have earned a lot of money. I've gone over the people involved and have come up with a few. Carina has lots of money, as does Jim Brody. Vera might be in good financial standing, but she probably isn't connected to all this, and then there's Bailey. Do you think Vera or Bailey are participants in all this?"

"Fair question, it's worth investigating their backgrounds. As for Jim, he's an outstanding citizen who supports the community in a number of ways. What would he have to gain?"

"You're in a better position than I am to know that. He's affable, charming, outgoing, and I learned today he also supports that lodge at Lake Plantain."

"Do I hear a *but* coming?"

"Uh-huh. I'm not as certain as you and Meredith are that Jim's a wonderful guy. It's as though he's trying to pave his way to Heaven with good deeds."

"I'm surprised you'd make such a harsh assessment. The man has worked hard to get where he is."

"Haven't we all?"

"I guess so, but there isn't one wrinkle in his life, that I know of."

"Then you might want to remove those blinders and take a closer look at the man and his company."

Jack opened his mouth to protest, and I raised my hand.

"I have no grudge against him. I do think there might be more to him than good deeds. As a policeman, you realize people have a secret or two they don't want anyone to find out."

"Boy, he really likes Brody."

Bun was right, Jack admired Brody. Why?

"Have you and your wife had any dealings with Jim, other than his support of projects in Windermere?"

"He supports the policeman's ball, and our efforts to gain the trust of our residents. I first met Jim when I was a rookie. Jim had opened his company in a small barn on King Road at that time and was doing well. He assisted us officers in our goal to raise enough money for children's education. Thanks to his efforts, we raised the funds needed. To my knowledge, the man has always been fair and honest in his dealings. You're a customer of his, aren't you?"

"Yes, since I started my business." I sipped from my cup, wondering if Brody had been more interested in bringing attention to his new business and branding it than helping cops reach their goals. "All I'm saying is you might look deeper."

"What makes you think he has something to hide?"

I shrugged a shoulder. "I met him at the rabbit show. He was pleasant, with an engaging way about him. A smooth talker who knows how to sell. Anyway, he offered me the opportunity to apply for a grant from his company. I wasn't crazy about the idea, but I filled out the paperwork and submitted it to him. He said his grant committee would review the application when they met later that week and he'd be in touch." I went on to say Brody refused the grant the very next day, without any input from his committee.

"It struck me as peculiar that he hadn't presented it to them. But then, I believe things happen for a reason. Maybe it wasn't meant for me to have grant money. I don't resent him for it, I just find his behavior odd, and that something wasn't right about the whole thing."

Thoughtful, Jack relented. "Okay. I'll give him a

look, then. Let's get back to Carina. How was she while you were with her tonight?"

"Upset, crying, and about to share something with me. We were interrupted by Adelle. She thought I had caused Carina more angst than she already had, and tried to get rid of me. You arrived in time to save us from an argument."

Jack's bushy eyebrows arched as he listened.

I heard a tiny snort and glanced at Bun. *"He shouldn't be surprised that you would take a stand. I don't know what his problem is, maybe he's off his feed."*

Unlikely as it was, since Jack was a tad fluffy around the middle, Bun's comment caused me to hold back a laugh. I pretended to cough.

"Why would Carina hire a man like Seamus to dig through Evelyn's paperwork? I'd think Bailey would want to get her hands on the document."

In agreement, I said, "True, and how would Carina know someone like Seamus? It's not as if she'd hang out at a bar to chat with him. He's not in her class of people."

His hat in hand, Jack rose. "I should get back to the station. You've given me plenty to consider."

At the door, he glanced at me. "Stay out of trouble, Juliette."

Alone, I looked in on the rabbits and returned to the house.

Bun, not one to hold back, immediately offered his opinion. *"Carver thinks Brody is a prince of princes."*

"That's one way to look at it. Jack is a smart cop, he's thorough, and I trust him. If Brody, Vera, or Adelle need to be researched, Jack will do it."

"I don't understand what Adelle really has to do with Carina. I did see her at the birthday party. I had forgot-

ten about that, there were a large number of guests that day. And, all those kids were screaming, as only girls will."

"They were excited. Dig deep, see what you can remember, then let me know."

"Okay. I'm sleepy after all this activity. I'll see you in the morning."

"Sleep well. Thanks for being my backup."

"I'll always protect you."

He hopped into his room, sank into his new cushion, and fell asleep. I was making notes on what had taken place when my cell phone pinged. I read the text message and grabbed my coat and car keys.

Leaving Bun behind, I returned to Carina's house. Except for the light next to the front door, the house was dark.

Unwilling to awaken Adrian, I tapped the door with the knocker rather than use the doorbell. Standing in the cold, I waited for Carina to answer the door. When she didn't answer, I tried the door handle, thinking she might have left the door unlocked. Something was wrong. My concern for Carina and Adrian heightened.

Unable to gain entrance from the front, I ran around the side of the house using my tiny flashlight to light the way. On the deck, I cupped my hands around my eyes to peer into the kitchen. The night-light was too faint to see much. The beam of my flashlight brightened the room and I saw Carina crumpled on the floor, her eyes closed.

I dialed 9-1-1 and requested that a rescue and the police respond to Carina's address. While on the phone, I tried the kitchen sliding door and found it unlocked. Wary, the sight of Carina lying so very still prodded me to enter the house. I crept across the floor and knelt next to her inert body. Relieved to find her pulse, I bent down to put my cheek near her nose, and felt her breath. I leaned back on my heels.

Flashing lights bounced off the walls and through the windows of the open floorplan of the house. Flipping light switches, I rushed to the front door to greet the rescue crew. As they went toward the kitchen, I saw Jack Carver on the doorstep. His expression ominous, I backed up and swung my arm out in invitation for him to enter.

"You can't mind your own business, can you, Juliette?"

"Now is not the time to lose your temper and lecture me." Turning my back to him, I marched to the kitchen.

A team of two men worked on Carina. Two others brought a stretcher into the room and loaded Carina onto it. One rescuer placed an oxygen mask over her nose and turned the cylinder knob to allow the oxygen to flow. Then they rolled her through the house to the ambulance.

"I'll look in on Adrian," I murmured to Sheriff Carver. With a brief nod, he followed the men outside.

I walked from bedroom to bedroom on the second floor. I found Adrian asleep in the bedroom three doors down from the top of the stairs. Totally relaxed, the little girl appeared angelic. I tiptoed away.

Jack waited at the bottom of the staircase. "Is the child all right?"

"She is. I thought for sure she would awaken."

"Does she have someone to look after her?"

"I'm not sure. I don't know any of Carina's friends other than Adelle. I'll call her to see if she can care for Adrian until Carina is back on her feet. When I realized she was breathing, I had already called for all of you, and let her be. You made good time getting here."

"I didn't see signs of an assault. I'll go by the hospital to get an update on her condition."

I dialed Adelle's number. Worried over Carina's situation, Adelle agreed to take Adrian to her home while Carina was checked over and said she would arrive shortly. I gave a thumbs-up to the sheriff, who then left, and I awaited Adelle's arrival.

Alone, I took the opportunity to rifle through Carina's personal papers. In the midst of it, Adelle knocked on the front door, which sent me into a panic. She had arrived sooner than I had anticipated, leaving me without enough time to find anything that could help Jack. I jammed papers back into the desk drawers, quickly fumbled through Carina's Kate Spade handbag for the house keys, and pocketed them.

I hurried to greet Adelle with a soft hello and prepared to leave.

A concerned look on her face, Adelle said, "I'll wait until Adrian is up and get her ready to go to my house. My own kids will be happy to see her, and I'll keep her at my house until Carina is sorted out. Keep me posted, won't you?"

"I will. Thanks for helping, I know Carina will be relieved to know Adrian will be okay."

The door closed behind me. I heard the lock click into place. Thankful Adrian would be looked after, I was certain the child would be fine. I drove from the house to the hospital and found Jack in the reception area.

"How's Carina?"

"The doctor is still with her."

I darted a glance at his half-empty coffee cup.

"Would you like some?" Carver asked with a half grin. "You look like you're about to take mine."

"Yeah, I could use it about now." I checked my watch, it was nearly two o'clock in the morning. A long day stretched ahead of me if I had no sleep, which I knew was a probability.

We walked the high-sheen-polished hallway to the coffee shop. Both of us pensive, I helped myself to a jug-style carafe of strong brew, paid for it, and sat at a nearby table with Jack.

"What brought you to Carina's house?"

I pulled the text message up on my phone and held it out for him to read.

"You were sure this came from Carina, then?"

"It's her number at the top." I pointed to it.

"Anybody could have used her phone to get in touch with you."

Tired, I said, "Not everyone thinks the way you do, Jack. I don't suspect every person I come across to be a perpetrator of some deadly crime. I figured Adrian was asleep in bed, and Carina must have been alone as well. I assumed she wanted to pick up where we left off."

"Reasonable enough, I guess."

"When I arrived, the house was dark. It was creepy." Goose bumps popped up on my skin at the recollection. "I went into her backyard to enter from the deck. I was nervous about going inside. Then I saw Carina lying unconscious on the kitchen floor."

"So, you broke in?"

Indignant, I snapped, "I did not. The slider was unlocked."

He grimaced and said, "You should have called us then and there. It might have been dangerous to enter the house. You should know better."

"Must you lecture me? It's over. Let's move on."

"Fine," he groused.

We returned to the waiting area and sat in silence.

CHAPTER TWENTY

At odds once again, there was no doubt an argument brewed between us. If Dr. Sommers hadn't walked into the room just then, we'd have had words. Ones that shouldn't be said aloud and couldn't be taken back once they were spoken. In light of Sheriff Carver's aggressive grumpiness, I found myself on the defense a lot lately.

Dr. Sommers greeted us. "Sheriff, Miss."

We rose and shook his hand. I held my breath for fear he had bad, very bad, or downright horrible news for us.

"I've finished examining Mrs. Richland. Her blood test results show she's become anemic, dangerously so. When she regained consciousness, we discussed what has been happening in her life lately. She's under extreme pressure, some self-inflicted, some not." He stared directly at Jack when he spoke of her health. He then looked my way. "I'm glad you are here, Mrs. Richland asked for and would like to see you." He flicked a glance at Jack and then added, "Alone."

Uncomfortable in the atmosphere that had now become worse than before, I said, "Uh, okay."

Dr. Sommers motioned as he spoke. "She's in the second room down that corridor, on your left. Don't stay long. We'll keep her for a day or so for observation and to work up a treatment regimen."

"I won't take much of her time." I trotted off and didn't look back until I'd reached Carina's room.

Sommers and Jack were in the midst of what appeared to be a heated exchange. Bun's words came back to me. Maybe Jack *was* off his feed.

When I walked in and sat next to Carina, she opened her eyes and said, "Thank you for sending the rescue. I must have scared you half to death."

"You did until I realized you were still breathing. Then I called in the cavalry."

She smiled bit, and then sobered. "Where is Adrian? Does she know I'm here?"

"She's with Adelle and will stay with her family until you're well enough to return home. Honestly, only children can sleep through such things." I went on to explain Adelle's plan and said I'd update the woman, so she could let Adrian know what was happening.

"What's going on with this anemia situation?"

"I was quite run-down after Paul's death. I had no appetite, was sleepless, and inundated by all that goes with the grief process and the legalities that need to be dealt with. I'm in the same state of health now. I must tell you about Evelyn, but you have to promise to keep it to yourself."

"If you're in danger, I can't promise not to tell Jack Carver. Otherwise, I won't say a word."

"Evelyn began blackmailing me after Paul died. As a couple, Paul and I had a certain social standing in the community, and even now, I still have that. Mainly, I think it's because of Paul and the programs I continue to participate in for the community. She knew our secret and Paul paid her to shut her up. When he was gone, it became my problem to deal with."

"Evelyn was cruel."

"And unfeeling. For a long time, she had no money and decided she would earn an income conceiving and carrying babies for those who couldn't. Anyway, we lived elsewhere then and never told anyone that I hadn't delivered Adrian. She'd blackmailed Paul all that time and it became worse when she moved to Windermere. Somehow she figured out that nobody knew of her part in our having a child. Paul and I were private about our lives, and for Adrian's sake, we didn't want the world to know how she'd been conceived."

"I see. Was that what you argued about at the party?"

"She threatened to take me to court for custody of Adrian if I didn't continue to pay her as Paul had always done. I became angry and said she'd get nothing more from me. I knew she'd call my bluff by spreading rumors about her, Paul, and worst of all, Adrian. My only hope was to let her think I was serious. I had planned to call my attorney to make sure I had nothing to worry over. Then we found her body in the woods. I did not kill her, Juliette, I didn't."

"I know you would never do such a thing. Besides, you didn't have a moment to yourself all day, let alone enough time to kill Evelyn." I reached over, gave her hand a gentle squeeze, and said I couldn't stay much longer.

"You've been a great help. When you came over, I wanted to tell you all that, but Adelle came in and things went downhill. Then Sheriff Carver showed up and made things worse."

Before I could ask her what Adelle's involvement was in all of this, a light tap sounded on the door and Dr. Sommers entered the room.

"Mrs. Richland should rest now. You can visit again once she's feeling better." I nodded as he turned to Carina. He said a room was ready and that an orderly would take her to the second floor for the night.

"I'll be back. Get some rest, Carina, and listen to what Dr. Sommers recommends for treatment."

She nodded. I made my exit with Dr. Sommers on my heels.

"Miss Bridge, if you wouldn't mind waiting a moment. Mrs. Richland can recover from this, but she should have counseling as well. I know she was a model at one time, that Paul Richland was her husband, and he died in an accident. I was the doctor on duty when he was brought to the emergency room. A woman showed up, claimed she was Mrs. Richland, and was given access to him. Not long afterward, the second, and real, Mrs. Richland arrived. It made for a messy situation, since I had just explained to the fake Mrs. Richland all that had happened to the man."

"Why tell me all this?"

"Because you seem to genuinely care about her."

"She's had a difficult time these last few years, and the fake Mrs. Richland didn't make it any easier." I kept Carina's confession to myself and said if she needed anything at all, he could call me. I dug a business card out of my inner pocket, wrote my cell phone number on it, and held it out to him.

"Thank you."

"You said she'll be here for a day or so?"

"She'll stay with us until I think she's ready to leave."

I nodded and went home.

Dawn had crept up to the horizon as exhaustion crawled over me. Bleary-eyed, I greeted Jessica when she popped through the door, bright-eyed and wide awake.

Surprised at my appearance, she asked, "What happened to you?"

"I've had an all-nighter." I told Jess what had taken place and slumped farther into the soft-cushioned living room chair. Bun sat in the doorway, his ears tipped forward, yammering about food.

"Make breakfast, will you? I have to feed Bun."

"Okay."

I took Bun's food from his cupboard and added fresh veggies to it. I refilled his water bin and whispered that we'd talk later.

"Are you talking to Bun or me?"

"To Bun. I always talk when I feed him." I looked down, Bun looked up, and I winked. His whiskers jittered.

"If you want to rest, I'll take care of the rabbits."

"I'll do it, but if you want to give me a hand, that would be helpful. I'll nap after the chores are finished."

Jess handed me a steaming cup of coffee and said, "If you say so. What do you want to eat?"

"Toast."

"No protein there. How about an egg to go with it?"

"Sure, thanks."

Unwilling to argue with her or anyone about anything, I remained in the chair, set my coffee cup on the side table, and relaxed.

"Wake up, wake up!"

I forced my lids open and glanced down. Agitated, Bun trailed back and forth in front of me.

"What?"

"You've been asleep for quite a while. The sheriff is in the barn with Jessica. And we have a birthday party to get to."

"You're right, thanks for waking me. I'll go see what Carver wants this time. We almost had an argument at the emergency room while awaiting Carina's diagnosis. She'll be fine, though she scared the bejeepers out of me. Jack was on the verge of a tantrum and if this case isn't solved soon, I might lose my mind, let alone my temper."

"Like I said, he's off his feed. Remember when Petra

was unwell? She was off her feed and cranky as all get-out."

"I didn't know she was cranky, but she wasn't hungry in the least."

"I tend to forget you don't speak rabbit. Not everyone has the power to communicate with humans like I do."

"Mm, good point." I freshened up, changed my clothes, and walked out to the barn. Jason, Jack Carver, and Jessica were there. Jason put away the supply order he had accepted from Jim Brody's company. He handed me the invoice and asked, "You okay?"

"I sure am. Thanks for handling this for me."

His face brightened with a look of satisfaction, and he wandered away, a bag of feed on his shoulder.

Jessica went to greet her next patient. Jack and I were alone. He looked tired, causing me to wonder if he'd had any sleep after leaving the hospital.

"Tired?"

"I slept for an hour or so after we parted ways last night. I came by to tell you Mrs. Richland is doing well. I also wanted to apologize for being surly these past few weeks. The powers that be have been breathing down my neck and want this murder investigation solved immediately. It's clear that they've forgotten how difficult finding a killer can be. They've probably been watching reruns of *Law & Order* on TV." He rolled his eyes.

I snickered and said, "If only life were that simple. Now, if you had a script to go by, you could wrap things up in an hour, too."

When he smiled at the idea, I realized he was

under pressure of his own, like Carina, yet in a different way. On the verge of sharing what she'd told me, I held my tongue. I'd made a promise and wasn't about to break it.

"What did Carina say last night?"

"She wanted to thank me for our assistance last night."

"You were in there for some time."

"She wasn't feeling very well, so I stayed to assure her Adrian would be taken care of. Oh, gosh, I should give Adelle a call."

"No need, I met with her and gave her the news. She was relieved and said Adrian is fine. You can pass that along to Carina when you visit."

"Have you been in to see her?"

"I was warned off by Dr. Sommers. It's rare that I allow anyone to keep me from doing my job, but he insisted. It would be a shame if Adrian became motherless. I can wait until her mother has recovered and is back home."

"Nice of you, Jack."

"Meredith had a hand in that decision. She pointed out how overbearing I can be at times."

Holding back my opinion of the way Meredith ruled the roost with a velvet-gloved hand, I murmured, "You think?"

"Mm, well, make sure you tell Carina her daughter is fine. I'm not sure if Adelle plans to take her for a visit. I guess you'll be doing the birthday event at her house today?"

"Bailey and I will set up around noon. The party starts at two o'clock." I glanced at the wall clock. If I dawdled much longer, I would be late.

"You never spoke of the relationship between Adelle and Carina?"

"I was on the verge of asking about her when Dr. Sommers asked me to leave. He didn't want me to tire Carina any more than she already was. I will see her later today and ask about it. I'll call you."

"That's decent of you. I'll get going and run checks on the people you mentioned yesterday."

Relief rolled over me when Jack went about his business, and I heaved a sigh. I'd felt my pulse rate increase and my nerves tighten until he apologized. Even then, I was careful of what I said. It never sat well with me when I had to be secretive, especially with law enforcement.

CHAPTER TWENTY-ONE

"**Y**ou handled that well. I'm surprised Jack offered an apology. Meredith is a stronger woman than I'd thought."

"I agree. I hadn't really thought that about her, but I guess she's more than able to handle Jack."

"*You're visiting Carina today?*"

Noting the time, I nodded. "After the party is over. I really need to get a move on if we're to arrive at Adelle's on time."

"*I know I'm not allowed in the hospital, though I should be. I'm good for the patients. I'll wait in the van while you visit Carina.*"

"We'll leave the party and return here so I can unload the supplies and get all you rabbits settled. I'm glad you understand that I can't take you to the hospital without permission."

When Jason entered the barn, I asked for his help to load the van, and said that while I was gone Jess would handle anything he might be unfamiliar with.

"You don't need to worry, the farm is in good hands. Oh, uh, should I leave the other rabbits outside the usual amount of time? The temperature is dropping."

"Bring them in after an hour or so. I'll return when the party has ended. Thanks, Jason."

The van loaded, I started the trek to Adelle's. Her home, modest in comparison to Carina's, was still a decent-sized house set on a half-acre of land. She greeted me as I opened the van door.

"Hi, I was just about to call you."

My heart pounded. "Is something wrong?"

With a shake of her head, Adelle assured me all was well. "Adrian has asked when her mother will be coming home. I hoped you could tell me. Adrian's enjoying her time with the kids, but she is concerned for her mother."

"As far as I know, Carina will be released when the doctor feels she's ready."

"Thanks, I wasn't sure what to tell the child, she's been through enough with the tragic death of her father."

"Mm, they both have. I'll start unpacking the rabbits. Bailey was right behind me and might want a hand with her equipment."

"I have the refreshments and games under control, so if you need me, just give a yell. Keep me posted on Carina, okay?"

I said I would and began setting up the rabbit pen. I waved to Bailey as she bustled back and forth from her van carrying the staging for the puppet show.

Blue skies, puffy white clouds, and sunshine were the order of the afternoon. We chatted and laughed over what the day might hold for us in the way of activities for the children and I mentioned the gossip of their moms.

"I never hear any gossip." Bailey sounded legitimately disappointed.

"I don't hear it very often, I'm too busy with the kids and rabbits. Do me a favor, will you, and listen to what's being said if you have a chance? I'll do the same."

"Sure, why not? We might hear something of interest."

"You never know," I said, as she went off to ready her puppets.

Prepared for the onslaught of the scads of children that I was certain would arrive shortly, Bun and I casually walked the grounds. We noted the gate that led to the house next door. Not too far from Adelle's driveway, I saw the dwelling through the trees. Unlike Carina's neighborhood, the homes here were closer to one another and less private.

At the corner of Adelle's house, I heard hushed, yet angry words spoken between a man and woman. I slowed my pace to eavesdrop. It was poor manners, but I had to listen, so there you have it. I edged closer, leaned against the wall, and removed my sneaker. I shook it lightly, taking time to empty out a nonexistent pebble while the conversation continued.

His voice held disbelief. "You can't possibly think I'll put up with this, do you?"

"Lower your voice, the neighbors will hear you. I only want to know what your plans are for the future. I don't think I'm asking for much. You owe me and you know it." The woman's low voice sounded familiar, but she murmured and I wasn't certain if I was right in my assumption of her identity.

I slipped my sneaker back on and took my time with the laces.

"He's pretty mad. But, she's going to blackmail him for what he's done. Uh, what has he done?"

With a shrug, I pressed my fingertip to my lips so Bun would stop yammering the way he does at the worst possible moments.

The man's voice had grown angry and a tad louder. "This has to come to a stop, I won't stand for it."

"If Evelyn did it, then so will I. She had a notebook with names of people and the sums they owed. I saw it once when I was at her house. When she noticed my interest in it, she took it off the desk and locked it in a drawer."

"And look what happened to her? Besides, what do you want from me?"

"Don't play dumb, you know exactly what I want. And, you'll give it to me or I will destroy you."

"Old Jimbo is getting his comeuppance."

"Shh." I'd finally figured out who was talking to whom and hand-palmed my forehead. How could I not have known? But then, so many people adored Jim Brody, it never dawned on me Evelyn might have held a secret over Jim's head, making him pay. Surprised that this particular woman would pick up where Evelyn's blackmail scheme had left off, I wondered if she really had seen the notebook. There weren't names, just codes that Jack's people had figured out.

Their conversation drifted away as did they. Disappointed that I couldn't hear more of what was going on between them, I started across the yard toward the rabbits' pen, Bun at my side.

"Can I talk now?"

I nodded.

"Good, then I'll just go after them and get the skinny on what is going to happen between them. He'll be paying up, don't you think?"

"Yes, but stay with me."

Moments later, Adelle approached me. "Are you all set, Jules? The guests will arrive any moment now."

"The rabbits and I are ready. I even brought Petra to entertain them with her backflips and tricks. She was supposed to compete in the rabbit games at the show, but she became ill the week it took place. Jessica and I had taught her some pretty cool moves that the children will enjoy." I looked past Adelle and asked, "Where's the birthday girl?"

"She's anxiously waiting at the front door to welcome her friends. There are more coming than had initially responded to her invitations so be prepared to handle a crowd."

"I will, thanks. You have a sweet home. And a great backyard, too."

"It's a lot to keep up with, but I manage. After my husband died, it was tough, but Carina has been supportive and together we manage to hold our lives together."

"I'm sorry to hear your husband passed away. You and your daughter were in the same situation as Carina, then?"

"He died long after Paul did. Carina was good to me, as I was to her. Our girls became very close and have remained so. They're almost like sisters."

"That's great, then. Carina speaks highly of you and relies on your friendship. How did your husband die, if you don't mind my asking."

"We owned a boat. He went fishing one night and never returned. When he didn't show up, I called the police and he was found floating in the water. His death was considered accidental. Carina and I pretty much need each other. She didn't have the financial issues I'd been left with, though." She grew pensive for a few moments and then smiled. "Things are better now, much better. My kids and I live well, comfortably, even."

"Is your daughter close in age to Adrian?"

"No, she's a bit younger. They met in dance class, which is how they became friends, but they aren't in the same grade at school."

My brain was in overdrive as I did the math. Hmm. Maybe I was off target here, but somehow pieces of the puzzle had started falling into place. That's when a horde of children arrived.

With no time to think about what I'd discovered, I greeted the little darlings who came to the rabbit pen while others took to the puppets that Bailey had bouncing around on the stage. Not only did she have marionettes, she also had her hand puppets. She was ready to entertain.

Petra tolerated the children well, did some jumping and running flips for them, and flew over the small fences I had set up for her. The kids clapped their hands in glee and asked for more.

Well into party mode, time passed, kids ran around the yard, watched the puppet show and then gathered for cake and gift giving. I watched them and studied Adelle as she took care of Adrian and Tricia. Too bad Adelle had taken the chances she had, if I was right, there was only one place they would lead her, and that was straight to prison.

Adelle Philby was a killer, I was sure of it. She had murdered Evelyn Montgomery and I thought I knew why. How could I prove it? I crouched inside the rabbit pen and petted Bun while I dialed Jack on my cell phone. When he answered, I said, "Meet me at the farm in an hour." I cut off the call before he could utter a word. I ordered Bun to remain vigilant while I loaded the rabbits in their travel cages and gave them a snack and some water.

Bailey wandered over and asked if she could help. I nodded and thanked her for asking. "Wow, these kids had a great time today. You were as busy as I was."

"They were a noisy bunch, all that energy, I would love to have that much." She stepped back, laughed, and then remarked, "On second thought, maybe I wouldn't. Some of them sure were wild, and where the heck were the mommies?"

"Why, gossiping, of course."

Her chuckle turned to laughter as did mine. The joy of it lightened the burden of knowledge I carried.

"Do you need a hand with your equipment?" I asked.

"Not really, I can handle it, besides you have live critters to take care of. We'll go get paid and then you can head home. I'm sure you don't like to leave your furry friends in those small cages, do you?"

"Not for any longer than they have to be. I kind of have free-range rabbits."

She snickered, and we walked toward the house. Adrian met us at the door, leaned toward me, and whispered, "Thank you for taking care of my mom."

"You're quite welcome." That happiness might not last long and there were surely going to be problems that would arise if there was enough proof to convict Adelle. Sad as it made me to think her children would be motherless while Adelle was imprisoned, I had to tell Sheriff Carver what I knew.

Adelle had our payments handy and gave us both envelopes with cash in them. We thanked her while congratulating her on a great birthday party and then left. As we parted, Bailey asked if Mora had been apprised of our decision to entertain at the lodge. I said she had and mentioned we should work out a skit that put her puppets and my rabbits together in an act. Where the idea had come from was anybody's guess, but it sounded doable. I walked across the yard and caught sight of Adelle as she watched me.

I drove to the farm, Jason and I set the rabbits up in their hutches and I left Bun in his room. With that job over with, I freshened up, changed my clothes and answered my cell phone.

Jack said, "I'm sorry, Juliette, I can't get to the farm right now. I'll catch up with you later, okay?"

"Fine, I'm going to the hospital, then."

He hung up without another word and I set off to see Carina.

Traffic was backed up due to an accident. It took me longer than I expected to arrive. About to enter through the automatic doors, I felt a tap on my shoulder. Startled, I turned and looked up at Jim Brody.

"Are you here to visit someone?" I asked, and stepped aside for an orderly who guided a wheelchair in ahead of us. The person in the chair appeared frail.

His smile wide, Jim said, "Yes, I am, are you?"

"I wouldn't be here otherwise." I shivered at the thought of how much time I had spent in this place after I'd been run off the road and left for dead a few years back. Curious, I asked, "Who are you visiting?"

"Carina Richland."

"I'm sure she'll be happy to see you."

We made our way to the elevators after asking for Carina's room number. Uneasy in this building, I knew my problem was the length of time and pain I had endured as a patient. I wondered if I would ever shake my response to this place, or any hospital.

We got off on the same floor and walked to Carina's room together. Jim hadn't asked where I was going, and seemed a bit surprised when we entered the room.

"I wasn't aware you knew Mrs. Richland," he murmured with raised brows.

"I've known her for some time now."

I greeted Carina with a smile. Dr. Sommers stood by the bed speaking to her. Jim and I backed away and stood near the door, offering them privacy. The doctor was in the midst of discussing Carina's future care and needs.

"You'll recover if you follow the treatment I've set up for you."

A glimmer of hope in her eyes, Carina promised she would do so and thanked him. He turned to leave, caught sight of us, and motioned for me to join him in the corridor. He passed Jim Brody without a glance. Hmm, interesting.

Two doors down from Carina's room, Dr. Sommers stopped.

"You'll be happy to know Mrs. Richland will be released tomorrow morning. Can you pick her up at nine o'clock?"

"I guess so. She's better, then?"

"Though her stay has been brief, she's willing to get well and that's a positive sign. The real test will be when she's at home. Patients don't always follow the recovery path they've been given. With time and follow-through, she can regain her health. If not, she'll end up back here, and nobody wants that, especially Mrs. Richland."

"You've set up treatment for her that will require what, exactly?" I had to know in case there was another incident such as this. Not that I was her caretaker, or ever would be, I just didn't want another situation like this to arise.

He explained what was in place for Carina to take advantage of if she seriously wanted to be healthy, then Dr. Sommers bid me good-bye.

Slow to enter Carina's room, I heard the conversation between her and Jim Brody. I stood just short of the door and eavesdropped.

"You shouldn't have come, I don't want to see you."

"I had to know if you were going to be all right."

"My health should be of no concern to you. Now, get out and stay away from me."

I could hear the anxiety in her voice growing by the second. Still, I hesitated.

"Carina, you know why I'm really here. I have every right and you're aware of it. Don't push me away, it won't end up well for you."

Was that a threat? Fearing things might get out of hand, I coughed and then walked in.

With a smile, I said, "The doctor thinks you're going to be fine. He's assured me if you follow his advice, you'll be healthy in no time flat. That's great news, Carina, and Adrian will be ecstatic when I tell her."

Stress pinched her facial skin as Carina valiantly tried to look as pleased as I sounded. "Yes, yes, she will. I can hardly wait to get home."

"Good, then I'll pick you up at nine in the morning. Dr. Sommers said you would be ready to go by then."

Jim looked my way and said, "I'll have a car sent to pick her up, if you're too busy at the farm, that is."

Panic filled Carina's eyes.

"Not at all, Carina and I will be fine, won't we?"

She nodded.

I looked Jim over for a second and then said, "Thanks for the offer, though. It was generous of you."

"I don't mind at all, but if you insist, the honor is yours." He turned back to Carina and wished her well.

I closed the door behind him and sat next to Carina's bed. With her hand in mine, I said, "Don't ever be afraid. You're much stronger than you think."

"You heard, then?"

"Some of it. What's his connection to you?"

She pushed her body farther upright and I adjusted the pillows. She exhaled and relaxed.

"My secret, that's what."

"Meaning?"

"He's my brother-in-law and Adrian's biological father."

As if I'd been sucker-punched, I gasped aloud. "You've got to be kidding?"

"This is no joking matter, honest."

"If you would rather not discuss it, I understand. I have no wish to upset you."

"If you don't mind listening, it would feel good to get it off my chest."

I got comfortable in the chair and let her talk.

Paul insisted they move to Windermere some years before. Carina hadn't wanted to give up her career and kept working until she decided to let modeling go and concentrate on Adrian. The move had proven fruitful for Paul. As a stock market trader, his work was done on the computer, and his clients were located all over the world. The one thing Paul had held back from her had been his brother.

"I hadn't any idea Paul had a brother, let alone that he had lived in Windermere. It did strike me as odd that Paul would want to move to New Hampshire. We were busy New Yorkers. He convinced me that relocation would be good for us and for Adrian."

"How did you meet Jim?"

"He's actually Paul's half-brother. Jim's parents divorced, and Jim's mother married the man who was Paul's father. Anyway, before we moved here, Paul and I couldn't conceive a child and ended up with a surrogate who lived in New York at the same time we did. She had been recommended by someone Paul said he knew."

I kept the mounting slew of questions from escaping my mouth and let her go on.

"I was desperate for a child. When Evelyn Montgomery entered the picture, it was as if my prayers had been answered. Evelyn was more than willing to carry our child for a price. Surprised by her astronomical fee, I wasn't certain the idea was sound. Something about the woman didn't sit right with me." She became silent for a while and then said, "Everyone in Windermere thinks Jim's a great guy, but I know a different side of him." With a look of distaste, Carina swished her hands to brush away the flavor of the words.

Willing her to tell me more, I urged, "Go on."

"Could I have some water, please?"

"Certainly." I poured a glass of water and handed it to her.

Her hand shook slightly, but the determination to tell me the story was written on her features. Enthralled, as though watching a soap opera marathon, I settled in.

"Paul insisted we go ahead with the surrogacy and I complied. As the situation became clear, Paul realized he didn't have what was needed to conceive a child. That's when Jim came along and was introduced to me as Paul's brother. Imagine my surprise.

"Jim, being the 'good guy,' said he would do his part, so we could have a child. Paul was grateful, after all they were half-brothers. No matter what my concerns were, Paul was determined to give me the child I so dearly wanted and insisted he wanted a baby as badly as I did. By then, I felt I was being unreasonable about the entire affair and gave in."

"What happened then?"

"They proceeded with the process and Evelyn carried our child. We fell in love with Adrian the moment she came into the world. We felt like a complete family. All went well for some time. Paul's business acumen was amazing, we raised Adrian and I relished being a mother. Jim met with Paul now and then, until they had a disagreement. Paul refused to discuss it, but said Jim was no longer welcome in our home or our lives."

"That must have been a shock."

Carina nodded, and said, "Since I couldn't convince Paul to talk to me about what had caused the rift, I let it go. It wasn't worth arguing over, at least I thought so at the time."

A nurse knocked on the door, interrupting Carina's story. I said I'd wait in the corridor until the nurse was finished.

It seemed like forever, but the nurse finally exited the room. Ready to hear what else had taken place, I heard Jack's voice behind me.

"How is she doing?"

"Very well. You can't come in. Carina's coming along nicely. She's been telling me about her, Paul, and Evelyn." I left out Jim Brody's part for fear we'd quarrel.

"I wanted to find out how she was doing, nothing more. I'll leave you to it. If there's useful information to be had, call me." Jack began to walk away.

I nodded as the nurse left the room. I opened the door and saw Carina had fallen asleep. I tiptoed out and caught up with Jack at the elevator doors. At his questioning look, I said, "She's asleep. I think I tuckered her out. I've got a lot to tell you."

"Of course you have," Jack said in a dry voice. "How about a cup of tea in the snack shop?"

"Sorry, I can't. Jason's on his own at the farm. I have to get back before he thinks I've deserted him."

The elevator stopped, and the doors slid open. A few visitors entered as we exited. With his keen stare on me, Jack took me by the arm and said, "I'll be by later. If Mrs. Richland has offered even a tidbit that would aid me in finding Evelyn Montgomery's killer, then I want to know."

"I'll tell you everything when you come by. See you then." We parted company outside the hospital. I shivered a bit, unsure if the brisk wind that blew across the car park had chilled me or if it was due to Jack's serious attitude.

My best bet would be to write down Carina's

story. It would help me figure out the importance
of what was said, and somehow, I knew all of it was
paramount to the investigation. A fine thread connected the murder, Jim Brody, Carina, and the
others in some way. I prayed I'd get the proof
needed to solve the mystery without placing myself
in danger. If a threatening situation arose, Jack
would then lecture me until I lost my temper, and
that's never pleasant.

I arrived home later than I'd anticipated. Jason
was gone, the rabbits were fine, and Molly hadn't
arrived yet, which left Jessica in charge. She met
me at the clinic door, assured me all was well, and
asked what had taken so long.

"Do you have any other patients today?"

"No, the last one left a while ago. Come help me
organize the rooms. You can explain while we
work. My appointments are stacked for Monday."

While we brought order from chaos, Jessica
shared the humorous moments of her examina-
tions without leaving me a second to tell her what
had transpired throughout the day. I chuckled
now and again, my mood on the upswing. It occurred to me how other people's problems wore
me out, were detrimental to my health, and
caused others to take responsibility for a business
that I owned. Maybe I should refrain from things
that didn't concern me? Nah, where was the fun in
that?

Finished, we entered the house. Bun waited in
his doorway and said, *"This better be good, I have been
quite worried that you were in trouble."*

"Sorry it took me so long, Jess. Carina wanted to

talk so I listened. Jack was at the hospital and has said he'll stop by tonight. Gosh, I'm so tired I can't think straight."

"A good night's rest will put things back into perspective."

I set the table, ladled stew into bowls, and added chunks of bread to a plate. We sat down to eat, and I explained my lengthy absence. Nourished, I leaned back in the chair, sipped a glass of ice water, and waited for the storm of questions.

"You must be joking."

I shook my head. "Not in the least. Once Carina started to talk, she couldn't stop. Like a fountain, her story flowed on and on. She wanted to say more, but a nurse came in and must have medicated her, because she was asleep when I returned to the room again. I will pick her up early tomorrow and take her home."

"How early? Do you need my help with the rabbits before you go?"

"I don't think so. Carina will be discharged by nine or so, which means the rabbits will be fed and the cleaning done before I leave. Thanks for offering, though."

Pensive, Jessica fiddled with her spoon, set it down, and said, "You travel a troubled path, you know that, don't you?"

"Funny you should say so. I had similar thoughts not too long ago."

"You might consider the toll it takes on you, and the rest of us, when you become so involved that you're reckless."

She meant well, I knew that, but being an inquisitive and tenacious person, it might be impossible to walk away from such avid curiosity. I said I'd take her words under advisement and gave Bun a wink when Jess looked away.

We cleared the remains of supper. Before she left, Jess urged me to be careful.

CHAPTER TWENTY-TWO

I recognized the phone number that popped up on my cell phone screen. It belonged to Sheriff Carver. I answered the call and listened to his excuse.

"I can't come by tonight. I know you've got information to share, I could see that when we spoke at the hospital today. Just jot down some notes before you forget what Mrs. Richland told you. I have my hands full here."

"What's wrong? You sound upset." No, more like angry than upset, but who was I to say?

"We were in the process of transferring Seamus and Colin to the county jail. The driver of the bus was in an accident and the prisoners have escaped. Lock your house up tight, or better yet, stay with Jessica for the night."

"O-okay. I'll be careful. Bye." I could feel my nerves tighten and stretch thinner by the second while considering what to do and where to hide. Assured the two men would seek me out before they left for parts unknown, if they were smart enough, that is, I heard Bun's voice behind me.

"We should ride this out, don't you think?"

"By waiting for them to arrive and possibly choke the daylights out of us?"

"Hmm, that's a possibility, but running never solved anything. I tried that when I lived with Margery. She always caught me, and I paid for my foolishness."

"This is a different set of circumstances. While Margery was cruel to you, Seamus is seriously vicious." I paced the floor, tapped my lips with my index finger, and asked, "Where can we go that won't put others in danger?"

His ears twitched, then stood straight up as his whiskers began to jitter.

"How about Carina's house?"

"Adelle might be watching the place in Carina's absence."

"Then let me think about this." Bun hopped along with me while I continued to pace. Suddenly, he stopped.

His ears and whiskers repeated what they'd done before. *"I bet they wouldn't find us at Evelyn Montgomery's house. What do you say?"*

Staring down at my smart, furry friend, I nodded. "I'll toss some stuff in a bag, and then put your food in a knapsack." Running up the stairs, I called over my shoulder, "I won't be a minute."

I haphazardly packed an overnight bag, went downstairs and set the knapsack on the table. While Bun chattered about his needs for our stay at Evelyn's, I tucked already measured food bags into the sack before I stuffed his bowls and several toiletry pads on top. I'd zipped the knapsack closed, then scooped Bun off the floor and helped him into the sling I'd swung across my body. Our safety was paramount and Bun was smart to recommend Evelyn's. I doubted the prisoners would consider us to ever be there.

Though certain neither man would bother with my rabbits, I worried about them. I opened the front door and ran into Adam.

"You're leaving for Jessica's, then?"

I nodded.

"Good, I'll be nearby to make sure no harm comes to the farm. Now get going."

"Thanks."

"You've got your cell phone, haven't you?"

I held it up as I raced down the steps and across the yard, and got into the car.

"I wonder why he didn't catch onto your lie."

"Me, too. He can tell when I'm not truthful."

The roads were almost empty of vehicles as we drove to Evelyn's.

"How will we get in? Sheriff Carver must have locked the place up tight after that last incident."

"We'll figure something out." I left the car a few houses away from Evelyn's. Bun craned his neck to see where we were going. His senses were much keener than mine, and he'd let me know if we had company.

I tried the bulkhead door. The handle rattled, but never gave when I pushed and pulled. I'd hoped it was stuck, not locked, but I wasn't that lucky. I crept past the bulkhead and studied the basement windows. I leaned down and touched the glass. The window moved slightly and the lock rattled. It was loose. I shoved the window frame with my foot. The window swung inward, the metal lock tinkled when it landed on the basement floor, and Bun jumped free of the sling.

On the ground, his nose wiggled frantically. His ears tipped forward, and his whiskers were completely still. I waited for the go-ahead.

"We can go in. Nobody's here. Will you fit through that window? You're still a bit fluffy, Jules."

Great, I was being judged by a rabbit. Huh. I gave him a look, and uttered sarcastically, "I'll be fine."

"You go first, I'll keep watch."

I tossed our bags inside, heard them thunk when they landed on the floor, and turned onto my stomach to enter the window feet first. It took some doing to get in, Bun had a point, I was a tad fluffy. The front of my clothes were a messy mixture of moist dirt and grass that had collected on them as I wiggled my way inside.

"Okay, come on, I'll catch you. Hurry."

Bun soared through the window and landed in my arms. His ears flopped against my open mouth as I caught him. I put him down, wiped my mouth in case rabbit hair had flown in.

"You could have let me know you were coming."

"We have company. I couldn't wait."

That's when I began to shake. Who had arrived? Were Seamus and Colin here, too? All this anxiety was enough to give me a headache. Sweat poured down my face as reality set in. I'm not much for sweating, but fear does that to me.

"Are you okay?"

I whispered, "It depends on who our company is. Do you know?"

"They weren't talking. I was unable to see anyone, I only heard footsteps, so I have no idea. Sorry, Jules."

"Maybe somebody was walking past."

"Wishful thinking, I'm afraid. I heard their feet on the pavement as they came closer to the house. Maybe we were too hasty in our decision to hide."

"You said 'their' feet? More than one person?"

"Two people, at least."

"Okay, let's go upstairs to the front door, in case they come in through that window." I pointed to it.

We left our baggage behind, then rushed to the stairs and made our way up, me on tiptoe, Bun on soft padded paws. The house was in the same condition as Adam and I had left it. Crime scene tape remained in place from Adam's assault, the rooms were dark, and turning on a light wasn't an option.

At the front door, we huddled just beneath the doorknob. I undid the door bolt and waited. Exhausted and nervous, I wiped sweat from my face, pushed the hair back from my forehead, and wondered who Bun had heard.

I sucked in a breath of air and held it when footsteps sounded on the stairs.

"Did you hear that?"

I patted his head and whispered I had.

"It's them, Seamus and Colin. I can hear them whispering. Can't you?"

I hadn't until they were in the living room. Bun was right, it was them. Criminy, we'd walked into a treacherous situation. I reached up, turned the doorknob, and opened the door a crack.

Colin whispered, "How long do you think we'll have to stay here?"

His voice deep and low, Seamus said, "How do I

know. We were told to stay put, and we will until we're paid for our part in the plan. Then we'll leave town. I've had enough of this."

Sideways, Bun and I sneaked out the door as silent as ghosts while the two men discussed their predicament. Luckily, they hadn't heard us. We all need to be thankful for something, and I was thankful for this.

Scrambling as close to the exterior of the house as we could get, Bun and I escaped the clutches of the two despicable men, who were rash enough to hold us against our will until they reached their goals of money and skipping town.

At the end of the driveway, Bun jumped into the sling that dangled from my neck. I hadn't removed it when we entered the house, but it was dirty. A matter Bun reminded me of.

"Eeew, this thing is nasty. Did you have to drag it through the dirt and grass?"

"Sorry, I wanted to get indoors before we were seen." The tip of my sneaker caught on the raised edge of the concrete sidewalk. I stumbled, and fell to my knees. My jeans tore across my right knee and the skin began to sting. No time for the injury, I kept going. "Are you okay, Bun?"

"Uh-huh. What happened? Are you hurt?"

"I think I skinned my knee. I'll check it when we're home."

I opened the car door, set Bun and the sling on the seat, and got in. We hightailed it away from Evelyn's without looking back. Rattled to the bone, my hands shook. I gripped the steering wheel and stopped at a red light after we turned onto the main drag. My phone was in my pocket and, glad it hadn't fallen out during our adventure, I dialed Jack.

"This better be important."

I drew a breath and blurted, "Seamus and Colin are at Evelyn's house. They're waiting for someone to bring them money to aid in their escape. Hurry, I don't know how long they'll be there."

The line went dead. I shook my phone and said, "Hello?"

No one answered. I determined Jack wouldn't waste time with a reprimand or questions, but would act on what I'd said.

It had grown late. Weariness enveloped me as I left my car in front of the barn. A police cruiser arrived, and Adam parked in the driveway.

Long-legged, he was at my side before I climbed the front steps. The porch lights were on and I could only imagine the sight I must present. Bun hopped next to me. Taking the stairs two at a time, he sat in front of the door and studied me, then Adam, and me again.

"I think we're in a tight spot."

Without a word, I led the way into the house. Bun jumped onto his pillow and sank down with a tiny sigh. Normally, I would have thought it cute. Right now, I wished it was me, instead of him, nestling into softness to nod off. I filled his water bin, left a smidge of alfalfa hay for him to snack on, and returned to the kitchen. Adam lounged against the living room door casing and waited.

"Sheriff Carver sent you?"

He nodded. "What were you doing at Evelyn's house?"

It wasn't worth lying about, so I told him it

seemed a good place to hide from Seamus and Colin.

His face never changed, his eyes didn't flicker, he simply stared, leaving me uncomfortable. Bun was right. We were in a tight spot. Crikey.

"Would you like something to drink?"

"No, thanks, and I'm not hungry, either. Tell me what happened."

I motioned to the living room, sat in my favorite armchair, and gave him the story.

"You have the worst luck of anyone I know. Why didn't you go to Jessica's?"

"I didn't want to put her in danger. I almost went to Carina's house, but thought the neighbors might call you people. Jack has enough to handle without me being charged with unlawful entering."

"Hm, well, the sheriff has officers at Evelyn's house. They have taken Dumb and Dumber into custody. Do you realize how fortunate you were that they didn't find you?"

"That goes without saying. We used our best stealth techniques to leave that house and the neighborhood."

With a snort of disbelief, Adam asked, "Stealth techniques?"

"Yup."

"I'm beginning to think the gray hair Sheriff Carver has is mainly due to you."

"So he says. Are you here to babysit? Or, did you come by to check in as Jack requested?" I was so tired, I could have dropped in my tracks. Would he leave, or was I stuck with him until Jack ordered him to?

"I'm here until told otherwise. Get some rest, you're exhausted. It's not my place to tell you how to run your life, Juliette . . ."

"But?"

"If you let us do our job, you'd undoubtedly be happier and less stressed. I know the sheriff would like that."

"You're right."

He looked hopeful. "I am?"

"Yes, it isn't your place." I got up, marched upstairs, and slammed the bedroom door. Who, if not me, would have gotten the information they needed to make an arrest? And, who had managed to get Carina to talk, had found the paperwork they were in search of, and had rescued Bun from those two idiots? Me, that's who. Gritting my teeth, and in filthy clothes, I flopped on the bed and sank into softness. My muscles relaxed, and my eyes were nearly closed when a rap on my door sent me off the bed in a single bound. What now? Anger had replaced exhaustion. I was in a mood no one ever wanted to witness.

I flung the door wide and snapped, "What?"

Adam stood still, took in my appearance, and backed up. "The sheriff is downstairs and wants to speak to you."

"Can't it wait?"

"Afraid not."

CHAPTER TWENTY-THREE

With a grimace, I stepped past Adam and stomped down the stairs.

Adam stood behind me when I stopped a few feet short of the sheriff. "This had better not be a lecture."

"If it is?"

"Then you will have to wait. I'm too tired to listen to your dire warnings, and don't dos."

He pressed his lips together. I wasn't sure if he was annoyed by my remark, or if he hid a smirk over the don't dos. Either way, I didn't care.

"If you'll take a seat and relax, I'll tell you why I'm here."

"Fine." I dropped into the nearest chair and drummed my fingers on the tabletop.

The two policemen sat adjacent to me. "It was brave of you to escape Evelyn's house before being found. Adam mentioned why you chose to hide there. It wasn't a bad idea, especially since you wanted to protect Jessica. Seamus and Colin might not have gone to Evelyn's place if they hadn't been so desperate to get paid and leave town."

Unappeased, I considered the difficulty Jack had when he admitted I had done something right.

"Is that all?"

"No, it isn't. When those two entered the house, did they mention who was supposed to pay them?"

I shook my head. "They never said who it was. Why?"

"They aren't talking."

I shrugged. "What does that have to do with me?"

"Would you come to the station to see them?"

By this time, Bun had come from his room to sit at my feet and rested his head in the curve of one ankle.

"Really? You want me involved after all the ranting you've done to make me stay out of your investigation?" Cranky, I was very cranky. I knew I raved and should have acted more mature. Just not tonight. From the look on Jack's face, I knew I was out of control and endeavored to keep my temper in check.

I'd had enough of being prodded in the direction Jack wanted me to go so he could gain traction in his investigation. Then, when he didn't like my initiative, I was warned off.

"Jules, you've been of enormous help. I warn you only when I fear you'll be in danger."

"What makes you think these guys will talk to me? Seamus wants to strangle me, and Colin, well, he'll do whatever Seamus tells him to. I'm not a fan of theirs and they feel the same in return. I'm sure they won't confess to me, of all people. If you have a sound plan, then spit it out, or get out." It appeared my anger had sneaked out again. Hm.

"Okay, let's talk about that."

"I'm listening."

Jack outlined how he wanted my conversation to go with the criminals. I took in every word without interruption, question or rejection. Though his idea might be viable, I considered it a waste of my time and his. I figured both prisoners would refuse to speak to me, other than to curse my soul, that is, and said as much.

Jack gave me a long, narrowed stare. "Don't you think it's worth the effort?"

"What I think is that I need some sleep. I have a farm to attend, animals that need me and don't lecture me, and I should let you do your job." I glanced at both men in turn.

I wanted him to grovel, but knew it would never happen. It wasn't my fault he couldn't get these creeps to name their financier. I heaved a sigh, and said, "I'll come by after I've seen to the rabbits and dropped Carina at home."

With a relieved expression, Jack nodded in agreement. "Adam will stay for the night."

"It isn't necessary. I'll lock up tight."

"If you're sure."

"I'll see you then, Jack." I looked at Adam and thanked him, then watched them walk out to their respective vehicles.

As they drove off, I bolted the doors, checked all the windows, and even locked the door leading to the breezeway. Jack hadn't said as much, but he was worried the person with the money would likely come looking for me in case I'd figured out who it was. Carina wasn't the one, but I knew in my heart that Adelle was.

I shook my head, waited until Bun turned in, and climbed the stairs. Sleep was out of the question as I tossed and turned and sought connections that made sense.

A journal that I kept in the nightstand drawer was perfect for writing what was happening now. I fluffed the pillows and slouched into them while I scribbled all that had taken place these last few days. I read the notes over, edited and clarified them, and added thoughts at the end. I wrote a separate page of questions, and then reviewed it all.

With more questions than answers, it seemed I went around and around without the ability to break the circle. One final answer, that's all it would take to find the connection that would enable Jack to catch the killer. Just one, I was sure of it.

The sky turned a pale gray. I gave up the sleep idea and readied for work. I ran a brush through my hair after I'd freshened up, dressed in work clothes, and took the journal downstairs to read while coffee perked.

I tossed the journal on the kitchen table and hit the start button on the coffee maker. Rummaging in the refrigerator, I found a stop at the market was in order after the rest of my responsibilities were met today.

Bun had risen, chomped the breakfast fare I'd

set out for him, and between bites, he said, *"Anything else happen while I slept?"*

"Not a thing."

"That's a relief."

"It sure is. I could use a break right about now."

Eggs and sausages sizzled in pans, slices of toast popped up in the toaster, and Jessica knocked on the breezeway door.

I'd forgotten to unlock it. When I let her in, she asked a bunch of questions that made me wish she had waited until we had eaten. Over breakfast, we discussed the evening before, ending with my proposed stop at the police station this morning.

Aware of her thoughts on my recklessness, I said all would be okay because I'd be in the station surrounded by police officers. My reasoning seemed to placate Jessica because she agreed it was the safest place for me to be.

We cleared breakfast remnants away before going into the barn. Bun supervised the other rabbits' breakfast fare that I served, Jess went about her own business, and then I did my daily workload.

A truck load of supplies arrived. I opened the barn doors and helped with the order. Bales of hay were brought in and stacked. While the driver, Ben Moore, didn't have to help me, he always did.

I handed him the invoice payment, and knowing Ben worked for Jim Brody, I asked after him. With a concerned expression, Ben said, "He's got some problems right now."

"Nothing serious, I hope," I remarked.

The man stepped close, glanced over his shoulder, as though someone other than me and the rabbits might hear him, and murmured, "Seems he's run into financial trouble."

"You won't lose your job, will you?"

With a shrug, Ben warmed to the subject. "If he can't get his situation under control, that could happen. He's a good man to work for, generous and all, but . . ." He shook his head, and then clamped his mouth shut as if he'd said too much and left.

Pensive, I closed the barn doors when he drove away and heard Bun say, *"What do you think of that, huh? Old Jimbo is having money trouble. Makes you wonder, doesn't it?"*

"Indeed, it does." Time had flown, and with the amount of chores and responsibilities that filled the day, I had no time to ponder Jim Brody's problems. Where might I get some information on the subject? Instantly, Mora Lindsey came to mind.

Mora handled all that went on for the senior citizens' activities held at the lodge and elsewhere. She would have an inkling of what was going on with Jim since he supported that piece of real estate. I decided to call her later and then focused on work.

Two hours later and soaked with sweat, I had done what usually took three hours to accomplish. The rabbits were fed, their caged hutches were clean and restocked, and a few of the critters were in the play area. With just enough time to shower and change, I went through the breezeway and hurried up the stairs.

Refreshed and dressed in clean clothes, I dealt

with my hair as best I could and then went to pick up Carina. I'd parked the car outside the revolving doors and dialed Adelle's phone number. She answered on the first ring. "Carina's coming home today. Could you bring Adrian home? I know she must be anxious to see her mom."

"What great news. Adrian mentioned her mother this morning. I'll drop her off for you. While I have you on the phone, thanks for doing the birthday party. The children enjoyed themselves."

"You're quite welcome. The kids were thrilled with the entertainment. I'm glad you were pleased."

An orderly wheeled Carina out through the doors. I opened the passenger's side door and assisted her when the wheelchair came to a stop. "How are you today?" I asked, and gave the orderly a nod before he wheeled the chair away and left Carina in my care.

"I'm happy to be going home. There's no rest in a hospital, absolutely none."

I smiled when she did, and drove her home. Carina was silent during the ride. I wondered what ran through her mind.

Her face brightened as we reached her neighborhood. "Will Adelle bring Adrian home later?"

"Yes, she will. She told me Adrian is anxious for you to come home. This will be a nice surprise for her."

I parked in front of her garage. The front door opened, and Adelle came out with a smile on her face. How had she gotten in?

"Looks like you have a welcoming committee of one."

"I know Adelle was rude the other night, but she does look out for us."

"Everyone needs help now and then."

I left her with Adelle and drove to the Windermere police station. With no clue of what would happen, Jack had convinced me to give his idea a try.

I gave my name at the front desk. I was told Jack was expecting me and could go to his office.

When I approached his office, I noticed the door was ajar. Jack beckoned me in and pointed to a chair where I could wait while he finished his phone call. He hung up and asked, "Are you ready for this?"

"I guess so. It better work, Jack. Must I be locked in a cell?"

"It's necessary if we want them to talk. They aren't cooperating in the least. Seamus has asked for an attorney. He'll get legal counsel that's offered by the state, and while I've put in a call for one, nobody has arrived yet. Don't worry, you won't stay there too long. I'll give it an hour and then a guard will return you to me. You're up to this, Juliette, I'm confident in your ability to get them to confess."

"Right." I wasn't as sure as Jack seemed to be. "Let's get to it, then. I have a business to run. Oh, uh, I received a delivery from Jim Brody's company today. The driver helps me take the merchandise into the barn. While we did so, he mentioned Jim has financial problems. Did you hear about that?"

He shook his head and nodded to the guard who stood at the door with a pair of handcuffs dangling from his fingers.

I gasped when I saw them and vehemently re-marked, "You aren't going to cuff me."

The guard grinned, as did Jack, who then added, "It has to look real. This is Deputy Tom Marchand. He'll be available if things run amuck."

Oh my gosh. What had I been foolish enough to agree to?

Tom marched me to the holding cells. On our way, he whispered, "Make sure to struggle against my grasp when we reach the cell door, then I'll shove you inside. It's in our favor to have steel bar cages as cells instead of the ones with solid steel walls that completely isolate prisoners. Those will be installed next winter. As it stands now, we only have six cells and put more than one person in each of them when it's necessary. McKenna and Bedford will be in two separate cells across from yours."

"O-okay." Authenticity might be the key to a confession, but manhandling was not in my play-book, and neither was close proximity to Seamus and Colin.

We reached lockup and I went into struggle mode when Tom gripped my arm after he'd re-moved the handcuffs.

I demanded loudly, "Let go of me." I tried to pull my arm from his hand, but the man was play-ing for real and his hold grew tighter.

"Don't give me a hard time. You got into this sit-uation all by yourself, and now you can hang out with the other the criminals." He opened the cell door. I jabbed my elbow into his ribs and noticed the surprise on his face. In an instant he shoved me into the cell. As I caught my balance, he closed and locked the door.

With his back to Seamus and Colin, who watched us, Tom winked at me. I rushed toward him and reached through the bars, but couldn't get my hands on him. He then ordered me to settle down.

"You're going to pay for this," I yelled at him as he walked away.

He'd brushed my threat aside and left me on my own. I knew cameras recorded what went on down here. I stamped my foot, then stomped across the floor and flung myself onto a hard bench.

"Well, well, if it isn't Miss Goody Two-shoes," Seamus sneered, and then continued. "You got caught at Evelyn's house, didn't ya?"

"Shut up, and mind your business."

His laughter was as unpleasant as his disposition. I glanced at Colin, who gave me a nod, but kept his mouth shut. I ignored Seamus, pushed up into a sitting position against the wall, and sat cross-legged in a yoga pose.

"What did you get caught doing, if it wasn't breaking into somebody's house?" Seamus seemed to enjoy my discomfort behind bars. Talking, even if he sneered, was exactly what Carver and I had hoped for.

"What do you care? You're in the same spot as I am. You were arrested for breaking into Evelyn's house. It wouldn't have been the first time, either, if I remember correctly," I said in a grudging tone.

"Yeah, but me and Colin almost got what we wanted before that happened. You and that cop got in the way. Now you're here with us." Seamus snickered and turned to Colin. "I told you she wasn't perfect. You were supposed to care of her, but you didn't. You'll get another chance if things work out for us."

I goaded him. "Big talk from someone behind bars."

"Not for long. We're gonna be transferred soon. A friend, who owes us, has set things in motion for us to live the good life and it ain't in jail neither."

I rolled my eyes. "Sure, sure, like that will ever happen."

"It will, everything's in place. You just watch. Oh, yeah, you'll still be here and won't get to see it, but we'll be free." He broke into another round of gritty laughter.

With feigned disinterin the conversation, I studied my fingernails and said, "I don't believe you. Nobody would be stupid enough to make it possible for you and Colin to escape."

He stepped closer to his cell bars, pressing his paunchy gut against them. Low voiced, he bragged, "You'd be surprised at what can happen with the right connections. We aren't as dumb as the cops think."

Narrowing my eyes, I asked, "Would I?"

"Never in a million years could you figure out who that person is. Our contact has been right in front of your nose and you never got wind of it."

Okay, now he had my interest. I continued to play my role. "I'm sure I don't know what you're talking about."

"No, 'cause you're the dumb one. Our work ain't finished yet, there's one more thing to take care of. Then we'll be paid handsomely for our part in what's been goin' on."

I sighed, pretended to pick at lint on my jeans. "Evelyn was nothing but a miserable blackmailer. She gathered secrets about people, important people, and used them to her own advantage. You know what I think? I think she might have been as miserable a soul as you are, Seamus."

His eyes gleamed with malice as his expression turned cruel. "Her business meant nothing to us, and in the end she got what she had comin' to her."

"If it wasn't you who killed her, then you probably don't even know who did." I shrugged a shoulder while taunting him, and said, "It doesn't matter to me. Like you said, I'll spend time behind bars for my part in this whole mess."

His laughter rang out. "You behind bars is a dream come true. I never did see such a meddlin' woman as you."

"Hm, well, I've heard enough. Why don't you just shut up now."

"Ain't you interested in our plans from here on out?"

"Not really."

"You say that, but the look on your face says otherwise."

Had I given myself away? Nah, I'd been nonchalant, and acted disinterested. Maybe too much so. I changed tactics and went to stand near the cell door.

"Okay, fine. Spit it out, you know you're dying to brag about what you and Colin have on your agenda."

"We'll be paid in full for our part in Evelyn's death. We'll also blackmail the person who hired us for the rest of, uh, their life. While we are sun-nin' ourselves on a beach in South America, the police won't be able to touch us."

He'd nearly slipped up but had caught himself in time. "Be realistic, do you think this person will continue to pay blackmail money once you two leave the country?"

"Yeah, 'cause otherwise I have information that goes to Sheriff Carver."

"I can't imagine anybody would be that stupid."

"You were stupid enough to get caught, weren't ya? What makes you so sure that wouldn't happen to, uh, that person?"

"Maybe you're right." I shrugged a shoulder again and leaned against the bars.

Footsteps sounded on the stairs. Tom came into view and said to me, "Back away from the door. You're going to see Judge Fowler."

I gave him as rotten a look as I could summon and stepped back three or four paces. He opened the door, another officer entered the cell with him while I was handcuffed. Taken away, I listened to Seamus sing his version of Johnny Cash's "Folsom Prison Blues."

At the top of the stairs, and far enough away from the jail cells to be out of sight and sound, Tom unlocked the handcuffs and escorted me to Jack's office. His partner went off on his own.

Jack looked up when I entered the room, and I took a seat in front of his desk while Tom stood in front of the door.

"Tom tells me you got right into your role. Was it worth it?"

"I believe they're being funded by a woman. I

couldn't get him to say as much, but every time Seamus spoke of their contact, he hesitated as if he struggled to keep the word 'her' from slipping off his tongue. He bragged about what was going to happen and how their life would be all roses and sunshine after they were freed during their transfer. They are being transferred, right? Seamus wasn't playing me, was he?"

"No, he didn't play you. A shuttle will carry them to the prisoner intake center in Concord. I don't know how they got word to whoever will execute their escape, but I can tell you right now they won't get away this time."

"I see. Seamus is confident they'll escape and spend their days on a beach in South America while continuing to blackmail this person. Sounds a bit wishful if you ask me."

"Let's have lunch before you go back and try to get more out of them."

His enthusiasm didn't sit well with me. After all, I was the one in a cell. "Is it necessary? I do have a farm to get back to. Jess is busy all day, which leaves Molly and Jason on their own."

"Just for an hour, I promise. Tom, you're dismissed."

Adam arrived with sandwiches from a deli a block away from the station. He handed out the food, took a seat next to mine, and asked how I was doing.

Silent for a moment, I finally said, "How would you feel being locked up?"

"Be a sport about this, Juliette. We need your help. Our methods aren't working, and I know you can get what we want from them."

"Sure of yourselves, aren't you?" I said around a mouthful of a ham and cheese grinder. "Seamus almost slipped when he mentioned their connection, but he won't make the same mistake again. Colin might talk if we were alone."

Sheriff Carver put his sandwich down, looked at Adam, and said, "When Juliette is returned to her cell, make arrangements to bring Seamus into the interrogation room." Carver turned to me. "Now tell me why you wanted me to meet you after the birthday party on Saturday? We never did talk about that."

Adam nodded, finished his own sandwich, and left Carver and me alone. It took several minutes to apprise him of what I'd overheard at Adelle's house. Carver didn't ask any questions, but took in all that I shared.

In an abrupt turn of conversation, Carver asked, "You like this kid Colin, don't you?"

"Not so much like, as I feel sorry for him."

Carver opened his mouth, I put my hand up and said, "He never thought he'd be in this position or that things would get to this point. He's not a bright kid, but has a good heart. He was supposed to dispose of me, Jack, and he didn't."

His expression one of surprise, Jack discarded his lunch and leaned forward with his elbows perched on the desk. "You listen to me, this boy knew what he was doing was against the law and he did it anyway. He didn't harm you because he couldn't bring himself to do it. Had Seamus been there, Colin would have done it. He's easily swayed and intimidated by Seamus. Don't you feel sorry for him, no sirree."

"Fine. I'll do what I can to get him to talk. Since the cameras record all that happens in the cells, and someone watches what goes on, I'll run my hands through my hair when I've gotten a confession. If, after a half an hour, there isn't any progress, I'll go sit on the cot and you can get me the heck out of there. I don't have all day, Jack."

"Fair enough. I appreciate your taking the time to help me. Like I said, we've done everything but beat the daylights out of those two, and that isn't an option."

"Good thing, they'd only sue the city for mistreatment."

Adam returned, handcuffs in his hand, and asked if I was ready.

"About as ready as I would be to have a root canal." I put my hands out and watched him snap the handcuffs onto my wrists. I glanced over my shoulder at Carver. "See you later."

Gathering a bundle of paperwork, Jack nodded and walked down the corridor toward an interrogation room. I wondered how many there were and asked Adam.

"Three altogether. The other two are upstairs. An elevator and staircase lead to the second and third floors. By the way, don't be nice when we get to the cells."

"I know the drill."

We took the flight of stairs down to the cells, and again I struggled against confinement. This had become old real fast. The ominous clang of the cell door closing tended to vibrate through my bones. It left me uncomfortable and somewhat worried.

Tom entered the corridor to assist Adam in escorting Seamus out of the cell block. I leaned against the wall and stared at the burly man when he walked past. He sneered at me and was about to spit when he was pushed along. Things had gotten nastier. God help me, I had to make this work quickly.

I gazed at Colin. He stared at me and then began to turn away.

"Why didn't you do as Seamus ordered you to?"

"You mean kill you?"

"Yeah."

"I don't kill or maim people or animals, Jules. It isn't right."

But stealing is? I almost said the words. Instead, I said, "You don't have to be part of this, you know. After you guys succeeded in the last getaway, the sheriff will double or triple security when you're transferred so you won't escape."

Hesitant, he seemed to think things over. "How can I get out of this? I've broken the law. Sheriff Carver doesn't have sympathy for people who do that. Isn't that why you're here? Because you broke the law?"

"You're right, I did. But I didn't kill anyone and haven't been charged as an accessory to murder."

Colin asked, "What were you arrested for?"

"Breaking and entering and resisting arrest. I broke into Evelyn's looking for papers once too often. This last time, the police noticed my car and were waiting for me. Have you been in front of a judge yet?"

"Soon, that's why the sheriff has us set up for transfer. We're supposed to be held at a prison waitin' for trial. I never killed Evelyn and didn't have nothin' to do with that neither. I don't think Seamus killed her either."

"How did you come to that conclusion? Seamus is violent."

"He ain't a killer."

I stated the obvious. "Yet, he wanted you to kill me."

"Only because he refused to do it."

"Who ordered my death? I have a right to know."

He stared at the floor. "I-I can't tell you. Seamus would be mad, real mad."

"I promise I won't say a word to him. It'll be our secret. Why should you be blamed for something you had no hand in. Prison isn't like jail. It's a harsh environment, where only the toughest survive." I'd made it up, I had no idea what prison was really like and didn't want to know. Though, I was aware it wasn't a place for those faint-of-heart souls.

"You and the sheriff are friends, aren't ya?"

I shook my head. "I wouldn't say friends, more like he yells at me all the time for not minding my own business. Sheriff Carver isn't capable of solving crimes, his officers do all the work and he takes the credit. Some sheriff, huh?"

With a tiny snicker, Colin nodded. "How long before you get taken away to a detention center for women?"

I lifted a shoulder and tried to appear stupid. It must have been easy to convince him because he admitted, "She's planned the whole thing. If you're in the same bus as us, maybe you can get away, too.

Prison ain't no place for you, Jules. Who'll take care of your rabbits?"

"Good question. Poor Bun will be brokenhearted. Where will your escape take place?"

"Just before we hit the highway going north. There's a wicked curve and an accident will block the road. It will look serious and the guards will get outta the bus. Somebody's supposed to come on board and get us out."

It sounded like a movie scene, a poorly scripted one. Who would deal with the bus driver? Would the guards leave the bus unattended? Not likely. Whoever was in charge had no intention of allowing these two men to escape. If nothing else, they'd rot in prison or be shot as they ran away. Maybe some hired henchmen would do their part, but the whole idea that the head honcho would assist in freeing them was ludicrous. While Colin mistakenly said the person was a female, I wasn't quite convinced. Hadn't I been assured they weren't as dumb as the cops thought? Maybe Colin played me, or maybe he was telling the truth. If a woman was behind all of this, it certainly wasn't Carina, but more than likely Adelle. I had seen her belligerence firsthand.

I'd had enough of trying to get one of these men to tell me who was behind Evelyn's death. A confession wouldn't happen, and I wasn't the only one who thought so. I was about to sit on the bench as a sign that I wasn't successful, when Tom entered the room followed by Adam. They escorted Colin out to who knows where and left me on my own.

I settled on the bench to wait for what came

next. A few minutes passed before Sheriff Carver clomped down the stairs and stood outside the cell. "Looks like we had no luck. Sorry to have put you through this Juliette, but it was worth a try." He unlocked the door and I joined him in the corridor.

"Where's Seamus?"

"Judge Porter has arrived and their lawyer has, too. Then they'll be transferred as soon as possible. You should go home."

On our way to the front door, I repeated what Colin had said concerning the location where they would make their escape. Carver nodded, thanked me, and returned to his office while I went back to Bun and the farm.

On my way, I called Mora, and asked if I could stop by her office. She agreed.

"I'm nearly there. I'll see you in a few minutes, Mora."

CHAPTER TWENTY-FOUR

I left the car near the front door of the Windermere Housing & Senior Center. The grounds
were neat and well cared for, the shrubs manicured to a fault. The buildings were enormous,
with apartments on three levels and a center attached to one end where elderly residents went for
games, entertainment, luncheons, and all sorts of
other get-togethers.

Impressive as it was, I never wanted to have to
reside in a place such as this. No green hills, no
forest, no privacy to speak of, and no rabbits to
enjoy. But then, being young and healthy, I was far
from needing someone to help look after me.

I wended my way along the brick walk to the
wide double front doors. I was greeted by a woman
at the reception desk, who smiled and asked how
she could help me. I said Mora Lindsey was expecting me. The woman rang Mora's office to let
her know I'd arrived. Not long afterward, Mora
came to the desk and together we walked through

the wide hallway to her office. On our way we had passed through a large sitting area that held a lovely grand piano.

"That is beautiful. Who plays it?"

Mora glanced at the piano. "One of our staff entertains the residents and two of the residents can also play. One of them, Mr. Grayson, has talent and used to work as a professional. Mr. Bernard plays by ear."

Her well-appointed office featured a mahogany desk, a leather chair, carved bookcases, a wide-screen computer, two high-backed elegant chairs with a dainty Queen Anne round table between them, and exquisite paintings on the walls. I took it all in, and before I could remark on how beautiful the office was, Mora handed me a cup of tea. She set a small, delicate dish of cookies on the table between us and sipped her tea. She set the teacup and saucer down and asked, "Is this visit about Jim Brody?"

Right to the point, that's what I liked about Mora. "Yes, as a matter of fact, I heard about his difficulties just this morning. It's unfortunate to have happened, don't you think?"

"I agree with you. He should have been paying more attention to that end of his finances, though. You knew Evelyn Montgomery, didn't you?"

I nodded and sipped from the teacup, nibbled a cookie to buy time, and wondered what on earth Evelyn Montgomery had to do with Jim Brody. I wanted to find out what I could about Jim's financial business. I was unsure how it included Evelyn Montgomery. Or did it?

"We only knew each other through the rabbit

competition. From what I gathered, Evelyn was well known on the rabbit show circuit." Uncertain where the topic was headed, I kept my end of the conversation neutral.

"Jim should have known better, that's all I can say, he and Evelyn had been friends for ages, why he didn't see what she was up to is a mystery." Mora leaned forward, then slid to the edge of her chair, and conspiratorially said, "His family must be upset to learn she had cleaned out the grant coffers. Surely they're aware of it now. I think all of Windermere knows."

"Why would Brody allow a woman such as Evelyn to be involved in any part of his business?" How did I not know about it? Jack must know. Why hadn't he mentioned it? Was he protecting Brody? The questions flew through my mind in the time it took to eat the remaining bit of my cookie.

I set the teacup down. "He and Evelyn knew each other, but from what I've heard about her, I didn't think Evelyn had friends, not one."

"His parents have great influence over Jim's business practices and might have insisted he give Evelyn a job."

With a light gasp, I stared at Mora. "They wanted Evelyn to work for Jim?" Could they have been aware of Evelyn's connection to Paul, Jim, Carina, and Adrian? I couldn't ask Mora, but I could, and would, ask Carina. How private did Paul, Jim and Carina keep Adrian's conception? Again, I had more questions than answers.

Mora nodded. "I'm not certain, no one has admitted it as yet. Jim's doing damage control and much of what's now come to light had been kept hush-hush. You don't think Jim had any inkling of what was going on with the account, do you?"

"I have no idea. But, I spend so much time at the farm, that I rarely get wind of gossip."

"Come on, Jules, you must know what goes on around town. You're in the perfect position to hear things. Women love to talk, and all parties are rampant with tittle-tattle, even those for children. The kiddies run around like little lunatics while their moms share the latest dirt on everyone."

I'd always been so busy with the kids and my rabbits, that I'd heard nothing other than the disagreement between Carina and Evelyn. Mora wouldn't believe me if I denied it, though. "I admit that I have heard some stuff, but nothing lately."

"I know you have quite a workload, and keep a close eye on those bunnies of yours. Especially while those little demons race around and do as they please. You have enough to keep you occupied."

"That's for sure." I handed Mora the teacup, which she filled again.

"How is Carina Richland doing? I heard she was taken to the hospital."

"She has a severe iron deficiency, and will continue treatments for it. She's home now and feels better."

"I always wondered if she'd start dating or would remarry, but not a word has been said that I know of. Carina keeps her business to herself."

"She does. Paul's death was difficult for her and Adrian. They have been working through their grief, but not everyone goes through it the same way." Because it was common knowledge, I didn't mind sharing that much with Mora. Nothing more would get past my lips, not one word. Mora had said more than I had expected, but that didn't mean I would.

"Sheriff Carver has those two criminals in custody, huh?"

I nodded. "Thank goodness for that."

"You didn't stop by to gossip. What can I do for you?"

"Since Jim Brody supports the lodge for the elderly to enjoy during the summer and fall, I wondered if you knew if he'll be able to continue to do so now that these problems have arisen. I only ask because Bailey Kimball and I recently discussed doing a show for the residents at the lodge. Our rates are reasonable, and the elderly adore the rabbits as well as Bailey's act."

"It would be a pleasure to have you both entertain. According to my boss, you've both done some sort of program for our residents before, just not together. I always search for quality entertainment for them to interact with, and you two are great for that type of engagement. It's getting late in the season, but we have a celebration coming in November. If you can fit it into your schedules, I'd be delighted to have you two with us."

"Wonderful, I'll bring Petra, she's a long-haired angora rabbit who does tricks. I think her talents would amuse everyone. I'll let Bailey know and if you give me the date with the particulars of the event, we'll get back to you right away. How's that?"

"Give me a minute to look up the date and time for you. It's up to you girls to decide how you want to handle your setups. We'll be indoors, and the lodge has ample space." She went to her desk, opened her calendar, and jotted the date and length of time for the event. I pocketed the sticky note she peeled off the pad.

"As for Jim's continued support, I haven't discussed it with him or our management team. It's bound to become a hot topic because Jim has done more than support the lodge. He funds many of our other events and insists his company pick up the tab for those who can't afford medications. He's been most generous to our residents and staff over the years. I hope things get straightened out."

"It amazes me that Evelyn actually worked for him. She wasn't very well-liked."

"I saw her at a fundraiser Jim hosted for a charity he supported. Now that you mention it, I did notice the tension between them."

"Hmm, when was this?"

"About three months ago. Evelyn didn't appear happy when they were having a chat. Jim seemed short when he answered her, and being curious, I mentioned it to him later. He said there had been a mix-up of sorts and then excused himself. There was probably more to that situation than I thought. Jim is a good man and I took his word for it."

"I must be going, the rabbits await. Thanks so much, Mora. Keep me posted on the outcome of Jim's problems."

She promised as I crossed the room and went out the door. I hurried to the farm. I'd been gone far too long, and Bun would be nervous, as would Jessica. Molly would have arrived by now along with Jason. I heaved a sigh. So far, the day had been filled with more than I had considered possible.

On the way home, Mora's information went round and round in my head, like an out-of-control recording. She undoubtedly knew more, but was fond of Jim which meant she wouldn't get into the nitty-gritty of his life. It wouldn't be beneficial to do so, and who could blame her for keeping the residents her main concern. If word got out that Mora had mentioned more than she should have, the funds she needed might suddenly dry up. As for my grant money, no wonder Jim couldn't offer it to me. Evelyn had taken advantage of her position to cipher funds from his account into her own.

Sheriff Carver and I needed to chat. He definitely would have gone through Evelyn's bank accounts once he'd learned of her occupation as a blackmailer. It only made sense that he would do so.

I swung into the driveway, parked in front of the shop, and went inside. All was quiet, neat, and ready for a spinning class. I walked into the barn, found Jason at the sink washing his hands, and asked where Molly was.

"Her car is here, but she isn't in the shop."

"She and Jessica are out back, dealing with Walkabout Willy. He's quite the rascal. Got away from the pen and took off for about two hours. We looked everywhere for him and didn't want to have to tell you he was gone."

I started for the back door. "He did return, right?"

"Yeah, no worse for wear, but he must have gotten

into a bramble bush, because he's covered with them."

Outside, I could hear the two women discuss what might have caused Willy to become entangled in the brambles. I greeted them, took a look at the woebegone rabbit, and said, "He doesn't look too bad."

"He doesn't like being handled this way, but we have to clean his coat of thorns."

"If that was Bun, he'd let you brush him for days." I crouched next to Willy, rubbed the fur on his head, and gently scratched his nose. He responded with closed eyes and then he relaxed. "Bring him inside and put him on the rabbit table. I'll keep him calm and you can finish the job."

We entered the barn and took to the task of bringing Willy's coat back to normal. I looked at Jess and asked, "You don't think he ate anything out there that might disagree with him, do you?"

"Probably not. For the most part, rabbits know what to eat and what isn't good for them. Of course, there's always an exception to every rule."

Soon, Willy was back to normal and allowed into the interior play area. Molly and I examined the spinning class schedule. Jason jumped into the conversation about his own work and school activities, while Jessica tended to her patient roster.

When Jessica's itinerary was complete, I gave her a hand to straighten the examination rooms and restock them.

As we finished, she said, "I won't be here tonight, I have a date."

"Anyone I know?"

She laughed. "My parents are taking me out to dine."

"Look at this this way, you get to visit with them and have a great meal, too."

I left her smiling and went into the house to see Bun.

CHAPTER TWENTY-FIVE

The afternoon ended with Bun and me alone, and my telling Bun what I had learned from Seamus, Colin, and Mora.

"Your time was well spent, then. Wish I could have gone with you, but I understand that I couldn't."

"It would have looked odd to have you in the jail cell with me. Besides, you'd have been unhappy over the way Seamus treated me. He's not a nice person."

"No, he isn't. What do you make of Jim Brody's issues?"

"Evelyn could have been blackmailing him over something, what it was, I don't know, but it might have something to do with Adrian and Carina. It's terrible that she stole from the grant accounts. He might have to come up with money to continue the grant payments that are portioned out to students and other places. It isn't good publicity for his business, either."

"Evelyn had a good thing going, too bad she didn't

play the blackmail card well enough. It cost her dearly. I didn't like the way she treated you, or how she treated Carina at the party. A vicious and hard-hearted woman, that one. What else did Mora tell you?"

"She's worried about the situation Brody has gotten himself into. Certain she knows more than she would say, I couldn't finagle a way to get her to tell me. I can't blame her, though. Her first priority is to the residents and fulfilling their needs. Brody has been generous with them and the people who work at that facility."

"Carver will have looked into Evelyn's bank accounts. You always insist he's thorough. He does have her notebook, doesn't he?"

"He does and he's on my call list. I have to contact Bailey before I do anything else." I sighed, flopped into a chair, and said, "These last several hours sure have been hectic. I'm on overload."

"Relax, you'll find the truth will come out with or without us. When we're behind the wheel, and we can drive it forward faster than anyone else, you only need to let your brain sort through all that you have learned for that to happen."

Bun, as usual, was right. Pressuring myself for the answer wouldn't do any good. My subconscious would sooner or later hand over key information required when it was good and ready. I hoped it was sooner rather than later. Colin had said "she," but which she did he mean?

Forcing myself out of the chair, Bun and I went into the barn. Bun was the director while I hauled out the equipment I always used for parties and started to clean them.

"Shouldn't you put all the rabbits in one cage? It would be easier, you know."

"It's not a good idea. They enjoy their own cages and snacks on the way home, and have come to expect as much. There might be discord among them if they decided to fight over food."

"I guess that could be a problem. It was only a suggestion. You know how good I am at making suggestions."

Too bad most of his suggestions weren't worthy ones. I do admit that he could come up with a decent plan now and again, especially when we were in dire straits. I patted his head, smoothed his fur, and left him in charge while I continued to sanitize the cages.

It didn't take long to finish up.

"I guess we're done here for now."

I imagined if Bun had hands, he'd have brushed them off as if his part was done. While I had done the work, it was always fun to have Bun's company. I swiftly moved the van, locked it, and then locked the barn doors for the night.

I fed the rabbits their final meal of the day and added chopped fruit and additional hay to each hutch. Other than the spinning class activities, all was quiet, the rabbits were at ease, and I yearned to have the same for me and Bun. "Let's call it a day, shall we?"

"Good idea."

In his room, Bun feasted on his own supper while I ate a peanut butter and jelly sandwich at the kitchen table. I called Bailey, gave her the date and time for our gig at the lodge, and asked if that worked for her.

"It does, thanks for checking with Mora. This will be fun and could even lead to more engagements there."

Unwilling to mention Jim Brody and the possible loss of his funding for programs the old folks enjoyed so much, I said, "That would be nice."

We ended our conversation. My next call was to Mora. I didn't connect with her, but left her a voice message saying Bailey and I were able to entertain at the lodge.

I'd hung up and was about to call Sheriff Carver when he knocked at the door. I hadn't heard or seen him arrive. I must be slipping or just plain tired. Tired, definitely tired.

He entered the room after I beckoned him in and plunked his hat and coat on the hooks near the door. Oh my. He was staying awhile.

"I was about to make tea, would you care for something to drink?"

"No, but I do want to know what you're up to and what you're holding back."

"Gee, Jack, I was about to ask you the same thing." I leaned back in the chair and folded my arms across my chest.

His eyebrows drew together in the middle, just above the bridge of his nose. "What do you mean? I'm not withholding information from you."

"Were you able to look into all of Evelyn's accounts?"

"I was. It wasn't until today that I found the very last one. It contained an incredible amount of money, too. Have you any idea where she would get that kind of money? Other than her blackmail scheme, that is. Those funds were split between three local banks. This last account was in a bank in Maine."

"She stole some of that money from Jim Brody."

"She did?"

I stared at him for a moment or two before I said in a soft tone, "Jack, you most certainly knew she worked part-time for Jim as the distribution clerk for funding the grants approved by his board of directors. Please don't insult my intelligence by denying it."

His face sagged with disappointment. At least, that's what it seemed to me. I waited in silence, hoping he would explain. Our mutual silence didn't last long, but long enough for me to think he wasn't going to talk about Jim or anything else.

I pushed my chair back, freshened my cup of tea, and returned to the table.

"I found out about Evelyn's theft earlier today. I didn't mention it because I wanted to look into it before I said anything. Jim was foolish to hire her, I can't imagine why he did so," Jack said.

"His family might have wanted him to."

His brows rose as he contemplated what I'd just said. I fiddled with the spoon next to my cup and then admitted it was conjecture on the part of the person who had told me so.

"I am under the impression that Jim's parents have a hand in what goes on in his business. I wasn't aware of that, and have never heard anything about them. Maybe Evelyn was blackmailing one of them and said she would take a job with Jim as payment."

"That's a little farfetched."

I stared at him and remarked, "Not really. Consider how easy it was for her to get that position and take the opportunity to funnel money from his accounts into hers. It was perfect. He's a busy man who has trust in his employees, we all know that. Evelyn could turn on the charm when it suited her, believe me, and he was familiar with her besides."

"How do you know that?"

His disbelief in every statement I made irritated me beyond reason. Jack found it troubling that someone he thought so highly of hadn't been smart enough to see Evelyn for what she was. That Jim had been taken for a ride by the very woman he considered trustworthy and kind seemed unthinkable in Jack Carver's mind. Possibly Jim hadn't been treated to the unfavorable side of Evelyn that so many others had.

"I promised someone I wouldn't share that information."

"I don't care if you did, I want to know right now. It is pertinent to my investigation."

I sat up straight, put my elbows on the table, and leaned toward him. "And that would be how?"

"Tell me what information you have first, and then if it makes sense, I'll tell you what I know."

Geesh, had this become complicated or what?

With a roll of my eyes, I said, "This isn't kindergarten, you know." I explained the connection between Paul, Carina, Jim, Adrian, and Evelyn. It took a while to unwind their tangled relationships so Jack could work it out. I got up, reached into the counter drawer, and withdrew the journal I kept. I flipped to the page with connecting lines and dots to show him instead of trying to make it clear verbally.

He read it over, perused the other pages in the book, and then said, "You really have a knack for finding out the nitty gritty. You also give me gray hair, you know that, don't you?"

I nodded, held back a grin, and said, "Everything I know is there in that book. I wrote the entire thing out when I learned of it. I can't figure out who killed Evelyn. What I know for certain is that it wasn't Carina."

"You never cease to amaze and annoy me. Like I said before, you'd make one heck of a detective."

"And, as I've said, I'm a rabbit farmer with an avid sense of curiosity, nothing more."

We both relaxed and smiled a little.

"I'll take this book if you don't mind. I want to read it over and take some notes. By the way, who told you about all these connections?"

"You know better than to ask me that. I will not give you that name unless I feel things have become dangerous." I watched him think things over, then I asked, "Are the two goons in Concord?"

"Yes, they are. No one came to save their sorry butts, and no one planned on doing so. It was merely wishful thinking on their part."

"Huh, then be on the lookout for something that's supposed to come your way since Seamus can't make blackmail money off his contact while he's in prison. He told me he had information and if his contact didn't pay up, you'd receive something from him in the mail."

"Good to know. I'll be in touch."

With that, Jack was gone. I watched his departure and turned when Bun said, *"He sure got an earful, didn't he?"*

"The time had come for me to give him what we have found out. The only thing missing in this puzzle is the last piece of it. The killer has been under my nose all this time, and now I know who it is, I just don't know the reason behind the murder. Seamus was amused by the fact that I didn't know the why of it. I'm certain there is one more connecting line that will pull all of this together." I heaved a tired sigh.

"You'll figure it out, I just hope it isn't too late before you do."

CHAPTER TWENTY-SIX

The phone rang. Carina was on the line. I answered the call on a cheerful note, though I didn't feel like it.

"Hi there, how are you doing?"

"We're fine now that I'm home with Adrian. Why don't you come over tonight?"

This invitation was my chance to ask the questions bugging me. The ones that would solve the murder and connect the dots. "Sure, I'd like that."

"Good, I look forward to it, say, around eight o'clock?"

"Okay."

By the time I was ready to drive to Carina's house, the full extent of the complexities involved in this mystery had hit me. Why didn't she say why she wanted me to come over, and why didn't I ask? I took a deep breath, started the car, and dialed

Jack's number. He answered on the first ring. I explained where I was going.

"That isn't very smart, Juliette."

"That's why I'm telling you, so you can be ready should something happen. I certainly don't want to be the next victim."

It was at this moment Bun decided to offer his two cents worth of advice.

"If the sheriff isn't bright enough to figure out you're in danger, then we will deal with whatever comes along on our own. I will protect you, my superpowers are working just fine."

Huh. Superpowers. I needed superpowers, but there weren't any handy. "Are you up for this or not, Jack?"

"Of course. I'll be there with officers in tow. Any clue as to why she's invited you over?"

"Maybe it's to finish what she didn't tell me when I visited her in the hospital. I don't think Carina realized Adelle killed Evelyn, not at first, anyway. With the stress she's exhibited, she might have figured it out and possibly faced Adelle with it. The only reason I'll go there tonight is to ask her that very question."

"Don't take unnecessary risks. We'll be outside waiting."

"I'll put my phone on speaker, like I did when Colin came here. I'll call you before I enter the house, okay?"

He agreed. "I can feel another gray hair popping out of my scalp."

"Let's hope this works out, because if it doesn't,

Adelle will get away with murder and we won't be able to prove she killed three people."

"Why all three?"

"It's obvious that Adelle cares for Carina more than Carina realizes, and she's trying to protect Carina from those who would hurt her in any way."

"A bit simplistic, isn't it?" Jack prepared to leave.

"More like obsessive. See you later this evening, Jack. Make sure you're there."

CHAPTER TWENTY-SEVEN

Bun rode in the passenger's seat of my car as I drove to Carina's home. We arrived on time and I noted the house was ablaze with light from top to bottom.

I rang the doorbell while Bun hopped to the rear of the house. As with most people, Carina used her kitchen as a gathering place. It would be a great vantage point for Bun to hear what was being said. He had also promised to let me know when the sheriff and his men arrived. Superpowers or not, my furry friend had my best interests at heart.

Carina invited me in after she opened the door and pointed to the kitchen. "We can go in there, if you don't mind. I enjoy my kitchen and like the atmosphere of it. Besides, the coffeepot is handy, as is the fridge," she said jokingly.

I took a seat at the counter and looked around. As many times as I'd been here, I hadn't taken the time to study the décor. She was right, it had a homey feel. The rest of the house was more elegantly decorated.

"I do like this kitchen. You're right, it is welcoming." Okay, we'd finished that discussion, now for the hard part.

"The cops are here."

I glanced out the sliding doors and across the brightly lit grounds. At the edge of the light, I saw one of Bun's long rabbit ears flip forward. I turned away, comforted to know he was there.

"How are you feeling?" I asked.

"I've been following the treatment plan Dr. Sommers set out for me, and so far it's working. I do get tired, but nothing like before. I have to treat myself better, I guess."

"True, because if you don't, who will?"

She looked me in the eyes and stared. "You know, don't you?"

"I do."

"How long?"

"Not very long."

"Oh."

"Why don't you explain the whole situation to me?"

A movement to my right caught my eye. Adelle had entered the room.

"She isn't going to do that because it's none of your concern."

I turned to Carina and asked, "Is that how you feel? If it is, why am I here?"

Once again, Adelle interrupted any confession Carina might make.

"It was my idea. You see, I knew you heard Jim and me the other day. I even knew the moment you realized what I'd done to Evelyn. You are a nosy one, aren't you?"

"So I'm told." I kept an eye on Adelle, while I spoke to Carina. "How long have you known Adelle murdered Evelyn?"

"Not long. After we found Evelyn's body, I suspected Adelle, but had no proof. I hoped she hadn't killed Evelyn. That's why I asked you to intervene. I wanted to know for sure. I was afraid Sheriff Carver was going to arrest me for something I hadn't done. My first consideration in life is Adrian and her well-being. I couldn't go to jail, I just couldn't leave her alone in this world."

The fear in Carina's eyes told me more than any words ever could. She not only suspected Adelle, but soon realized she was right. It wasn't from anything I had done, which meant Adelle must have somehow confirmed Carina's supposition. Carina was caught in an evil situation.

Her friend was a killer, an obsessive woman who killed again and again without regard for her victims or the people she got to do her bidding. Seamus and Colin would likely pay for their part in these events by spending their future in prison, as would Adelle if I had any say in it.

"You ordered Seamus to take care of Paul, didn't you, Adelle?"

"What if I did? There's no proof to be had, so nothing can be done about it," she said with finality.

"And you had your husband killed, too, didn't you?"

"Why would I do that?"

"Because even then, he somehow realized that

you were obsessed with Carina and that she was being blackmailed by Evelyn. He faced you with his assumptions and because you had plans that didn't include him, you had him killed, am I right?"

Her eyes narrowed and her lip curled when she said, "What they say about you is true, you are a smart one. Seamus took care of the boating accident for me. He's darned good at what he does, too. Colin, well, Seamus leads him around by the nose. Imagine, that idiot actually thought I was going to help them get away so they could blackmail me? Stupid fools."

I had held my breath, and let it out slowly when I faced her. "Did you think for one second that Carina would continue whatever relationship you two have had now that she's aware you're a three-time killer, and that one of those killed was her very own husband?"

"She'll be fine, we're meant to be together. Always, aren't we, Carina? I had planned to blackmail Jim Brody for his part in trying to inveigle his way into Adrian's life when all Carina wanted was to be rid of him."

Carina looked at me, then at Adelle. Considering what would happen if she didn't agree, she assured Adelle that all would be the same between them.

A look of pleasure crossed Adelle's face, before she said, "Now it's your turn, Jules. Did you tell the sheriff your thoughts about me?"

"I did."

"What was his reaction?"

"He doesn't believe me. He always thinks I'm off base when it comes to crime solving, but I've hit the proverbial lottery this time around. I finally figured out the three deaths that are standing at your doorstep. Sooner or later, Jack Carver will come knocking and you'll pay the price for your actions."

That's when she punched me in the face and knocked me off the stool. Carina screamed. Woozy, I got off the floor and flew at Adelle using the moves I'd learned in self-defense class. We rolled on the floor struggling to get control of each other, when I was suddenly hauled off Adelle while she was dragged to her feet. Adam held me by my arms, while Tom and Jack handcuffed Adelle as she tried to free herself.

Her expression changed from the woman I had initially known to the unhinged woman she had become. I leaned back against Adam and relaxed as I caught my breath. Adrenaline still raced through my veins leaving me shaking and angry. I knew better than to assault Adelle again. Jack might grow another gray hair over it, at the very least.

Adelle yelled and screamed obscenities as she was taken away. Carina slumped against the sink and sobbed, while Jack came up to me and said, "Well done."

I gave him a halfhearted smile and remarked, "Ya think? Now, where's Bun?"

He nodded toward the open doors. Bun leapt into my arms. *"Good work."*

A week later, all the paperwork for my part in Adelle's arrest was completed at Jack's office. I gave a full written statement detailing what had taken place and how I had come to the conclusion she was a three-time murderer. Carina had gone in to see Jack and he said that she had done the same thing. Staring at the man, I relaxed in the chair.

"You are a bold woman, Jules, I'll give you that. I'm certain Adelle would have killed you with her bare hands if we hadn't been there."

"She would have tried her best. Though, I was determined to give her mine in return. Adelle seemed confident she'd get away with her crimes and that she and Carina would be together. It boggles my mind."

"Adelle will be a guest of the New Hampshire prison system for years, but I never did make the emotional connection between the two women. Did you?"

"I've spoken to Carina about that. She never considered Adelle more than a good friend and isn't sure how Adelle misconstrued her friendship for something more. Adelle's an unbalanced woman, which might be how she reached that conclusion. It's plain to anyone who talks to Carina about Paul that she was, and still is, deeply in love with him."

"I've been to the prison to speak with Seamus and Colin. They willingly gave Adelle up in order to assist the district attorney when he promised to shorten their sentences. Don't worry, Juliette, they'll still be in prison for a long time. By the way, I've also taken it upon myself to ensure Jim Brody receives the money Evelyn embezzled from the grant program."

"That was good of you, Jack."

Bun, sitting at my feet, had been quiet during our time with Jack. He tapped his foot on the floor next to my chair, and said, *"He could never have solved this without us. I hope he has come to realize what a brilliant pair of investigators we are. I sure hope we get another case soon."*

"I should get back to the farm, Jack." I reached down, plucked Bun off the floor, and settled him in the sling before leaving. About to head out the door, I said, "Bun and I are creative in the way we get to the bottom of things, Jack. You should be more appreciative of that." I smiled and walked out as Jack shook his head in dismay.

Connect with Us

Visit us online at
KensingtonBooks.com
to read more from your favorite authors, see books
by series, view reading group guides, and more.

for sneak peeks, chances to win books and prize packs,
and to share your thoughts with other readers.

facebook.com/kensingtonpublishing
twitter.com/kensingtonbooks

Tell us what you think!

To share your thoughts, submit a review,
or sign up for our eNewsletters, please visit:
KensingtonBooks.com/TellUs.

Grab These Cozy Mysteries
from
Kensington Books